FINDING YOU

D.G. TORRENS

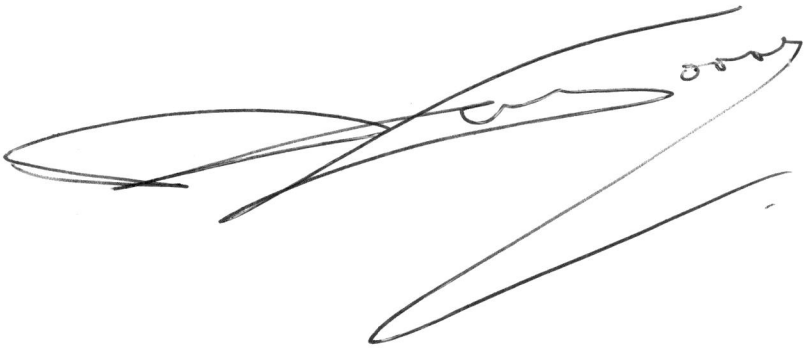

Copyright © 2018 D.G. Torrens
FINDING YOU

Edition 1.

ISBN-13: 978-1547131754

ISBN-10: 1547131756

Formatting by word2kindle

Cover Design by Probookcovers.com

Editor Chew Chen Yen

CONTENTS

QUOTE

Release me from your spell, for your power over me is strong.
You want me to want you, yet you do not desire me.
You weaken my resolve and render me powerless.
Release me from your spell, so my wounds can heal.
No more promises.
No more words.
For my heart can't take anymore...

~ D.G. TORRENS ~

ONE

*E*den's heart rose and fell with rapid breaths, awakening her from a deep sleep. She placed a hand on her chest and drew in a deep breath. Thoughts of Jacob whispered through her mind while a tsunami of emotions soared through her veins. She pressed her hand firm into her chest.

Jacob may be gone, but he consumes my heart as if he were alive.

Beads of sweat pooled on her brow. She brushed them away with a swipe of her fingertips and climbed out of bed. She stepped into her jeans and threw on a sweater. Bella caught her attention and raised a smile on her face.

"Don't worry, Bella. I'm okay," she reassured her loyal Alsatian.

Bella leapt out of her basket and ambled over to her, nudging her hand. Eden ruffled her ears and then made her way downstairs with Bella trailing behind.

"Hey, girl, come on, let's go for a walk," she said while reaching for Bella's lead off the hook.

Bella wagged her tail excitedly while Eden pulled on her parker and slipped on her trainers. She glanced at the clock on the wall and rolled her eyes. *Every day, I wake up at stupid o'clock and unable to fall back to sleep. Seriously, 4 a.m. I need to sort myself out.*

Eden loved this part of the day, the peacefulness and beautiful sound of the blackbird song echoing through the trees.

She closed the door behind her and strolled down the street towards the river. Thoughts of Jacob dominated her mind once more. *Memories are long when they hurt, unforgettable fragments hiding in the shadows of my mind and making unwanted appearances. I will never forget that tragic day – a day of pain my heart refuses to let go of. Jacob was the one! How could I ever love someone that much again? It is too painful when you lose.*

The pain of his unexpected death haunted her dreams. She could not forget the knowing look he displayed in his eyes while his life slipped away from her. At that moment, Jacob knew he was dying. A lone tear escaping from his eye as the realisation took hold while she cradled him in her arms would remain with her forever.

That was 12 months ago, and it still felt like yesterday. The pain of losing him was unlike anything she had ever experienced. Her love for him was irrevocable.

Eden thought about her upcoming twenty-eighth birthday, *we were supposed to be going to Italy...* An image of Lake Garda flashed through her mind. *It was my dream destination. I was really looking forward to it.* Tears clouded her eyes. Her thoughts directed her to the stranger approaching her at Jacob's funeral—a woman. The woman placed a hand on Eden's arm, looked deep into her tear-filled eyes and said, "I'm so sorry, Eden."

Eden did not recognise her and wondered how the woman knew her name. She glanced at the woman standing before her clutching her swollen stomach. Her own face drowning in her tears.

Eden cleared her throat, "I'm sorry. I don't think we have met before. Did you know Jacob well?" she queried curiously.

The woman's eyes widened. She froze. Without saying a word, she turned around and headed for a car parked nearby. Before climbing into the car, the woman stopped, glanced over her shoulder locking eyes with Eden one last time. She left Eden with a sense of dread. Eden will never forget the revelation that followed their brief encounter, a revelation she was not prepared for—Jacob was having an affair. Torn between staying with Eden and leaving her for his pregnant lover. Jacob's sister revealed all the following day. Eden was completely broken. She was still in love with him and yet hated him at the same time. Jacob was not that kind of man, or so she believed. Jacob was one of life's keepers, a genuine man and one that would never betray his fiancée. She realised soon after that she didn't know Jacob at all.

Bella brought Eden swiftly back to reality and tugged on her lead when they reached the river. "Okay, calm down, Bella," insisted Eden while unclipping her lead. Bella spun around happily and then ran off down the riverbank. She picked up her pace and followed Bella. June was in full swing. The early morning sun peeked through the parting clouds and wrapped its warmth around Eden's shoulders. She paused and glanced around her. The wildflowers gently blowing in the wind filled the riverbank. The river was shallow and its current gentle. A majestic swan glided past and raised a smile on her face. *Not bad for lonely*, she surmised.

"B-E-LL-A," she shouted.

"Come on girl, time to go home."

Bella came bounding up beside her. They turned on their heels and made the long walk back home. Eden sighed while pushing open the door; *I have an exceptionally long day ahead of me.* Bella ran past her straight into the kitchen. After feeding Bella, Eden ran up the stairs and took a shower.

She placed her hands palms down on the cold, tiled wall of her shower, allowing the warm water to cascade over her naked body. Thoughts of her impending meeting took pole position in her mind. *Today's meeting is to reveal the new journalist for Imperial Home Magazine— Well, there is nothing more I can do now except keep my fingers crossed. If selected as the new journalist, this could propel my career and elevate me to the next level.* Eden was both excited and nervous, "Journalist!" she said aloud, while stepping out of the shower and reaching for a towel. She had been an assistant for three years and was ready to move up a notch in her career. She knew she was the right person for the job and hoped the board could see it too. She had shared lots of stories and ideas with her boss, Andrea. Andrea was one of the journalists for the Magazine and Eden practically did her job for her.

Her mobile phone ringing caught her attention. Not wanting to miss the call, she ran to the bedroom and picked up her phone, "Hello," she answered.

"Eden, it's Blake. Can you come into the office a little earlier this morning? I need to go over a few things with you and bring you up to speed."

Eden's eyes darted to her wall clock, "Sure, the meeting is at 9 o'clock, so... I could be there by 8.15," she agreed.

"Great. See you then," finished Blake.

Eden selected a simple, pinstriped shift dress and sling-back shoes for her meeting. After dressing, she surveyed her reflection in her mirror. Her deep blue eyes trailed over her trim form and she smiled. *That will do*, she decided. She threaded her fingers through her long, dark tresses cascading down her back and added a touch of lip-gloss to complete her look.

"Today's the day!" she said aloud, while hurrying down the stairs. She ruffled Bella's ears and kissed her nose. "See you later, Bella."

TWO

Eden entered Blake's office juggling two large, Costa coffees.
"Morning, Eden," greeted Blake.

"Morning, Blake. Here you go, black with two sugars, right?"

"Yes, thanks. I need a strong coffee this morning. Eden, take a seat. I need to talk to you. We have a new client for next month's centre spread. He is extremely wealthy and a very prestigious client. I need you on this one. He lives out in Warwickshire and apparently has a mansion of sorts. Although, I have heard he can be difficult. Our client likes things done his way and will not compromise under any circumstances. I want you to interview him."

The corners of Eden's mouth quirked up, "Andrea will not be happy about this though."

Blake swivelled in his chair. "Andrea is not the right person for this client. I have already spoken with the partners and told them I need you for this interview. Look, I should not be telling you this–but hell, I cannot hold it in any longer. The job is yours. You are Imperial Home's newest journalist! This will be your first, official interview as Journalist."

Eden's jaw dropped, "No way! Really. Oh my God, this is the best news. Thank you, Blake. I needed this promotion. Nevertheless, I am worried that this will ruffle the collars of the other journalists. I mean, this will be my first day and you're handing me this new, prestigious client?"

Blake placed a reassuring hand on Eden's arm, "Don't worry about them. As far as I am concerned, this interview needs handling carefully. You are the best person for this assignment. You just let me worry about the rest of the team. You deserve it, Eden. You have worked hard. Everyone knows it was your challenging work and dogged research that went into Andrea's prosperous stories and client interviews over the years. You never once complained or dropped her in it. There are many who would have done in your position. You carried her for too long. You have something that the other journalists don't have. It is that something that we require for the success of this interview. This client has many connections and could bring an abundance of business to Imperial Home Magazine in the future. Therefore, we really need this to be successful. So, no pressure," teased Blake.

He added, "I thought I should advise you that Andrea will be leaving at the end of the month. I cannot go into detail; however, her capabilities and conduct were under question for some time. Andrea's contract was up for renewal. She is not happy with the added terms set out and decided not to renew her contract with us. There is no place for people who need carrying and rely on others to do their work for them. You were more than Andrea's assistant and practically did her job for her. That is not what this company is about. We are about teamwork. You above anyone else have proved that you are a team worker. You always have the magazine's best interest at heart."

Eden could hardly believe what she was hearing. Feeling ecstatic, her mouth curved into a smile. "We must celebrate at lunchtime. Do you fancy having a toast with me?" she suggested.

Blake's eyes gleamed, "Try keeping me away. Now, remember, act surprised in front of the board or I will be in trouble if the other partners find out I have told you already!"

"Don't worry, I will. By the way, who is this new client?"

"His name is Noah Ainsworth. I suggest you look him up on Google and familiarise yourself with him. He is quite the notable bachelor of mystery, by all accounts! I will schedule a meeting with Mr. Ainsworth for tomorrow. They will require you to do the interview at his home, accompanied by the magazine's photographer. It might take a few visits to get it exactly right, or should I say, right for Mr. Ainsworth. I will email you all the information on him after the meeting. Anyway, more about him later. Come on, it's almost 9 o'clock and we don't want to be late for the big reveal!" he winked.

Eden liked Blake. She had worked for him and the other senior partners for three years. Unlike some magazines, it had been a family run magazine since 1885 that believed in old-fashioned family values—teamwork or no work. It was one of the most prestigious and prosperous House and Home Magazines in the UK, having won many National Magazine Awards.

Eden felt privileged and proud to be working at the magazine. She loved that it celebrated the admirable beauty of English design. She always surveyed each issue with her intricate eagle eye. Every issue captivated her. It featured visually aesthetic layouts, resplendent country houses and hideaway mansions. She often came over dreamy eyed while glancing over the large, decadent, grade 11 listed mansions, and wondered what it must be like to live in one. The photographers did an incredible job of capturing the essence and beauty of each individual property. They brought them to life before the reader's eyes. Each property the magazine displayed was accompanied by a one-on-one interview with the owners of the homes. This was the most popular section of the magazine with their subscribers—a personal insight into how the other half lived. The magazine's detailed articles offered its readers elegant photo spreads that revealed the charming, decadent design choices and accent pieces that created their beautiful homes.

Eden had always been a fan of the magazine long before she became an employee. When she first purchased her small country cottage in Shenley, she often bought the issue for tips and ideas. The advice columns offered her useful advice from notable design experts and buyers guides for furniture and furnishings, as well as tried and tested tips. Imperial Home always featured quintessential English staples that were a hit with its readers.

Eager to climb the corporate ladder, it was now minutes away from her official grasp... Blake opened the oak doors leading to the grand boardroom. He stepped aside, allowing Eden to walk through ahead of him. Her breaths quickened as she stepped inside.

"Ah, Eden, please take a seat," urged Kennedy, one of the four partners of Imperial Home Magazine.

Eden smiled nervously, pulled out a chair and sat in front of the partners. Blake gave her a wink, then turned his attention to Kennedy.

"The floor is all yours, Kennedy."

"Eden, we have requested your presence here today to offer you the position of Journalist for Imperial Home Magazine. You will be part of an excellent team of Journalists, and you were by far the best candidate for the position. You come highly recommended by Blake. You have produced some impressive work during this year for Andrea. Our only regret is that we did not realise sooner that it was your work gaining all that recognition and not Andreas. Nevertheless, here we are. Of course, you can take your time to think about it if you wish. There is no need to give us an answer right away." He paused, handed Eden an A4 envelope and continued. "Your new contract-of-employment and salary details are all enclosed. If there is anything that you're unhappy with, then I am sure we can renegotiate." Kennedy sat back in his chair.

Eden rose to her feet and glanced at all four partners sat before her while drawing in a deep breath. "Yes. I accept! Thank you so much for giving me this opportunity. I won't let you down."

Blake beamed at Eden. He reached across the table and extended his hand, "Congratulations."

"What he said," chimed in Kennedy.

"Well deserved, Eden," said Liam.

"I ditto that," piped Paul.

Eden was in seventh heaven. *Finally, I am where I want to be in my career*. Her eyes darted from one partner to another, and she smiled, *I need a large glass of prosecco at lunchtime*, she decided. She wanted to jump on the table and scream with happiness; instead, she turned on her heel and made her way back to her office, maintaining her decorum.

Before Eden had a chance to sit down, Angie popped her head around the door. "Congratulations! I am so happy for you. If there is anyone who deserves some good luck in their life after everything you have been through–it's you. This promotion was a long time coming, Eden."

"Thanks, Angie. But how did you know?"

Angie winked, "Who do you think typed up your new contract of employment...You have no idea how much I wanted to tell you. Sorry, Blake had me sworn to secrecy."

"I totally understand and that is why you are Blake's P.A. I'm going to the pub at lunchtime to celebrate. I need a large prosecco. Care to join me?"

Angie's eyes twinkled, "Try keeping me away. What time are you heading out to lunch?"

"Let's say around 12.30. Blake will join us too. In fact, why don't you round up the rest of the team?" suggested Eden.

"Leave it to me. See you later," finished Angie.

Eden turned on her laptop and logged on. She did a quick Google search for her new client, Noah Ainsworth, and was surprised to see there were many pages listed on him. *How is it I have never heard of this man before?* She wondered. After 20 minutes on Google, she learned that Noah Ainsworth was one of Britain's wealthiest bachelors. Her eyes rested on an article dated three years before and she read the article from the Telegraph:

It seems Noah Ainsworth's people have hushed the press over recent speculation that his former girlfriend, was admitted to a psychiatric hospital amid speculation she was behind the bachelor's near-fatal, hit-and-run accident, although there is no confirmation at this time. An investigation is still underway, and Noah Ainsworth remains in critical condition.

Eden searched for more information on Mr Ainsworth's accident, but there was little to be found. *The whole incident seems to have been buried and brushed off as a terrible accident. There were a few reports in various magazines speculating over what they thought had happened - nothing more. It seems the press soon tired of it and moved on to their next victim. Noah Ainsworth never publicly spoke about his accident. It was off topic for anyone wanting to interview him. His people put out a brief statement to satisfy the public's curiosity. Very mysterious! It must have been one heck of an accident to put him in intensive care,* she mused.

Eden surveyed an image of Noah Ainsworth for some time. "He is

6ft 1-inch tall, sporting thick, dark hair and piercing emerald eyes. I cannot deny he is extremely handsome. I bet he knows it too," she mumbled.

Besides his obvious physical attributes, Mr Ainsworth is an admirable and successful businessman who has acquired an impressive empire over the last decade. Mr Ainsworth is a self-made man, single and never married. Eden glanced through the image gallery and there were very few personal images of Noah Ainsworth. *Okay, that's enough digging on Mr Ainsworth. I think I know enough. He is going to be a tough nut to crack. I am guessing he will have his own list of questions already printed out for me to ask.*

Eden had interviewed several people during her three years at Imperial Home for Andrea. They were usually the self-absorbed types with beautiful, majestic homes they were eager to display in the magazine. However, this was the first time that she would interview such a prestigious client as Mr Ainsworth. *Ordinarily, the woman of the house likes to head the interviews and give the tour of their elegant homes. The men like to take a back seat and leave their wives to discuss their interior design choices,* she mused.

Noah Ainsworth came across as an extremely private individual and made Eden wonder why he was willing to open his house and himself up to Imperial Home. *I can't find any personal interviews with Noah Ainsworth on Google or photos of him either. They were all corporate images at best. In fact, there was little to be found on Mr Ainsworth personal life and this intrigues me,* she concluded.

Eden spent the next couple of hours working on her emails and emptying her in-tray. By 12.30, she rose to her feet, grabbed her bag, and headed out the door.

"Angie, are you ready?"

Angie raised her head, "Yep. Just logging off. I will be right behind you."

"No problem. I will just give Blake a nudge. See you there."

Eden popped her head around Blake's door, "Are you ready?"

"I sure am. Let's go celebrate."

The pub was heaving when Eden and Blake arrived. Most of the publishing team were there and with drinks in hand. There was no sign of Andrea anywhere. This did not surprise Eden at all. A tap on her shoulder sparked Eden to pivot. "Angie! About time. What took you so long?"

Angie let out a harsh breath and placed her bag down on the chair in front of her. "Last minute phone call. I knew I should have left it— but you know me! I just couldn't leave a phone ringing. Anyway, I am here now."

"What are you drinking, Angie," chimed in Blake.

"I will have a Prosecco, please. Thank you."

Blake smiled, "One Prosecco coming up," he repeated while heading for the two-deep bar.

Eden studied Angie's face, contemplating whether to inquire about their new client. She fell silent until Angie piped up, "Come on out with it," she pressed.

"Have you heard about this new client of ours—Mr. Ainsworth?"

Angie beamed, "Oh yes, everyone has! The delectable and mysterious Noah Ainsworth and you, lucky lady, get to spend some one-on-one time with him. I have to confess, I am seriously jealous!"

Eden shied away from Angie's comment. Regretting bringing it up, she attempted to change the conversation. "Anyway, how is your house coming along?" she asked.

Angie laughed aloud, "I don't want to talk about my house. I want to discuss Noah Ainsworth. Come on Eden, you must be a little curious about him. A rich devilishly handsome man never married and living in that great big old mansion all by himself! Not to mention the questionable details surrounding his accident three years ago! He has got every single woman this side of Warwickshire talking about him." Angie's voice turned into white noise and Eden's attention was lost. She glanced around the heaving bar. Thinking of her new position. She could not wait to get home and look over her new contract of employment, which was currently sealed in an A4 envelope poking out of her handbag.

Angie interrupted Eden's thoughts with a tug on her arm, "So... are you excited to meet him?"

Eden turned her attention back to Angie, "I wouldn't say excited, but curious, yes."

"Just curious! You are a mystery to me, Eden Marshall," blurted

Angie while shaking her head. She added, "He is one man that I wouldn't say no to!"

Eden rolled her eyes, "You have a one-track mind. Look, I don't really care how handsome or rich Noah Ainsworth is. I have no interest in him or anyone for that matter. What I am more concerned about is making it through the interview unscathed—apparently, he can be difficult to interview. I am rather nervous about it, to be honest with you. But don't tell Blake that."

Angie placed a reassuring hand on Eden's arm, "Just be confident and don't let him detect that you are nervous. I have heard rumours that on the rare occasion he agrees to an interview, he is a tough nut to crack—he rarely gives anything away about his personal life. He always drives the interview and is never coerced or intimidated by interviewers. If he does not like the way it is going, then he will end it. I have a friend at Majestic Interior Magazine who had an unpleasant experience with him. He almost got her sacked from her job... I heard that he was not impressed with her directness and pushy attitude. So be careful."

Eden's brows snapped together, "Now I'm nervous, thanks, Angie!"

Angie chimed in, "Would you rather I not tell you and let you walk in there blind. I want you to be armed and ready. Just don't be too pushy. Try to make him feel comfortable and that way he is more likely to open up. Noah Ainsworth maybe wealthy and of great interest to the public, but he goes to great lengths to secure his privacy. He is an extremely private man and very guarded. He only lets people see what he wants them to see. He is an enigma to most people, and that is his allure. I mean, let's be honest here—Noah Ainsworth is one delectable cookie!"

Eden shook her head mockingly, "Thanks for the heads up. Did everything work out for your friend in the end?" she queried.

Angie nodded, "Yes, her pride was hurt, nothing more."

Eden swiftly changed the subject, "So, are you still dating that guy?"

Angie's forehead crinkled, "You mean, Andrew?"

"Yes, that's the one. I can't keep up with you these days!"

"No, two dates were enough for me. So, I am on the hunt again!"

Eden rolled her eyes, "Maybe you need to give these guys a chance. It takes more than a date or two to get to know someone?"

Angie shook her head, "Not for me. Anyway, my journey to finding the one is fun! Enough about me. How will you be celebrating your promotion this coming weekend?" Sadness clouded Eden's face. "No celebrations this weekend. It will be 12 months to the day on Saturday since Jacob's death. His sister and I are going to visit his graveside. A brief silence descended. Pain resurfaced at the mention of Jacob's name. Her eyes filled up and she discreetly wiped away a tear.

"I'm sorry, Eden. I should have remembered. However, to be honest, I am surprised you are going. If anyone had done to me what Jacob did to you, I don't think I would be visiting their grave," admitted Angie.

Eden sipped her wine and then looked at Angie. "Jacob was stupid. He made a mistake—a huge mistake. He was going to tell me before he had the accident. His sister told me he had never regretted anything more in his entire life. He had put off telling me for weeks because he could not bear to hurt me. In addition, before you say anything, Angie, I know how it sounds. Yes, he cheated on me. Yes, he made the biggest mistake he could have made. Nevertheless, when all said and done, Jacob was the love of my life. I held him in my arms while his last breath escaped from him. I watched as his eyes closed for the last time. I held him in my arms until the ambulance arrived. The way I felt about him never changed. He was the one. I will never forgive him for cheating on me, yet I cannot erase the four amazing years we had together either. Because at the end of the day that is what I have chosen to focus on. I do not want to be consumed by hate and bitterness for one regrettable indiscretion. I am visiting his grave for all the love he did give me, for all the happy times we shared and for the four years that we gave to each other. He was a big part of my life and my first love. I cannot just turn my back on that because it did not end the way I hoped it would. I still love him and miss him every single day. I will never allow myself to love anyone that completely again." Eden reached for her glass of wine off the table and gulped it down in one.

There was a tear in Angie's eye, "I'm so sorry, Eden. I know how much you loved him. I know how much it hurt you and still hurt's you that he is gone. You are an incredible woman and a far better woman than I am. Look, you know you can call me if you need to talk anytime," she apologised.

"Thanks. I am fine, really. Losing him will always hurt, but I am living with it. I have no other choice. Everything else that happened after the funeral ruined me for anyone else. I will never trust or love another man again. I will never allow myself to love someone that deeply. Right now, Jacob still has a hold over me. He still dominates my dreams and thoughts. Regardless of what he did - my love for him was real. The pain, the loss and the revelations afterwards are all mixed up in my head. I have Bella and I know Bella will never let me down!"

Eden and Angie spent the next hour mingling with the rest of the team before heading back to the office. Eden had two long meetings to get through before her working day ended. She printed off her presentation packs and headed to the meeting room for the first of her two meetings.

Finally, by 5.30, she was done and headed on home. The traffic was bumper to bumper out of Birmingham City and Eden braised herself for a timely journey home. She turned on her radio and sang along to, Shawn Mendes – 'Mercy.' The heartfelt lyrics penetrated her heart and forced thoughts of Jacob to the front of her mind. She felt his loss as if it were yesterday. *The pain cuts deep; I wish I could be released from his hold. Jacob may be gone, but my love for him remains. I am finding it hard to let go of my feelings and wonder if I can ever stop loving him. I miss you, Jacob—you still consume my heart,* she thought sadly.

After a long slow journey home, she finally approached her driveway and backed into it. She parked up, reached for her handbag off the passenger seat and climbed out. Eden walked up the crooked path to her small, two-bedroomed cottage and smiled when she heard Bella on the other side of the door barking excitedly! She opened the door and Bella bounded towards her, jumping up and down excitedly.

"Bella, do you fancy a walk?" Bella wagged her tail, ran into the hallway, and picked up her lead in her mouth off the table.

Eden dropped her bag in the hallway; clipped Bella's lead to her collar and headed straight out the door again. She needed to stretch her legs after her tiresome journey home. It was a beautiful summer night, and the approaching riverbank was busy with dog walkers and ramblers. Shenley River and the surrounding landscape was beautiful, peaceful, and her sanctuary from the City. Eden unclipped Bella's lead and let her run free. She ambled along the riverbank surveying the clear shallow waters, focusing on the pebbles submerged below. The calm river was alive with nesting ducks, and the tall reeds provided them with shade. Wild Canadian geese grouped on the far side for their annual molt while awaiting growth of their new wing feathers... Eden laughed while watching one chasing and pecking at another. She walked for over an hour while Bella ran in and out of the cornfields on the far side. She glanced down at her phone and checked the time. *We need to head back home,* she decided.

"B-e-l-l-a," she yelled. Bella was nowhere to be found. Eden let out a harsh breath, quickened her pace and trenched through the overgrown grass towards the cornfields. Beyond the cornfields were acres of private, beautiful green land that stretched as far as the eye could see. She searched all around her and could not see sight of Bella anywhere. Her heart pounded through her chest. She panicked and called Bella's name repeatedly. "B-E-L-L-A," she hollered. She stood still while glancing around her and listened out for Bella. Then she heard someone talking, followed by Bella's trademark bark! Bella appeared. She sighed with relief, "Hey, where have you been?" asked Eden. Bella weaved in and out of Eden's legs and ran towards the river. Eden spun around, startled when a man emerged from out of the cornfields. He was tall and overshadowed her. Eden froze on sight of him with her mouth agape.

"Is that your dog?" he inquired.

"Mmm... yes, is there a problem?" queried Eden.

The man studied her for a few seconds and made Eden feel self-conscious. His emerald, green eyes searched her face curiously.

Eden's eyes flashed with recognition, "Noah Ainsworth," she blurted.

"That's right. I see my reputation precedes me."

Eden composed herself, "I'm sorry. My name is Eden Marshall from Imperial Home Magazine. They have assigned me to interview you tomorrow." Eden extended her hand, "Pleased to meet you."

Noah glanced at her hand. His expression dulled, "Well, isn't this quite the coincidence?"

Eden retracted her hand and looked at him perplexed, "Excuse me?"

"Never mind." he added, "Your dog found his way onto my land beyond the corn. I was out walking when I stumbled across him. I thought he was lost until I noticed the collar and how well-kept he was. I surmised he must belong to a walker strolling the riverbank. It happens occasionally. I was just investigating and making sure I reunited him with his owner."

The corner of Eden's eyes crinkled, "My dog is called, Bella–she not he!"

Noah raised his brow, "I apologise. On closer inspection, I would have come to that conclusion," he gave a half-smile.

Eden turned around and called Bella, then turned back to Noah Ainsworth, "Well, thank you. I will make sure Bella does not run into your fields again. And just for the record, Mr. Ainsworth, I can assure you that bumping into you this evening was as much of a strange coincidence for me as it was for you. There was nothing deliberate about it."

Noah surveyed Eden briefly, "Noted! And by the way, Bella was no trouble."

Eden clipped Bella's lead on her and then spun around to meet Noah's gaze, "Again, I am sorry." She tugged on Bella's lead, "Come on Bella we need to go home."

Noah watched as Eden headed towards the riverbank until she was out of sight. *Eden Marshall is one very intriguing woman,* he surmised. Eden finally reached home and kicked off her shoes. *What were the chances of that happening–Mr Noah Ainsworth of all people...? Who the hell does he think he is? I have better things to do with my time than stalking a potential client!* she thought feeling annoyed with his insinuation.

She placed a large bowl of water down for Bella and retrieved the envelope from her bag. Once she was curled up on the sofa, she emptied the envelope contents and began to read. First, there was an official congratulatory letter followed by the details of her new role and a contract of employment. She started to read her new role with pride.

. . .

JOURNALIST RESPONSIBILITIES

1. Researching a subject and story
2. Writing/editing news stories and features in the publication's house style
3. Ensuring work is well-written, accurate and submitted to deadline
4. Conducting interviews, either in person or remotely
5. Attending seminars and conferences. Also, exhibitions and events to allow advertisers to meet their readership.
6. Sourcing images to accompany written pieces.
7. Meeting with colleagues to plan the content of the issue and the character of the publication.
8. Keeping up to date with trends and developments relating to the magazine's subject matter.
9. Networking
10. Pitch story ideas to the editor and cultivate sources.

She smiled while reading her new list of responsibilities. *Nothing there I have not covered over the last three years,* she concluded. Eventually, she moved on to her contract of employment and read it with a fine-tooth comb. "Wow!" she said aloud on reaching her new salary details. She jumped off her sofa and leapt into the air! *Finally, a decent salary and a company car...*

THREE

Noah Ainsworth worked out of his suite of offices situated on the top floor of his mansion. He had a tech team, a PA and his most trusted business manager, Max, to name a few. They all worked full time at his disposal from his home. His tech team kept him connected to all his offices around the world. His offices were adorned with the latest technology and computer software. There were many large screens adjacent in all his offices that linked with boardrooms around the world. He rarely visited any of his office buildings in person. He could attend any meeting at any time, right from his own personal suite of offices at home via conference call. Noah's need for solitude was warranted. His regular headaches and the steel plate in his cranium served as a reminder.

Noah had acquired a vast empire over the last decade and at just 29-years old, he was in his prime. His security was profoundly tight, and his tech team kept his empire safe from hackers. Luke was a genius who headed up the tech team. He was a computer wizard and often head-hunted by other firms. Nevertheless, Ainsworth Global Communications treated Luke and his team very well and their loyalty to the company was affirmed.

After coming off the phone to Imperial Home, Noah instructed Luke to find out everything he could about Eden Marshall. He allowed no one to enter his home without learning about them first. No matter how captivating they were. He liked to know every detail about them. He was security conscious bordering on obsession. Noah had every reason to be after his near-fatal accident several years back. Although, he was fully aware of Imperial Home's impeccable reputation and long, affluent client list. That did not account for the staff that flowed through its doors. It was not long before Luke produced a short file on Eden Marshall.

"That's everything we could find, Mr. Ainsworth," advised Luke handing over the file.

Noah took the file from Luke's hand, "Good work, Luke. Please close the door behind you."

He sat back in his chair and swivelled around to face the window. He opened the file and started reading. He glanced up to the passport-sized photo at the top of the page and his eyes rested on Eden's face. His eyes glimmered. *I am looking forward to my interview with her.* He studied her image for some time before moving on. He worked his way through the short file and smiled to himself. He was surprised to discover that she lived rather close at just three miles away in a small cottage in the next village! *Shenley, a quaint little cottage too. For a woman who works in the city, her choice of living is surprising. Why not a contemporary city apartment, I wonder? Better suited to a single, professional, and close to work. Mmm... you do not get more remote than Shenley, except Acton, of course,* he mused.

He continued to sift through her file. There was nothing in the file to indicate a security breach. He discovered that Eden studied Journalism at University for four years and went straight to Imperial Home on graduating *So, Eden has recently been promoted. She rarely takes time off for holidays. She owns her cottage, which she purchased four years ago. Her mother lives close to the city and her father has passed on. She is an only child and comes from a solid working-class family. I am guessing Eden Marshall prefers her own company as much as I do. Interesting, to say the least.* Noah closed the file, satisfied. He ambled into the adjacent office, calling for his loyal companion.

"Come on Duke, where are you hiding?" Duke limped from behind the heavy curtains and over to Noah. "Hey boy, how's your foot doing? Lie down, that's a good boy. Let me have a look at it."

Duke obediently lay down. Noah took his paw in his hand and felt around Duke's ankle. "That's coming along well, Duke. You will be bounding around the fields in no time at all. You are walking much better too. The tech guys have been spoiling you, I see!"

A few days previous, Duke stumbled and sprained his ankle, he had not been able to go out since then. Noah was missing his daily walks with Duke and decided he was ready to go out again. Duke was a large, white, Siberian Husky with beautiful, spellbinding eyes and currently the great love of Noah Ainsworth life! They were virtually inseparable, mostly. Noah made his way downstairs and Duke followed behind. "I need a good run myself today, Duke."

FOUR

*B*lake was waiting for Eden in her office when she arrived. "Good morning, Eden. I hope you are ready for your first appointment with Mr. Ainsworth this afternoon. I have emailed you his address and anything else you need to know. Just a heads up, don't rush in like a bull-in-a-china-shop or he will show you the door! As I mentioned yesterday, Mr. Ainsworth can be difficult. Although, this is a more insightful interview with him, there are topics that are off limit. He emailed me a brief list, which includes his mother/father and one or two others and whatever you do—don't mention his accident. Read them thoroughly and embed them into your mind! Off topic, remember. I will leave you to get yourself organised. Report to me after the interview. Good luck, Eden."

Once Blake left her office, Eden turned on her laptop and printed off her list of questions she had prepared for Mr Ainsworth. *I will avoid his romantic life and stick to his hobbies, likes and dislikes. Noah Ainsworth can add more if he wishes. The last thing I want to do is lose the magazine such a wealthy client on my first day as journalist,* she decided.

She left the office at 1.15 p.m. and headed to her interview. She soon realised that Mr. Ainsworth lived only three miles from Shenley Village. *That figures,* she thought, recalling her run-in with him by the river.

So, he lives in Acton, which is far more remote than Shenley. I never have much cause to visit Acton. He must own all the private land north of the river, she mused.

She followed her satnav's directions along narrow, winding, country lanes until she saw two, colossal stone posts propping up sizeable iron gates with a designation on it– AINSWORTH HOUSE. The gates were closed. She climbed out of her car and pressed the button. Eden stood back as the gates opened. She climbed back into her car and drove on. Each side of the lane was heavily wooded. She could not see a mansion or large house through the dense forest.

"Where is it," she said aloud. She continued driving up the lane, then took a sharp right. She stopped the car and stared ahead at the impressive building that came into view–her jaw dropped, "WOW!"

The 18th-century, Grade 11 listed, Victorian mansion with its Gothic Revival style park surrounding it, captivated Eden. *He must employ several cleaners to keep that place clean*, she concluded.

Eden climbed back into her car, drove up to the main entrance and parked up. She remained seated for some time to gather her thoughts before climbing out. *Okay, Eden, let's do this,* she braced. She made her way to the front of the large, impressive doors then rang the bell. The doors opened and a traditional butler greeted her.

"Miss Marshall, I believe?"

It surprised Eden that he knew her name, "Yes, I am Eden Marshall from Imperial Home Magazine. I have an appointment with Mr. Ainsworth."

The butler's expression remained stern, "Please, come in. Mr. Ainsworth is expecting you."

Eden walked through the doors and stood in one of the most impressive atriums she had ever seen. There were two, grand, opulent staircases leading from the left and the right meeting at the top. She could not take her eyes off them. She was lost in thoughts of fantasy, imagining herself in a beautiful gown gliding down the elegant staircase. *This is like something out of a Gatsby movie,* she marvelled.

The butler swiftly brought Eden back to reality, "Miss Marshall, please follow me."

She followed the tall, stiff butler through to a large, impressive library.

"Please make yourself comfortable, Miss Marshall. Mr Ainsworth will be with you shortly." The butler quietly left the room, closing the doors behind him.

Eden glanced above at the beautiful artwork majestically displayed on the ceilings. Her eyes rested upon the floor-to-ceiling bookshelves. There were several, beautifully carved, wooden ladders on each side of the room leaning up against the shelves. The ladders were on runners, which allowed a person to slide from one end to another. Eden surveyed Mr Ainsworth's collection of books with a permanently jaw-dropped expression. *An avid book lover myself, I am interested to see what Mr Ainsworth reads.* Her eyes trailed over a first edition book by Charles Dickens. *This is a rare special edition complete with three errors that makes this book sort after by Dickensian collectors. This book is extremely valuable*, she marvelled. She reached up to the handle of the glass cabinet, she was about to slide it open when Mr Ainsworth entered the room.

"STOP," he shouted.

Eden turned around, startled. She lost her footing, slipped, and fell. Mr. Ainsworth rushed up to her, placed his hand under her arm and helped her up.

"Just for the record, I do not like people touching my rare books. At least not without my prior permission. Is that understood, Miss Marshall?"

"I'm sorry. It won't happen again, Mr. Ainsworth," assured Eden, feeling mortified.

"You can call me, Noah, since we have met previously under"–

he paused for a moment and continued, "Shall we say conspicuous circumstances," he intoned while taking a seat behind a large, polished, walnut desk.

"Please, take a seat. Can I offer you any refreshments, Miss-?"

Eden cut him off, "You can call me, Eden and yes, I would like a tea please."

The corners of Noah's lips turned up marginally. He pressed a button on his desk. His butler appeared with his hands clasped behind his back, awaiting his instructions.

"Jackson, would you rustle up a tray of tea for Miss Marshall and me?"

"Right away, Mr. Ainsworth." Jackson left the room swiftly.

Eden's eyes fixed on a man standing by the entrance door. He was dressed in a dark suit and sported an earpiece.

Noah sensed Eden's curiosity, "That's, Martin, one of my bodyguards." He turned to his bodyguard and nodded. The bodyguard then left the room without a word.

Noah turned his attention back to Eden, "Now we have the formalities out of the way. I assume they gave you a list of subjects I do not wish to discuss?"

Eden studied Noah's face. His eyes were intense. For a moment, she was lost in them.

"Eden... was that a difficult question?" he pressed.

Eden's face flushed, "No. Not at all. Sorry. And yes, I was prepped in advance," she replied nervously.

Noah surveyed her briefly, stood up and glanced out of the window. "Bella... how is she?" he blurted, turning around.

"Bella is fine, thank you. Again, I am sorry about Bella's intrusion onto your land."

She was not enjoying the interview. *Noah Ainsworth is proving to be far more intimidating than I anticipated. It is not going to plan, and I just want to run from this house.*

Noah did not respond. He sat back down in his chair and crossed his legs. Sensing her nervousness, he changed his tone, "Okay Eden, the floor is all yours."

She shifted nervously in her chair, reached into her handbag, and took out her Dictaphone, "Do you mind if I use this?" she asked.

Noah's eyes shifted to the Dictaphone in Eden's hand, "I have no objection at this point."

Eden opened her notepad and looked at the first question. She cleared her throat, "You have an incredibly beautiful house. What was it about this particular house that led you to purchase it?"

Noah's eyes furrowed, "Really! That is your first question?"

Eden was confused. She was playing by the rules, treading carefully. *It was a decent first question—what's his problem*, she wondered. Eden glanced at her notepad and then back to Noah. His face was deadpan.

He continued, "Well... if you insist. I was in search of a property that offered me complete solitary. I am a very private man and in this digital age, it is almost impossible to maintain a private life. However, I manage to maintain my privacy, but it is not without its complications at times. I viewed this property just once and I knew it was the one for me. It was hidden away by a vast forest and not another property to be seen for several miles. That was the allure."

Jackson entered the room with a tray of tea and two freshly made cakes.

"Thank you, Jackson. I see Betty has been baking again. Please put the tray down on the table by the window."

Eden watched while Jackson obediently walked over to the far window and put down the tray.

"Will there be anything else?" asked Jackson.

Noah rose to his feet and walked from behind his desk, "No thank you. I will call you if I need anything."

Jackson left the room. Noah walked over to the table and took a seat. "Well... are you going to join me?" Noah asked, turning around.

Eden found Noah Ainsworth seriously annoying and intriguing at the same time. He was certainly unpredictable. She made her way over to the table and took a chair looking out onto the property grounds.

Noah poured the tea and handed Eden a cup. "Please, help yourself to sugar."

For a minute or so, an uncomfortable silence ensued until Noah broke the silence, "Eden, may I ask you a question?"

"Of course, what would you like to know?"

Noah walked around the library. Eden sipped at her tea, nervously awaiting his question. "Before they assigned you this interview, how much did you know about me?"

Eden felt embarrassed. She was not sure how to answer the question. In truth, she did not know of him before her assignment.

She turned to face him and drew in a deep breath, "I knew nothing about you before this interview. Only what my brief Google search revealed to me," she admitted.

Noah surveyed her embarrassment and flushed cheeks, "Mmm, that's interesting. So, no pre-conceived ideas about me then. I like that. As unusual as that it is to hear."

He walked over to Eden and extended his hand. She placed her hand in his and rose from her chair. "I have never liked interviews. I find them... well, intrusive at best. That is why I rarely agree to them. However, I have been coerced into this one by my management team. They believe I need to project a more—shall we say, approachable side. Good for business relations, they insisted. I have the best business management team in the UK, I believe. So, I reluctantly agreed. However, let's dispense with the boring questions, which I don't want to hear, and I am sure you are not too happy with. I am guessing that if you had a free reign that list of questions would look much different! Come on, I will show you around my house and we can talk along the way. It will be far more interesting for us both," he suggested sporting a wry smile.

Eden followed behind Noah into the dining hall. Her mouth fell open on sight of it.

"As grand as this room is, I can honestly say that I have never eaten or entertained in here," revealed Noah.

Eden's eyes trailed the width and breadth of the vast hall before her. She could almost imagine it filled with life. Then she turned to Noah, "May I ask why?"

"I feel more at home in the kitchen with Jackson and my cook."

Noah's response surprised Eden. *I was not expecting that in a million years. It does not fit with my image of him at all.* She made her way towards the large windows framed by the most elegant drapes she had ever seen, "Would you mind if I look around?" she asked.

"Go ahead, take as long as you like. I need to step out for a moment. I will be back shortly," advised Noah while leaving the room.

Eden glided her hand along the elegant-polished table until she reached the far end. She pulled out the high-back, ornamental chair and seated herself.

She glanced ahead and smiled, "Wow! This is incredible," she whispered under her breath. She heard the doors creak open and leapt from the chair nervously.

"It suits you," commented Noah as he approached Eden.

"I'm sorry. My curiosity got the better of me!" she confessed.

Noah paused briefly, holding her gaze before breaking off and turning around. "Come on, we have much ground to cover.

Eden hurried to keep pace with Noah heading down the corridor.

He took a swift right and then left down a few steps and through another set of less elegant doors.

"This is one of my favourite hideaways," he said while entering the kitchen.

A plump, friendly faced woman spun around with a wooden spoon-in-hand, "This is Betty, my cook," he introduced.

Eden smiled at Betty, "Hello, pleased to meet you."

Noah looked at Eden, "Take a seat. You are in for a culinary surprise. I took it upon myself to organise a late lunch for us."

Eden listened while Noah bantered comfortably with Betty. She noticed a more natural side to him emerging, a side she preferred.

"So, Eden–the fact that you are sitting here in my kitchen means Noah approves of you. This is quite rare, by the way," winked Betty.

"That's enough Betty," piped Noah, cutting her off.

"His bark is far worse than his bite. Don't allow him to intimidate you, Eden," Betty smiled mischievously and continued to serve up lunch. She added, "The dressing is my own secret recipe," she revealed while placing a dish in front of Eden proudly.

"It looks amazing, Betty," replied Eden.

Noah chimed in, "All salad and vegetables are sourced from right here at Ainsworth House. Carter, my grounds keeper is responsible. He is completely dedicated to fresh, home-grown produce. I am incredibly lucky to have found him."

"Maybe you need to tell him that from time to time, Noah!" piped Betty.

Noah's brows furrowed, and he scowled at Betty.

"I'm just saying," she finished before leaving the kitchen.

Eden was not expecting the day to turn out the way it did. *After everything I have heard about Noah, I half expected to be thrown off his property at some point during the day. Although, I sense he is secretive and there is probably no one who truly knows Noah Ainsworth completely. There is a huge invisible wall surrounding him, and it is the reason behind the wall that I am most curious about,* she thought.

"I need to walk the grounds for a short while after lunch. Duke will be getting anxious about now. You can stay here if you prefer, or you can join us. It will give you an opportunity to see the gardens," blurted

Noah. He added, "I thought a photographer was accompanying you today?"

Eden searched his curious eyes, "Yes, that's right, Stephen will join us later. Before he arrives, is there any area that is off limits to him?"

"Yes, the whole of the top floor. He is free to photograph the primary rooms on the first and second floor, however, he will be accompanied by one of my security men at all times," advised Noah.

Eden gave a half smile, "That's fine. I will send him a message advising him of that just in case he arrives after I leave. And yes, I will join you in the gardens. I could do with some fresh air myself. It is really hot today."

"That's settled then. While you are finishing your lunch, I will get Duke," commented Noah. He kicked back his chair and left the kitchen.

Eden was puzzled, *who is Duke? Maybe his son? I don't recall anyone mentioning he was a father. I certainly did not read about it anywhere,* she wondered. She finished her glass of wine. After washing her hands, she stood by the window waiting for Noah to return.

The kitchen door swung open, and Betty walked through. "Noah is waiting for you outside the main entrance with Duke. He must like you; he has never brought anyone into my kitchen before. And believe me, that is a big thing for him. He is not much of a people person. However, if you dig deep enough, you will discover an incredible person below his tough exterior. Enjoy the gardens and hopefully, we shall meet again, Eden." Betty continued to prepare for dinner.

Eden left the kitchen. She found her way to the entrance. She opened the doors and caught sight of Noah walking with a dog. Her lips curled into a smile, *well... I never saw that one coming!*

"Eden, meet Duke. My most loyal and trusted friend."

Eden knelt down and held out her hand, "Hello Duke. You are a beautiful one." Duke limped up to her and licked her hand ferociously. He sniffed all around her curiously and then limped off, attempting to run on his sore foot.

"Duke is a beautiful dog. What breed is he?"

Noah smiled, "He certainly likes you. Duke is a Siberian Husky. He is almost four years old. I have had him since he was 6 months old. Let's just say that we kind of found each other. Come on, I will take you down to my lake. It is really peaceful down there and Duke loves it."

Eden walked alongside Noah with a comfortable ease that surprised her. The warmth of the sun enveloped her shoulders and the only thing ruining the walk was her unsuitable heels. She stopped, slipped off her shoes and held them in her hand, swinging them as she walked. Noah paused and glanced down at her feet. Eden realised that it may be inappropriate and put them back on again.

Noah shook his head, "Please, if you are more comfortable barefooted then don't mind me." he assured her.

Noah liked Eden. She was not the superficial journalist he had been expecting, as most of them were. There was an air of innocence about her and a naivety he had rarely seen. *There is nothing superficial about Eden Marshall,* he surmised.

"What happened to Duke's foot?" enquired Eden.

"He stumbled over a rock on the far side of the lake a few days ago, while chasing a duck. Nothing is broken, just a slight sprain according to the vet. He was kept indoors for a few days and it drove him insane. He likes to be outside. He will be back up and running in no time."

Eden watched as Noah ran off ahead to catch up with Duke, who was rolling around on the bank of the lake. Noah lay down beside him and a rough and tumble ensued. Eden watched in awe and could not match the Noah before her to his public profile. They were quite different people. It was as if she was with a completely different person. She guessed that she had been given a glimpse of the real Noah Ainsworth, rarely witnessed by outsiders.

Noah climbed to his feet and Duke headed straight into the lake, "Duke, not now!" shouted Noah.

Eden laughed while watching Duke swimming around in the lake happily.

"I don't blame him, that's exactly what Bella would do, and I would probably have joined her too!" piped Eden.

She added, "It is so hot today, touching 30 degrees. Let Duke swim in the lake for a while. It will cool him down. If I were out with Bella today and had a lake at my disposal, I would jump in there without question!" she admitted while turning away from Noah and fixing her eyes on Duke splashing in the lake.

"Oh, I see—a rebel is in my midst!"

Without warning, Noah snuck up behind her, picked her up and threw her into the lake!

Duke swam up to her, Eden emerged aghast!

Eden swept her hair back off her face, "Oh my God! I cannot believe you just did that..." she added, "Well, I am here now. She turned her back on Noah and splashed about with Duke for a while before emerging from the lake, dripping wet followed by Duke. Noah noticed the way Eden's dress clung to the curves of her body, revealing her toned silhouette beneath it. His eyes shifted swiftly to Duke and he smiled while Duke shook the water off his fur.

Eden turned to Noah, "I am guessing you have a towel that I can use?"

A discreet smile emerged from Noah's lips, "Of course! There are also clean clothes for you to change into," he offered.

Noah called Duke to his side, but he ignored him and waddled up beside Eden, nudging her hand.

"Traitor," blurted Noah.

Eden ruffled Duke's head, "Hey Duke that was fun, right." Duke barked and continued walking alongside Eden until they reached the house.

Noah extended his hand, leading Eden around the side of the house. He paused at an old wooden door allowing Eden to walk through first. Noah closed the door behind him, and a stout woman appeared from another room.

"Eden, this is my housekeeper, Esther. She will see to you."

Noah turned to his housekeeper, "Esther, please escort Miss Marshall to the guest suite on the second floor. She will need towels and a change of clothes," instructed Noah.

Esther nodded and indicated for Eden to follow her.

Eden turned to Noah, "Thank you."

"I will be waiting in the library when you are ready," advised Noah while heading towards another room at the far end of the corridor.

Eden upped her pace to keep up with Esther, "I bet Noah keeps you busy?" said Eden, attempting to be friendly.

"Mr. Ainsworth is an articulate man who likes things just so," replied Esther curtly, not turning around.

Detecting Esther was not the conversational type, Eden followed her the rest of the way in silence.

"Here we are, Miss Marshall. Would you like me to run you a shower or bath?"

Eden studied Esther's expressionless face briefly. "Mmm, no thank you. Just a towel and some dry clothes will be fine. I can shower once I get home," she advised.

"As you wish," replied Esther.

Esther pushed open the large double doors, which revealed an impressive, high-ceiling room. Eden stepped inside and glanced around. "Wow, this is beautiful!"

Esther passed two large, embossed towels to Eden, "The bathroom is through that door and the closet is through those doors at the far end of the room. Take your pick. The closet is well-stocked with various sizes and all garments are new. Mr. Ainsworth likes to be prepared for every eventuality. I see that in this instance his foresight has paid off. I shall leave you to dry off and change. If you need anything, just press that button over there," she pointed.

Eden waited until Esther left the room and then flung herself down onto the super-sized four-poster bed. She clutched the beautiful, silk throw in her hand and closed her eyes briefly; "Who lives like this... it's not real!" she said aloud. She climbed off the bed and walked over to the double doors leading to the closet. What was waiting for her behind the doors was nothing short of exasperating? Eden pushed open the large heavy doors and stood back with her jaw-dropped, "Oh my God... This isn't a closet! This is a department store. Her eyes trailed the clothes rails and shoe racks set out elegantly before her. Noah had thought of everything. There was a choice of sizes in every outfit, every shoe size imaginable and accessory display cabinet covering everything from belts, jewellery, and handbags.

"I must be dreaming," she mumbled while walking over to a rail filled with dresses of every style and for every occasion. She flicked through the rail until a pretty summer dress caught her eye. It was a simple, white brocade, knee-length dress with thin straps. Perfect for a sizzling summer day. She searched for her size and slipped it on. Eden spent the next ten minutes trying on some of the beautiful shoes displayed in the shoe racks. She settled on a white and baby blue, mid-heal, sling-back sandal and reached for a thin blue belt from the cabinet, which matched the blue in the sandals perfectly. She walked over to the large, opulent lean-to mirror resting against the back wall and ran her fingers down the sides of the dress. Her eyes rested on her hair and she gasped. She wrapped it around her fingers with one hand and searched through the drawers with the other until she found a hair clip. After securing her hair in a knot at the nape of her neck, she headed down to the library.

Noah paced the wooden floors of his library impatiently. He spun around when the doors creaked open and drew in a deep breath on sight of Eden. His eyes widened as she emerged before him. Noah was speechless and he could find no words.

"I see you have found something that fits," he commented.

Eden looked down at her dress and then back to Noah nervously, "yes, thank you. You have an impressive collection of clothes in the guest suite. I will be sure to have it cleaned and returned to you."

"There is no need. The dress is yours."

Noah turned to the window, not saying a word. He then turned back to Eden, "Well, I think this concludes our interview for today. We shall reconvene tomorrow if that suits your schedule," he advised.

Eden was surprised and expecting to continue with the interview for a while longer. "That's fine with me. I enjoyed your lovely house today, but the highlight for me was, Duke! Is there anything about today you would rather I did not include in my write-up?" she asked.

"I think it's safe to assume that throwing you in my lake would be best left out of the interview!" he suggested.

"Sure. Consider it done," she smiled. Then added, "What about the photographer, he will arrive soon?"

Noah's finger traced over his right brow, "The photographer will not need me. My security men will assist him during his visit."

"Okay, if you are sure." Eden reached for her handbag and then turned to Noah, "Well, I will be going now. What time should I be here tomorrow?"

Noah did not reply straight away. He pressed a button and remained silent. Eden shifted on her feet, awkwardly awaiting his reply. The doors to the library opened and a man walked in wearing a tailor-made suit and a crisp white shirt.

"Ah, Max, I would like you to meet, Miss Eden Marshall."

Max walked over to Eden and shook her hand, "Pleased to meet you, Eden."

"Likewise, Max," she replied.

Noah chimed in, "Max is my personal business manager and takes care of everything for me. He will assure that you have the time you need to conduct your interview with me over the coming days. We shall continue the interview at 11 a.m. tomorrow. Assuming that works for you?"

Eden gave a half smile, "Yes 11 a.m. works for me."

Noah turned to Max; it was clear that Max was not impressed. "Please cancel tomorrow's conference call. You can reschedule for later in the week." Noah glared at Max.

Max raised an eyebrow.

"That will be all Max. Thank you." Max left the room and Noah continued, "You must excuse Max, he does not like my schedule to be upended so abruptly."

"You really don't have to re-arrange your schedule. I am happy to work around it," suggested Eden.

"It's done now. I shall see you here at 11 a.m. tomorrow morning and bring some flat shoes," insisted Noah.

Eden made her way to the door and Noah halted her, "Eden, bring Bella with you tomorrow. Duke could do with some like-minded company," he demanded before turning around and picking up his mobile phone. Eden offered a nervous smile and then left the library.

Jackson was waiting in the atrium for Eden. He guided her out of the door silently. Eden thanked Jackson and headed to her car. She paused before climbing in, her eyes trailed over the colossal building before her, *not what I was expecting at all! I cannot figure Noah Ainsworth out. He is an enigma...*

FIVE

oah wound up his conference call with his New York office and reclined in his chair. Max appeared disgruntled and paced the floor, "Okay Max, what's on your mind?" demanded Noah.

"I don't like it - there I've said it. I think that on this occasion you are making a mistake, Noah. I have always been honest with you, and I think Jim Peters is the wrong person to head the New York office. I do not trust him. He is not the right replacement for Jeremy."

Noah jumped off his seat, walked over to the bar, and poured himself a whisky. He sipped at it slowly while pondering over Max's words. "Why, Max?"

Noah's face hardened. A look that Max knew all too well–Max nervously cleared his throat. "Well, the word from New York is that Jim cannot be trusted. He sold out his last company. This did not come up in our searches at the time and that is why I am just hearing about it now."

Noah studied Max briefly, "So, you are telling me that Jim has been in my employ for three years and you are only finding this out about him now?" roared Noah.

Noah added, "Jim Peters has been an asset to Ainsworth Global over the last three years, nothing he has done suggests any foul play as far as I can see. I have ears to the ground on every single person in my employ and not once has Jim Peters name come up negatively. However, I do not doubt you, Max. What I suggest is that Jim Peters is kept a close eye on. If you find anything that suggests he is a liability to Ainsworth Global, then I want to be the first to know. Keep your eyes and ears to the ground and make sure your connections in New York do the same."

Noah turned his back on Max and Max left the room without saying another word. He knew Noah needed to digest this latest information. He was a thinker, a forward planner and where business was concerned, he never acted on impulse. He was a meticulous planner and thought everything through to the very last detail before taking action. Noah Ainsworth did not make mistakes.

Noah called Duke, who came bounding over excitedly. He knew it was time for a walk and ran in and out of Noah's legs, "Come on Duke, I need some fresh air."

Noah walked the footpaths through his land for over two hours. Eden Marshall dominated his thoughts. It had been a long time since anything, but work had dominated his mind. He could not get her out of his head. Her piercing blue eyes hypnotised him. The genuine innocence of her smile and her naivety were spellbinding. *Eden Marshall— now you, I was not expecting.*

Noah's thoughts drifted back in time—a time he wished he could erase from his memory bank. He stopped abruptly in his tracks, massaging his temples with the tips of his fingers. The intense pain was tearing through him, crippling him. He stood rooted to the spot until the pain subsided and then continued to catch up with Duke. His crippling headaches were a constant reminder that his life could end at any given moment. Snapshots of his past flashed before him. The unexpected series of events that took place three years before. He had not seen them coming—he walked in blind to the most horrific scene imaginable. The signs had eluded him, but they were all around him. Keeping it out of the press was down to his trusted manager and friend, Max. He knew Max had curtailed a public circus of events and for that, he was forever grateful to him.

Duke came bounding up to him, "There you are. Come on boy, it's time we went home. Duke heeled and remained by Noah's side all the way home. Duke could always sense when Noah was in pain. He became protective and refused to leave his side.

Duke helped him through the worst time of his life. With the sudden reminders of that period in his life, Noah pushed all thoughts of Eden out of his head. He would never allow another woman to get that close to him again.

Jackson was waiting for Noah when he entered through the side door. "Jackson, could you see to Duke for me and get me my tablets please," asked Noah while rubbing his forehead.

"Of course, Mr. Ainsworth. Are you feeling okay?"

"Just my usual headaches, Jackson. I will be fine."

Noah made his way upstairs to the top floor where his bedroom was situated down the corridor from his offices. He sat down on his bed and cradled his head in his hands for some time.

Jackson appeared with a tray. "Here you go, Mr. Ainsworth. This should sort you out in no time. If there is anything else that I can do -"

Noah cut Jackson off mid-speech, "Thank you, Jackson. I think I will have an early night."

Jackson nodded and left the room. Noah swallowed his tablet with a little water and lay down until his throbbing headache subsided. Twenty minutes later, he was feeling much better and headed to his shower room. He slipped off his clothes and stepped into the wet room. He turned on all three shower heads and placed his hands against the marble-tiled walls. His cultivated body pressed hard against his hands while the warm water cascaded over his broad, muscular shoulders. He stood up straight and washed himself down before stepping out of the shower and reaching for his towel. His stomach was rumbling now. He was feeling much better and realised that he had not eaten since lunch. Changing his mind, he headed for the kitchen.

"Noah! Jackson said you were having an early night?" questioned Betty.

"I changed my mind. I took a shower, and it woke me up. So, what's for dinner?"

Betty's lips curved into a smile, "Homemade steak and kidney pudding."

Noah sat down while Betty dished up dinner for them both and Jackson. Betty sat opposite Noah and studied him curiously, "Are you okay, Noah? You don't seem yourself this evening."

"I'm fine, Betty, really. There is no need for concern. Nothing a good meal and conversation with two of my favourite people won't cure!"

Betty knew that Noah meant what he said. He always ate his meals with Betty and Jackson. This was one of the things Betty and Jackson loved about him. Noah was not pretentious at all. He was most comfortable in the kitchen and strolling his land with Duke. He was not much of a people person. Mainly because most people in his opinion always had an agenda and he was finding genuine people were becoming increasingly rare. Betty often advised him that this was due to his position in life. Betty was like the grandmother he never had. At 62 years old, she was wise and made sense of most things for Noah with her humble wisdom. Jackson, on the other hand, was a man of few words—but when he did offer pearls of wisdom, they were powerful and long-lasting.

Noah was a different man these past three years. Betty and Jackson have witnessed his dramatic change. They had been in Noah's employ for over eight years and stood by him through the worst time of his life. He trusted Betty and Jackson above anyone else.

"Eden is a beautiful young lady, Noah. Will she be coming back?" pressed Betty.

Noah's brows knitted together, "Betty, she is just a journalist. She will be conducting her interview for Imperial Home Magazine over the next few days. So yes, she will be coming back," he replied curtly.

"Mmm, Just a journalist—got it!" commented Betty sporting a mischievous grin.

Noah did not engage Betty in further comments and Jackson glared at Betty, willing her to be quiet. Betty began humming to herself while clearing the table.

Noah turned to Jackson, "You have taken none of your holidays this year, Jackson— why?"

"Well, I have not felt the need to. As you know, I do not have any family of my own. I prefer to spend my time reading on my day off or walking the fields. I am not much of a socialiser. I consider you and Betty my family."

Noah looked at Jackson endearingly, "I am very lucky to have found you, Jackson." Noah gave him an affectionate slap on the back and left the room.

SIX

*E*den lay curled up on her sofa stroking Bella lying beside her. Noah dominated her mind and raised a smile on her face. Her phone ringing interrupted her thoughts. She picked it up off her coffee table and swiped to answer, "Eden, it's Blake. How did it go today?"

"Blake! What a surprise."

"Sorry Eden, I couldn't wait until tomorrow."

Eden climbed off her sofa and paced the room. "Well, it went far better than I expected. Although, Mr. Ainsworth certainly guides the interview his way. He is an extremely intriguing man, to say the least. I did as you advised and allowed him to lead the interview. He showed me around part of the house and then we walked around his gardens with his dog, Duke. Like you said, he is extremely private and gives very little away regarding his private life. He has asked me to come back tomorrow to continue the interview."

"This is great news, Eden. Did Stephen capture the best of the house? We need some impressive images for the feature as we have reserved the centre spread for Mr. Ainsworth."

"I believe so. Stephen sent me a message as he arrived after I left. From what I can tell, he did an astounding job. Apparently, Stephen said that Mr. Ainsworth security guided him around the parts of the house that were accessible to him. The whole of the top floor of his house was off limits, though."

"Okay, thanks, Eden. I will catch up with Stephen tomorrow at the office. It appears that Mr. Ainsworth is comfortable with you. I knew you were the right person for this. Great job and keep up the excellent work. What time will you be heading over to Ainsworth House tomorrow?"

"Eleven a.m. Do you want me to come into the office first?"

"No, I suggest you prepare well for the interview and head straight over there. Call me when you are done," finished Blake.

"Sure, will do. Speak to you tomorrow." Eden placed her phone on charge and wandered into the kitchen to pour herself a glass of wine. Her glass almost dropped from her hand when her phone began ringing once more startling her. She put her glass down, hurried to the living room, and reached for the phone off the table, "Hello."

"Hey Eden, its Angie. Sorry to call you so late. Nevertheless, I could not wait until tomorrow. So how did it go today?"

Eden slumped down in her chair and rested her feet on the footstool, "Well, Mr. Ainsworth is an exceptionally intriguing man. He didn't throw me off his property, so I guess you can say it went well."

Angie huffed, "Oh, come on, you can give me more than that."

Eden laughed down the phone, "Okay, well, mmm–"

Angie cut her off mic-sentence, "Oh my God, you like him!"

"I do not... well, not in the way you're thinking anyway. Yes, Noah Ainsworth is, well, fascinating and very mysterious. He is captivating."

"You like him, Eden. Just admit it. I can't say I blame you. If anything, I am seriously jealous. Those eyes of his are mesmerising to say the least."

Eden piped up, "Are you quite finished. He is attractive and yes, I will admit he has my attention. You should see his house, Angie. I have never seen anything like it in my life. It surprised me to discover that he is not as standoffish as his public persona portrays him to be. In fact, there is quite a warm, down to earth side to Noah, that I am guessing rarely emerges outside Ainsworth House. Anyway, I hope that satisfies your curiosity. I am going to drink my wine and unwind now. I will catch up with you at the office," finished Eden.

"You bet your ass you will!" said Angie.

Eden leapt to her feet, made her way to the kitchen, and retrieved her glass of wine from the countertop. She took a large gulp and once again, Noah Ainsworth dominated her mind, sending tingles down her spine. She sipped at her wine and then closed her eyes briefly, fixating on the contours of Noah's chest. She recalled his fitted, crisp white shirt clinging to his chiselled form. She felt the hairs on the back of her neck stand on their ends and inhaled a deep breath.

Bella thrust Eden back to reality with a nudge. "Okay, Bella, just a quick walk. You will have plenty of time to run around tomorrow. You have been summoned to Ainsworth House no less." Bella barked and spun around eagerly. Eden grabbed Bella's lead, clipped it on, and then headed out of the door. She walked Bella around the village for 30 mins and headed back home. *Tomorrow is another intense day at Ainsworth House, and I want to finalise the interview. With it being Friday, it would be a perfect way to end my week,* she decided.

Eden's mobile phone vibrated on the kitchen worktop. She glanced at the message flashing across the screen. It was Jacob's sister. She swiped the screen and read the message:

Hi Eden, just checking you were still on for Saturday.

Ping me a message to confirm. Love Laura. X

She replied swiftly and confirmed she was going to visit Jacob's grave. A sense of foreboding swept through her veins like a tidal wave. She left her phone on the table and made her way upstairs for a much-needed shower. All good feelings of her day dissolved and a dark cloud looming reminding her of Jacobs's premature death superseded them. Feelings of that day gripped her like a vice. She brushed away a tear with the stroke of her hand and stepped into the shower.

Today is the first day that I have not thought about Jacob once— until now. Ordinarily, Jacob flashes through my mind at least ten times a day. It is time I moved on for my own sanity. Jacob's gone and I am still here... she concluded.

SEVEN

*R*ight after the conference call with the New York office, Noah headed downstairs, leaving Max with a list of instructions to execute immediately. He was agitated, as things were not going well. He paced up and down, mulling things over in his mind. Duke paced the floor with him while attempting to nudge his hand. Noah glanced at his loyal companion and smiled, "You are right, Duke. Let's get some fresh air before Miss Marshall arrives. Maybe it will clear my head and present me with some clarity."

Noah was just about to exit the main entrance doors with Duke, when Max came bounding down the stairs, "Noah, we need you upstairs–NOW!" he urged.

"What's the problem, Max?" Noah pressed, turning around.

Max's brows furrowed, "It's Caspian Communications– they have just released a new primetime Ad that challenges Ainsworth Global Communications directly..." Max paused and recoiled at Noah's fearsome expression. He noticed the vein popping out of his neck.

Noah raged, "DAMN YOU CASPIAN!"

He took the stairs two by two until he reached his office with Max trailing behind.

"Caspian has everyone in the business talking about this one,

Noah. We cannot ignore it. We need to come up with a counter Ad ASAP," urged Max.

Noah watched Caspian Communications' latest advert playing out on primetime television. It was a direct insult to Ainsworth Global Communications and a personal insult to Noah. He watched the advert unfold before his eyes. He clenched his fist and slammed it down hard on the table. He rose to his feet and turned to Max, "I want you to round up the marketing team right now. We shall reconvene in one hour," ordered Noah.

The doors opened and Jackson stepped in, "Miss Marshall has arrived and is waiting in the library."

Jackson's words did not register. Noah stared right through Jackson.

"Mr. Ainsworth...?" pressed Jackson.

Noah ignored Jackson and turned to face Max, "NOW MAX. What are you waiting for? I need the team assembled ASAP. Caspian will regret making a mockery of me," he roared. Then he turned his attention back to Jackson, lowering his tone, "Thank you, Jackson. Please advise Miss Marshall I am on my way."

Eden paced the library; *I am more nervous than I thought I would be today.* Bella made herself at home and plonked down onto the hearthrug. *I need to delve a little further into Noah's personal life. I have no idea what kind of response I will receive. You got this, Eden,* she thought. The door bursting open startled her.

"Miss Marshall, I'm afraid I will have to postpone our interview today. We can continue next week." Noah paused and handed Eden a business card. She looked at it and noticed it was his business manager's card and not his own personal card. Noah continued, "Please call Max directly to rearrange an appointment for next week. Sorry for any inconvenience. I trust you know your way out?"

Bella caught Noah's eye. He knelt down and ruffled Bella's ears. "Sorry, girl." He turned on his heel and left as quickly as he arrived.

Eden stood alone in the vast library, feeling annoyed. A different Noah presented himself today and one she did not care for too much either. Eden picked up her bag and turned to Bella, "Come on, time to go." Bella jumped up reluctantly and followed behind her as they exited the library. She smiled on sight of Betty approaching her.

"You can't leave just yet. I have cooked you and Mr. Ainsworth lunch and prepared a little feast for Bella too."

Eden walked over to Betty, "I'm sorry, Betty. Noah has cancelled our interview for this afternoon."

Betty whispered, "Well... I don't like to see decent food go to waste. There is no reason why you cannot stay for lunch. Come on, I insist."

Eden followed Betty through to the kitchen where Jackson and Carter were already seated. Duke was lying down at the far end. He sprung to his feet on sight of Bella. Bella ambled over to Duke and allowed him to circle her before lying down. Eden smiled while seating herself at the table. Jackson glanced at her curiously and then continued eating.

"Don't let Jackson intimidate you. He is a man of few words and a puppy at heart," Betty winked at Jackson and turned her attention to the array of pots on her worktop.

"I'm not sure about this, Betty. I got the distinct impression that Mr. Ainsworth wanted me to leave."

Betty served a plate of creamy pasta in front of Eden and chimed in, "Don't mind Noah. I had already cooked you both lunch and I shall tell him I bullied you into staying. How's that?" Betty playfully nudged Eden's arm, plates up some pasta for herself, and sat down beside her. Eden's eyes rest on Bella and Duke, raising a smile on her face.

Carter piped up, "Looks like they have hit it off."

Eden agreed, "They sure have. It's a shame they did not get to run the fields together today."

Betty chimed in, "Well, I am sure you could take them for a quick run after you finish your dinner. Duke still needs walking. He's already missed his morning walk."

Eden pondered on Betty's suggestion, "I guess I could, Bella is certainly going to need a run too after that dinner."

"Well then, that's settled."

Jackson whispered in Betty's ear, "I know what you are trying to do. Stop meddling. Mr. Ainsworth won't thank you for it..."

"Oh, be quiet, Jackson. If left to his own devices, Noah will grow old alone. A little direction is all he needs."

Eden could not make out what Betty and Jackson were whispering about. She finished her dinner and turned her attention to Carter, "Do you know where Duke's lead is?"

Carter pointed towards the hook on the back of the kitchen door. Eden took Bella's lead out of her handbag and reached for Duke's lead off the door hook.

"You won't need the leads," said Jackson. "Duke does not like being leashed. All the land you can see is owned by Mr. Ainsworth—no need for leashes," he reiterated.

"Thank you, Jackson. It's just precautionary in case we run into strays or foxes." Eden stood by the back door and called Bella and Duke. They both jumped up excitedly and left with Eden.

Betty observed Eden for a few moments and sighed, "She would be perfect for Noah if only he could see it too."

"Jackson's right, Betty. You should not interfere with Mr. Ainsworth's personal life," advised Carter. He added, "After everything that happened to him three years ago, a woman is the last thing he needs in his life. He is better off alone, in my opinion."

Betty turned around after closing the door, "You are talking rubbish, Carter. Noah has no idea what is good for him. He has locked himself away from the world and barely leaves this over-sized house. That is no life for a young man. He is just scared, that's all and who can blame him. Noah is like the son I never had, and a little helping hand now and then won't hurt anyone."

Jackson and Carter shook their heads and dug into their dessert. They knew when to shut up! Once Betty started on something, there was no stopping her.

Eden's lips curved into a smile while watching Bella and Duke playfully chasing each other across the fields. *I cannot believe how well they have taken to one another*, she mused. Glancing across Noah's land as far as her eyes could see, Eden gasped as the green land merged with the blue sky in the distance. *Wow! This is awe-inspiring and completely breath-taking*, she thought. After an hour of walking, she checked the time on her mobile phone, "Bella, Duke..." she shouted. Hearing their barks in the distance, she made her way back to the house. Bella and Duke caught up with her and walked alongside.

Noah stepped into the kitchen and searched for Duke, "Where's Duke, Betty?"

Betty sheepishly lowered her eyes. Jackson and Carter decided it was time to vacate the kitchen fast!

"Mmm, well, Duke is out walking with Miss Marshall and Bella. I insisted they stay for lunch as I had already prepared it before you cancelled your appointment with her. I don't like to see good food go to waste."

Noah's face hardened, "Betty, I know you think you are doing right by me, but please, don't interfere with my personal life. I have no interest in Eden Marshall and never will have." Betty's eyes darted towards the back door and then back to Noah. He spun around and saw Eden standing in the open doorway. Duke and Bella strolled in and plonked themselves down on the floor. Noah glared at Betty. Betty hurried out of the kitchen. Eden did not react. She placed Duke's lead on the hook and called Bella to her side.

"I shall leave, now. Please thank Betty for a lovely lunch. I will be in touch with Max about wrapping up our interview next week." Eden reached for her bag off the chair and left. Jackson was waiting outside. He led her towards the front entrance.

"Thank you, Jackson."

Jackson offered Eden a sympathetic smile and closed the door behind her.

Noah remained rooted to the spot in the kitchen. *Damn it... I should have chosen my words more carefully.*

EIGHT

*E*den forced all thoughts of Noah Ainsworth from her mind. *Like I would be interested, anyway. Who the hell does he think he is?* She cursed while banging around in her kitchen, feeling agitated by his comments to Betty the day before. She buttered her toast and ate it hurriedly, knowing that Laura was due to pick her up at any moment. Bella weaved in and out of her legs, almost tripping Eden over.

"Sorry, Bella, I have to go out this morning. No walk for you until later. Come on, you can go in the garden for a few minutes, but make it quick or you will have to hold it in until I get home." Bella jumped up and down. She followed Eden to the back door and ran out as soon as Eden opened it. Eden ran upstairs and made a quick change into a simple, knee-length summer dress. It was hot outside, and she could already feel the heat from the summer sun. Alerted by the doorbell ringing, she ran downstairs and opened the door.

"Morning Eden. Are you ready?" greeted Laura.

"Almost. Just let me call Bella in from the garden."

After getting Bella in and locking up the house, she left for the cemetery with Laura.

"So, how are you feeling about today?" pressed Laura.

"To be honest, I'm not sure. I am confused right now. I need to see Jacob and yet I feel as if I need to let him go too. I am also feeling guilty for wanting to get on with my life by moving on. If that makes any sense," confessed Eden.

Laura placed her hand on Eden's arm, "Look, Eden, I know how much you loved my brother. I also know how much he loved you despite his affair. He knew he had made a mistake–a huge one. However, I agree, you and you do need to move on with your life. You are young and beautiful with your whole life ahead of you. There is someone out there for you. Someone that will treat you the way you deserve to be treated. It was unforgivable what Jacob did to you. I know I would not be so forgiving if I were in your shoes."

Eden remained silent while pondering her thoughts. "I have to ask Laura– have you seen Jacob's baby?"

Laura shifted uncomfortably in her seat. "Yes, I have seen Jacob's son. I didn't tell you before because you were in mourning and I didn't want to upset you."

"He has a son?" chimed in Eden. She paused and turned to glance out of the window, discreetly catching a tear emerging down her cheek.

"He is called Simon and was born three months after Jacob passed. He is adorable and looks just like Jacob. I stay in touch with my nephew's family so that I can remain close to Simon. He is the only connection I have to Jacob now," Laura explained.

Eden looked at Laura, "I fully understand. I would have done the same in your position. It was a difficult time for all of us. I am just happy Jacob gets to live on in his son."

Laura took a right, then an immediate left, and drove through the wrought-iron gates leading to the vast cemetery. She parked up her car and they both climbed out.

Eden sighed, "I can't believe it has been a year already. I am going to say my last goodbye to Jacob today. This is going to be my last visit."

"I understand and I think you are doing the right thing. You really do need to move on. I will let you have some private time before we leave today."

Laura knelt down in front of Jacob's grave. She began clearing the dead flowers away and replaced them with fresh cut summer flowers. "I miss you, Jacob. I wish you could have seen your son just once. He is the image of you." She climbed to her feet, placed her hand on Eden's arm and then made her way back to her car. Eden inched closer and remained in quiet contemplation for some time. Tears shimmered in her eyes, "Jacob, I need to let you go now. I really loved you, despite everything that happened in the end. I hope you are in a good place. You will always hold a special place in my heart. I just want you to know that I forgive you." Eden stood up, leaned forward, and placed a kiss on the top of Jacob's gravestone. "Goodbye, Jacob." She wiped her tears away with a brush of her hand and headed back to Laura's car.

"You okay?" queried Laura.

"Actually, I am. I think I am going to be just fine," assured Eden.

Laura turned to Eden, "So, what now for you?"

"Well, I received a promotion at work, so I will throw myself into that for the time being. As for my personal life—I have no idea right now. But one thing I do know for sure is that I need a long, overdue holiday."

"Well, I can't disagree with that," agreed Laura.

Laura dropped Eden home with a promise to stay in touch. Eden felt freer than she had since Jacob's death. Bella greeted her excitedly at the door. She collected her post off the floor and ambled into the kitchen while flicking through her letters. Not expecting any visitors, she almost dropped them when the doorbell whistled through her house. She placed her letters down on the worktop and headed for the door.

"A delivery for Miss Marshall," greeted the young man holding a beautiful spray of flowers. He continued, "Please sign here," he pointed.

Eden's eyes widened. She signed for the flowers and took the card out from the top. She closed the door behind her, peered at the card, and read it.

> To Miss Marshall,
> Sorry.
> N.A.

"SORRY," she shouted. She stomped off into the kitchen and placed the flowers down on the table. She fumbled in her lower cupboard for a vase. "This will do. He could have at least signed it,

Noah, or Mr. Ainsworth... But no, that would have been too personal for him," she cursed aloud.

Eden spent some time arranging the flowers in her vase and then put them on the window ledge in her living room. *Seriously, this man has issues!* She surmised. Eden was just about to head upstairs to change when she heard someone flicking her letter box repeatedly. "What the hell..." she mumbled.

She opened the door and glanced down. Her mouth curved into a smile and Bella came running past her, barking happily.

"So, what do I owe the pleasure, Duke?" Duke barked and followed Bella into the house. Leaving Eden standing on the doorstep searching for Noah, who was nowhere to be seen. Then she spotted an off-roader parked on the far side of the street. The driver's window wound down to reveal Noah. Eden had no idea how to react or what to say. She was completely dumbfounded.

"Is it safe to step out of my car?" shouted Noah from across the street.

Eden rolled her eyes. She shrugged her shoulders, turned around and entered her house, leaving the front door wide open. Noah smiled to himself and climbed out of the car. He walked up the path to Eden's front door and paused, unsure whether to enter. Eden hollered from the kitchen, "Well, are you going to stand there all day?"

Noah closed the door behind him and wandered through to the kitchen. Not turning around, Eden continued with what she was doing. Then she spun around and glared at Noah, "How did you know where I lived?" she blurted.

"You were not difficult to locate. I have my ways."

"Of course, you do," she mumbled, turning her back on him again.

Noah continued, "Look, Eden, I don't normally do this. Clearly, you don't want me here. Therefore, I will just say what I came to say. I apologise, for what I said yesterday." Noah paused, and then called Duke to his side, "Come on boy, time to go home." Duke sneaked off into the living room and plonked himself down on the hearthrug beside Bella. Noah followed swiftly, "Duke, come on, it's time to go. Now is not the time for your antics." Duke barked, refusing to budge. Bella inched closer to Duke!

"Well, it looks like you are staying for dinner then. Duke has no intentions of moving anytime soon," piped Eden.

Noah remained silent, looked at Duke and shook his head. "Really, Duke." He left him to it and followed Eden through to the kitchen. "I don't want to put you to any trouble," he commented.

"You are here now, and I don't think we have much choice in the matter. It seems our dogs are quite taken with one another."

"Yes, they do don't they. This could be a problem if we don't nip it in the bud," chimed in Noah.

"Well, I will let you break the news to them both!" she chuckled while handing Noah a bottle of red wine to cork.

Noah's eyes follow Eden as she moved around the kitchen with grace. Admiring her lithe, toned form, he drew in a deep breath. *I am seriously regretting my words yesterday. Eden is unlike any woman I have ever met.* She turned around with two plates of Greek salad and sat opposite Noah. He glanced into her eyes briefly and was temporarily mesmerised. Eden shifted nervously in her seat and broke the silence, "I hope you like the salad."

Noah took a mouthful and smiled, "Almost as good as Betty's," he teased.

Eden rolled her eyes, "I have to agree with you, Betty is a superb cook, and you are lucky to have her. She clearly thinks the world of you."

"Yes, she does. However, sometimes she interferes where she does not belong."

"Ah, I see, like your personal life, for instance?"

"Exactly, which leads me back to yesterday. Betty would love nothing more than to see me in a relationship. She worries I am going to grow old alone. I am not worried, of course, and I happen to like my life just the way it is. It is less complicated when you are alone. No distractions and no emotional stress," he finished. Noah averted Eden's gaze and continued to eat his salad. Swiftly changing the subject, he said, "This is a great salad.

Maybe, before I leave, we could give Duke and Bella one last treat before we break them up and take them for a walk."

Eden chose her words carefully. She began, "Two things, Noah. Firstly, I understand where you are coming from, as I too am happy with my single status in life and have no plans to start dating anytime soon. So, let us be clear on that. As you stated, it is a complication I do not need in my life either. I have Bella and she is all the company I need. Secondly, yes, we should take the dogs for a walk. I will let you break the news to them that they can no longer see one another!" The corners of her mouth quirked up. Noah raised his eyebrows and then called Duke. Bella followed swiftly behind him and they both sat side by side.

Noah turned to Eden who was looking at them in amusement, "Looks like you have your work cut out, Noah. There are going to be tears at the end of the walk!" she teased while reaching for Bella's lead and slipping her jacket on.

Eden locked the door behind them and meandered alongside Noah towards the river. Noah's hand accidently brushed hers and she felt a warm sensation take over. As soon as they left the roadside and turned onto the riverbank, they unclipped the leads and let the dogs run free. Noah jammed his hands in his jeans pocket and realised he had not felt this relaxed in an awfully long time. He turned to Eden and studied her for a moment, "So why Shenley?"

Eden's eyes rested on his face, taking in his chiselled jawline before answering, "It is quiet. A perfect escape from the city. I needed somewhere peaceful to come home to after a busy day at work. Somewhere for Bella and me to enjoy long country walks away from the city. Shenley ticked all the right boxes. It was a no-brainer."

The corners of his mouth turned up, "I get that. I felt the same way about Acton, too. It could not be more remote. That was the allure for me. You don't get more private than Acton."

Noah confused Eden. Now and then when he let his guard down, he was charming to be around. Then his guard would go up and he was as cold as they come. Eden laughed aloud on sight of Bella and Duke rolling around on the riverbank together playfully.

"I have never seen Bella like that with any dog she has met. This is quite bizarre, don't you think?"

Noah shook his head mockingly, "What to do!" Then he turned to Eden, "May I ask you a personal question?"

"Well, it depends," she replied.

"Depends on what," he queried.

"If I can ask you a personal question too."

"A deal."

"So, what do you want to ask me," pressed Eden.

"I am curious to know why you choose to be single?"

Eden stopped dead in her tracks. Her smile faded. She thought seriously about her answer and decided to be truthful, "I was in a committed relationship for four years. Sadly, he was killed in a car accident a year ago today. I hope that satisfies your curiosity!"

Noah was taken aback. He stopped walking and watched while Eden ambled in front of him. She did not turn around and left Noah Jaw-dropped and speechless.

Eventually, she stopped and turned around, "Well, are you coming or are you getting tired already," she teased.

Noah caught up and remained silent. *Eden Marshall is the most intriguing woman I have ever come across. I am not used to women being candid with me. Normally they are interested in my power, status, and money. But not Eden. I can see she is genuinely happy with her lot. I envy her for that. I have everything money can buy and yet I am not happy at all. I am not at peace with my life, or myself,* he surmised.

Eden spun around, the corners of her eyes crinkled, "My turn... What do you do for fun when you are not working?" she smiled coyly and continued walking.

Noah ambled alongside of her and pondered on her question, "You get to ask me one personal question—which many people would pay for that chance and you ask me what I do for fun? Seriously, Eden."

Their eyes locked, Noah inched closer to her, he could hear her breathing nervously, she averted his gaze and made to turn around. Noah reached for her arm and pulled her close to him. He searched deep into her eyes. She remained still, her heart pounding through her chest.

She wanted to pull away, but she couldn't. He leaned forward and pressed his plump lips on hers. She drew in a deep breath and parted her lips, allowing Noah's tongue to meet hers. She trembled, and he pulled away.

He stood back and held his hands up in the air, "I am so sorry. I don't know what just happened." He walked ahead of her, calling Duke.

She remained rooted to the spot, unable to take in what happened.

What the hell was all that about? Why didn't I pull away? Oh God, this is so awkward... she thought. This is the last thing I need - bloody complications!

Bella came bounding up to Eden, "Come on, girl. Time to go home." Eden clipped Bella's lead on and glanced over to Noah, who was doing the same to Duke. Noah caught up and stayed silent. She felt the tension in the air. A coldness emanated from him. There was no eye contact between Noah and Eden. Noah walked hurriedly ahead with Duke.

Fine, make it even more uncomfortable, Noah. No words needed. A 'goodnight' would have sufficed, though.

Eden reached her house and watched as Noah climbed into his off-roader. Duke ran across the road unexpectedly, "DUKE, COME BACK RIGHT NOW." shouted Noah. Duke circled around Bella before rubbing noses and heading back to the car. "Bad boy. Never do that again, Duke. You could have been run over," cursed Noah.

Eden watched as Noah sped off down the road. All she could see was his taillights disappear into the distance. "That was rude! No need for that at all. That's the last time I invite you into my home, Noah Ainsworth." Bella let out a moan and stood staring down the road. "Sorry, Bella. Duke has gone home now. Come on, you can snuggle with me on the sofa." Eden locked up the house for the night, made a quick change and slumped down on to the sofa, swiftly followed by Bella.

She was annoyed with herself because she could not remove Noah from her mind. *He intrigues me. Everything about Noah Ainsworth is mysterious. But most of all, he is unlike any man I have ever met.* She closed her eyes briefly and relived their kiss. *It was unexpected and sublime. He astounds me,* she mused.

NINE

*N*oah angrily paced his office. Max remained silent while Noah delivered his instructions to the New York office. After finishing his call, he turned to Max. "I need you to fly to New York, Max—today. I want you to find out who is responsible for the leak and then make an example of them. I want the person responsible removed from my employ as soon as possible," he demanded.

Max stood up and straightened his suit jacket, "I'm on it, Noah. Don't worry, I will sort this." Max left the office and closed the door firmly behind him.

Noah turned to his marketing team, "Sean, an update please."

Sean began typing speedily on his laptop and then looked up at the big screen at the top end of the office. "This is what we have come up with according to your instructions."

Noah took a chair, leaned back, and crossed his arms. The corners of his mouth quirked up as he watched the advert unfold. When it finished, he jumped off his seat and walked over to Sean, patting him on the back. "Excellent, pure genius. This is why you are head of marketing. Fantastic job, Sean. I want this aired primetime ASAP. A continuous running advert until I say otherwise. I shall leave the details with you."

"I already have our advert booked. It runs tomorrow from p.m.," advised Sean.

"Great, that should wipe the smile off Caspian Communications..."

Noah added, "If he wants an advertising war then he has one! "Noah left the office and headed for the kitchen to make himself a coffee. He searched the cupboard impatiently until a bottle came crashing to the floor.

Betty ran into the kitchen, "Noah, what on earth are you doing?"

"I am trying to make myself a coffee."

"Well, why didn't you ask Jackson or Esther?" she fumed while sweeping up the broken glass.

"Sometimes, I just want to make my own coffee, Betty," he roared then left Betty to it. Duke grumbled in his basket by the window.

"What's with Noah today, Duke?" blurted Betty. Duke's ears pricked up. He rested his head on his paws and closed his eyes.

Noah stormed into the library, slamming the door behind him. *Caspian is infuriating me. I don't like being bated. I need to think things through. This feud between Caspian and me is taking its toll. Although, I will never admit it.*

An image of Eden found its way to the forefront of Noah's mind. He smiled and felt instantly relaxed. *I am smitten. This is the last thing I need right now. I feel bad for the way I left her standing after I kissed her. What was I thinking? Walking off like that was unacceptable. I can't get her out of my mind. I must admit, her lips felt good.* He buzzed for Jackson, "Can you bring the car around to the front of the house please, Jackson. I am going out and taking Duke with me."

"Of course, Mr. Ainsworth."

Noah left the library and took the stairs two by two to his bedroom to make a quick change. He stood glaring at his wardrobe, "Mmm, Jeans and a sweater, I think." He grabbed a pair of black jeans and teamed it with a blue ombre fitted sweater. He ruffled his hair and sprayed a dash of Gucci on his neck. He paced his room, *What the hell am I doing. What has gotten into you, Noah? She probably won't answer the door to you anyway... No, but she will answer the door to Duke,* he mused.

Noah searched the house for Duke and found him in the kitchen, curled up in his basket. "Come on Duke, we are going for a ride."

Betty observed him furrowing her brows.

"Don't ask, Betty."

"I wasn't going to say a word." She turned around and carried on baking while Noah exited through the side door with Duke.

He climbed into his car, ordered Duke to lie down on the back seat, and drove off. "Okay, Duke, this is a long shot, so I need you to put your cute face on for me." Duke tilted his head and rested his head on his paws. Noah parked across the road from Eden's cottage and noticed her car parked in her driveway. *Well, it looks like she is in. I have nothing to lose but my pride.*

Duke sat up, wagging his tail excitedly when he realised where he was. He barked and pawed at the window to be let out. Noah knew he could rely on Duke to do the rest! He opened the door for Duke, checked the road both ways and then let him run across the road. He ran straight up Eden's path and flicked the letterbox with his nose, barking excitedly.

Bella ran past Eden and sat by the front door barking, "Okay Bella, I am coming." Eden opened the door; Duke rushed in and ran off into the living room with Bella where a play fight ensued.

Eden glared across the road at Noah's car, then turned on her heel and walked back into her house, leaving her front door wide open...

Noah took a deep breath, climbed out of his car, and crossed the road to Eden's house. He paused for a while and then stepped into the hallway and closed the door behind him. He stood in the doorway of the living room and chuckled on sight of Duke and Bella rolling around on the floor. He turned to the kitchen and caught sight of Eden in a white cotton maxi dress. Her hair fell past her shoulders and she was wearing no makeup. Eden had never looked more beautiful to him than she did right now.

"Coffee?" she blurted while searching for two mugs in the cupboard.

"Sure. Coffee sounds great."

An uncomfortable silence followed. Noah knew he needed to say something worthy of Eden's forgiveness. Eden's back was facing him as she poured the coffee. Noah walked over to Eden and spun her around. He searched every inch of her face and brought his hand up to her cheek. She stood still, unable to move—frozen in his presence. He grabbed her face with both hands and kissed her fervently on the lips.

Eden threw her arms around his neck. Noah could feel her heart pounding against his chest and loved the feel of her. He picked her up and sat her on the worktop. He took her hands in his and gazed into her eyes, "I am terribly sorry for my behaviour yesterday. The truth is, I was scared. I was not expecting you, Eden. I have never met anyone like you before. You have taken me by surprise, and I have not stopped thinking about you since the day we met," he confessed.

Eden was wide-eyed, and words failed her. She placed a finger on his lips, laced her fingers through his and led him up the stairs to her bedroom, closing the door firmly behind them to keep the dogs out!

Noah swept her up in his powerful arms and placed her down on to the large wooden bed. He kissed her neck slowly and reached for her hands, placing them above her head firmly. He slipped his fingers under her shoulder straps, eased off her dress to reveal her lithe, toned, naked form. He gasped while drinking every inch of her in. His deep emerald eyes traced her body while his hands coasted her inner thighs. She parted her legs and allowed his hands to wander. Her body contorted as his fingers found their way inside of her. Noah placed his other hand firmly on the small of her back, pressing her body close to his. He then eased himself inside of her. Eden flung her head back and moaned with pleasure. Noah felt Eden's inner warmth envelope him and he inched deeper inside of her. Eden closed her eyes while gyrating beneath him, sending Noah into a wild frenzy. He released his grip on her arms and arched his back while Eden placed her hands firmly on his buttocks, encouraging his movement harder and faster as they climaxed together... Noah's pleasure was evident as he groaned in a sublime moment of ecstasy. Eden's eyes were lost in Noah's as their fingers laced together. Eden's heart continued to pound through her chest as Noah's breath whispered along the length of her neck. Along, frenzied silence ensued while their hands explored one another's bodies, unable to release each other.

Noah was the first to move and slid to the side. Eden did not want the moment to end. Never in her life had any man made her feel the way she was feeling right now. She knew Noah had captured her heart, her soul, her everything.

Noah turned to Eden and smiled as he swept a strand of hair back off her face, "So, Eden Marshall, what do you do for an encore?" he teased.

Her mouth curved into a smile. She leaned forward and kissed him on the lips, "You will have to stick around and find out!"

Bella and Duke ran up the stairs barking, Noah leapt up and opened the door, "What are you two up to?" Bella and Duke ran into the bedroom and jumped on the bed. Eden laughed while wrapping a sheet around her. Noah picked up his jeans and stepped into them while Eden watched him. She wanted nothing more than to fall asleep in his muscular arms. Her eyes trailed his toned torso.

"I think they are hinting for a walk," said Noah.

"Yep, I sense that too," agreed Eden while reaching for her dress. She added, "I will just take a quick shower first."

After dressing, Noah sat down on the bed and relived the moment in his mind with Eden. *I am more than smitten. I can't fight my feelings and nor do I want to. For the first time in over three years, I feel truly alive.*

Twenty minutes later, they were walking along the riverbank. Duke and Bella were chasing each other through the cornfields, and Noah contemplated the delivery of his next words to Eden. He laced his fingers through hers and stopped her abruptly, spinning her around to face him, "I want to be honest with you, Eden. I wasn't looking for anyone. In fact, I was adamant I did not want anyone to complicate my life right now. However, I never factored you—not in a million years. You are something else. I really want to get to know you better." He paused and studied her for a moment. Eden's expression gave nothing away, and this unnerved him.

Then a smile formed on her face, "Well, it seems we are singing from the same hymn sheet!"

He picked her up and kissed her firmly on the lips, "Are you absolutely sure about this?" he pressed.

"I am sure."

"Once the press gets hold of this, they will have a field day. Maybe we should keep it from them for as long as possible," he suggested.

Eden nodded, "Agreed. I am not sure how I would deal with all the publicity. I like my privacy and a quiet life. Not to mention that I have just been promoted at work. Oh, God—my boss will go crazy if he finds out! He sends me on my first prestigious interview with one of the country's most eligible bachelors and I seduce him! Mmm... grounds for dismissal for sure!" she concluded.

"If I recall it correctly, I was a willing hostage to your seduction. But yes, if we are going to make this work, we need time to get to know one another properly before we become victims of the media," decided Noah.

Eden loved the feel of Noah's hand wrapped around hers. It felt strong and safe. He was nothing like the man they purported him to be in the press—far from cold. As she peeled the layers back little by little, a warm, deeply sensitive man was emerging—a man she did not figure on at all. A warm feeling circled her stomach. Turning to Noah, she confessed, "I never expected you either. Now you have my heart – don't break it."

He cupped her face in his hands and searched her eyes, "I promise you that your heart is safe with me. Now, let me cook for you tonight, at your place. It will surprise you what I am capable of when Betty's not around," he laughed.

"Now that's an offer I cannot refuse." She turned to Duke and Bella then back to Noah, "I don't think there will be any objections from these two either!"

Once back at Eden's cottage, Noah wasted no time in the kitchen while Eden watched on with great amusement. He searched her cupboards, reaching for the pasta and spices, occasionally turning around, and resting his eyes on her. Eden felt a warm glow deep inside of her. *I pray that I am not wrong about Noah. I can't face any more betrayal, not after Jacob.*

TEN

Jackson raised a curious brow when he caught sight of Noah and Duke quietly entering the house. "Good morning, Mr. Ainsworth," greeted Jackson.

"Good morning, Jackson," coughed Noah.

Noah stopped and turned around, "For goodness' sake Jackson, how many times do I have to tell you– call me Noah. Mr. Ainsworth is well... too formal. You are practically family, Jackson. So, no more Mr. Ainsworth–please," he reiterated.

"Very well Mr–" Jackson paused mid-sentence, "I mean, Noah. It will take some getting used to, I'm afraid."

Noah headed straight for the kitchen. Betty singing at the top of her voice greeted him. "Good morning, Betty."

Betty spun around with a devilish look on her face, "Why, good morning, Noah!"

"Before you ask, Betty, it's none of your business," piped Noah.

"I never said a word," chimed in Betty while continuing to sing around the kitchen with a big grin on her face.

Sean burst through the kitchen door, bringing Betty and Noah to an abrupt standstill. "Noah, where the hell have you been? I left you a ton of messages last night. Caspian Communications are furious.

Caspian called this morning declaring an all-out war with Ainsworth Global Communications!"

A victory smile appeared on Noah's face, "Good. So, what's the problem? Caspian chose this war–I am a mere participant. If he can't handle my choice of weaponry, then he should concede."

Sean remained quiet pondering Noah's words, "Everyone is talking about your primetime Ad, Noah. The media are all a frenzy. Dubbing this the digital war of the century! Caspian will not let this go. He will come back fighting harder and you know this. We need to be prepared," advised Sean.

"And we will be. Stop fretting. I already have something in the pipeline. Caspian won't know what's hit him. When he chose me for an enemy, he chose foolishly," finished Noah.

Sean shook his head and left. Betty continued clattering around the kitchen. Noah reached for a croissant off the table and left.

* * *

Eden's eyes adjusted to the morning light. She stretched her arms above her head and yawned sleepily. Recollecting the night before, she sat up and glanced at the empty space beside her. She turned to her bedside clock, "7 a.m. what time did he leave?" she said aloud. Eden climbed out of bed and rushed to the shower room. *I need to report to Blake by 8.30. I'm feeling nervous. I can't tell him. He will be furious. I hate lying to Blake. He has been so good to me. Well, technically saying nothing is not lying,* she surmised.

By 8.30, Eden was pacing the floor in her office waiting for Blake to arrive. When her door swung open, she spun around and came face to face with Blake, "Morning, Eden. Sorry, I'm late. Let me grab a coffee and then you can update me on Mr. Ainsworth." Blake disappeared through the door and Eden rifled through her notes and turned on her laptop. She sighed with relief when she caught sight of Stephen's email accompanied by an attachment of images. She glanced through the images of Ainsworth House and gasped, "Wow, these look amazing!"

Blake ambled through the door with two coffees, "Here you go, black, no sugar, right?"

"Yes, thanks." She took the coffee from his hand and sat back down in her chair. She turned her laptop around to show Blake the images, "Stephen has done an incredible job with these images. They are stunning."

Blake studied each image carefully, "Beautiful. You are right, Stephen did a superb job. So, tell me about Noah Ainsworth; did he open up to you at all?"

Eden paused and turned her laptop around to face her. She opened Noah's interview file and then pushed her laptop towards Blake.

"I think you will agree that Noah was quite candid and more so than the media is used to. He differs greatly from the way the press purport him to be. He is extremely private and operates his empire from his top floor offices within his home. He is very enigmatic and mysterious. For someone so handsome, rich, and single, he is surprisingly down to earth. Anyway, I would like you to read this and give me your feedback. I do think it will complement the images Stephen has taken and make for a fabulous centre spread. I do need to conduct the final part of my interview with Mr. Ainsworth, which should be concluded by tomorrow afternoon," finished Eden.

Blake was smiling from ear-to-ear. "You did us proud, Eden. Mr. Ainsworth called me last night singing your praises. I knew you were the right person for the job. I don't suppose he spoke of his accident or love life at all?" pressed Blake.

"Sorry, no, he didn't. Although, he was candid about his day-to-day life, he made it very clear that his accident, parents, and love life were off topic. However, I believe I have captured a more realistic image of Noah Ainsworth in my interview - an image seen by few. He is not the cold fish people think he is. It surprised me to discover that he preferred to eat his meals in the kitchen with his butler and cook. He admitted to feeling more comfortable in the kitchen. He has a beautiful dog that he is devoted to and often takes him walking, alone across his vast land. He is incredibly organised and surrounds himself with a very efficient team of employees who also work from Ainsworth House. The entire top floor of his home has been converted into offices. He is surprisingly close to the staff who run his house for him, like Jackson his butler, Betty his cook and Carter his grounds keeper, treating them more like family rather than staff. He does not appear to have many visitors, and he has no personal life from what I understand. He is all work and no play. Therefore, I am not at all surprised he is a bachelor and more importantly one of the top 50 richest bachelors in England. One point I will make though and that is, he was nothing like the man I was expecting to interview. He was a pleasant surprise."

Blake observed Eden. She shifted in her seat awaiting his response, "So, you will go back to Ainsworth House tomorrow, is that right?" queried Blake.

"Yes, I am just waiting for confirmation from his business manager, Max."

Blake rubbed his chin with his finger, "Okay, Eden, as tomorrow concludes your interview with Mr. Ainsworth, I want you to get inside his head. See if he will share his thoughts on love and marriage with you. It would make for great reading and our readers will love it. Noah Ainsworth is the most talked about bachelor in the UK and an insight into his thoughts on love and marriage would be an excellent way to end the interview. I am counting on you, Eden," finished Blake.

Blake left her office, and she was already feeling the pressure of her final interview with Noah. *No pressure then... I need to speak with him and soon. I don't want to push him away and I do not want to fall out of favour with my company either.* She picked up the phone and called Noah's mobile.

"Noah Ainsworth speaking," he answered.

"Noah, its Eden. Sorry to bother you. I have just come out of a meeting with my boss, and we were discussing your final interview with the magazine. He has placed me in an awkward position. I just wanted to let you know in advance. Basically, he wants me to ask you about your thoughts on love and marriage. Of course, you can choose not to talk about that." Eden silenced herself. She felt awkward and hoped he viewed her call for what it was—a heads up.

"So, let me get this straight. Your boss wants to know my thoughts on love and marriage for the benefit of his readers?"

"In a nutshell, yes."

"I see. Well then, let us give your boss something to get excited about, shall we? Drop by this afternoon around 2.pm," finished Noah.

"Yes, okay. I can be there."

"Good. I must go. See you at two."

Eden stared in disbelief at her phone before placing it on the hook. *That went better than expected*, she thought. About 15 minutes later, Blake startled her when he burst through her office door!

"Eden, have you seen this?" Eden stood up and walked around the table to Blake, who was holding out his iPad for her. She glared at the screen, let out a harsh breath, and felt her heart racing while reading Noah's twitter feed:

@N_Ainsworth
Feeding the curious minds of the masses—it is best to remain single until you find a perfect partner for your mind and soul. I believe I have at last found mine...

OMG... what was he thinking? This will spark a media frenzy. Reporters and journalists will bend over backwards to find out who the mystery woman is. Oh shit, I am not sure I am ready for this train ride!

"EDEN," shouted Blake while nudging her arm.

"I'm sorry, Blake. This is a shock. I had no idea. Then why would I? As I said, he is a private man. He has clearly put that out there himself before the press found out and speculated. To be honest, I don't blame him. The media will hunt a man in his position down for every single detail of his life. However, when it comes to his love life, practically half the women in the country want to know about it. This is only going to help sell this week's magazine and I am guessing you are going to sell out following that tweet," advised Eden.

"You are right. This is huge. See if you can get a little more information about the mystery woman at the interview, something, anything that he will allow us to print," pressed Blake before scurrying out of her office.

I can't believe what Noah has done. He is not an impulsive person and thinks everything through to the last detail. I hope he knows what he is doing, she worried.

ELEVEN

*E*den pulled up outside Ainsworth House and climbed out of her car. She wasn't sure how to feel right now. *I am feeling apprehensive of what the coming weeks will bring. News of Noah's love life has spread like a virus and is already trending on Twitter. All the Social Media gossip columns are theorising over whom the mystery woman could be. I cannot reconcile with Noah's decision to go public on Twitter about his love life. It seems so out of character,* she worried.

The door of the main entrance swung open, and Duke came bounding over to Eden, "Hey Duke. Sorry, Bella's not with me today." Duke continued towards the fields. Eden spun around and saw Noah standing between the two masterful columns outside the entrance. He looked every inch the powerful, handsome man that he was. He astounded her. For a brief moment, she was speechless.

"I saw you pulling up and thought we could talk more privately while walking," suggested Noah, breaking the silence.

Eden glared at him before chiming him, "What were you thinking? You have half the country talking about your mystery woman right now. For goodness, sake, Noah, you are even trending on Twitter!"

Without saying a word, Noah grabbed her hand and walked speedily towards the top field, out towards the woods. He paused and turned to Eden, "I would rather have put out an announcement than some nosy journalist snaps a picture of us and turns it into something less acceptable. I know what these hungry, freelance journalists are like. They stop at nothing, Eden, to get that one picture that will elevate their career. At least this way, I have put it out there myself. As for the mystery woman that everyone is talking about, well... that is up to you how long you wish to remain a mystery. I am not sure that I have ever felt this way about anyone before. You make me happy and for the first time in my life, I could not care less who knows about it."

Eden's jaw dropped. She was not expecting to hear that from Noah. The corners of her mouth turned up, and she pressed herself against him. He enveloped her in his arms, his lips found their way to hers and he kissed her hard. She felt his passion as deeply as her own. He picked her up and swung her around, "Come on, I want to show you something past the lake. I think you will like it. I thought it was the perfect place to end our interview. It's a long walk though and about as secluded as anywhere can be."

They walked past the lake and through the woods to the far end. Eden could just about make out a cabin or lodge of sorts positioned between two large, oak trees overshadowed by the dense woods. As they approached, she gasped. Her eyes trailed the beautiful, Scandinavian-influenced wooden lodge. A narrow wooden bridge arched over a bubbling stream leading up to the veranda circling the entire lodge. "Wow!" she blurted.

"This is my private place. You are probably thinking why I need this when I live alone in that big old house. The truth is that I needed somewhere to escape to when I needed to think clearly. Duke and I walk up here some nights. We light a fire and spend the night here alone and away from the rest of the world. More importantly, Max cannot find me here. I had this built just after I moved into Ainsworth House and no one knows it is here except for Jackson, Betty, and Carter. It is my personal sanctuary. Absolutely no one can find me here, and that is how I like it. Now, this can be our private place."

Eden followed Noah across the bridge to the entrance of the lodge. He unlocked the door and Duke rushed through first and took up position in his basket. Noah stepped aside to allow Eden to walk through.

"Oh, Noah, this is beautiful. I love the way the trees hide and overshadows it. It makes it so elusive."

Noah took off his jacket and hung it on the back of the chair. He walked over to Eden and slipped off her cardigan while kissing her neck teasingly. He then stepped back, "I suggest that we decide the best way to end the interview. An ending that would be satisfactory for your boss and then we can spend the rest of the afternoon getting to know one another." Noah took her hand and led her through to the kitchen. He took out a bottle of champagne and two glasses, "Stand back," he urged as the cork flew out of the bottle. He poured their drinks and then clinked Eden's glass, "Here's to new beginnings," he toasted.

"To new beginnings," repeated Eden.

They both sat down, side by side. Eden turned on her Dictaphone and wrapped up the interview. "So, Mr. Ainsworth, there has been a lot of speculation regarding a tweet you put out on Twitter recently. Could you elaborate on that and put our readers out of their misery?"

Noah laughed aloud. He found he was enjoying toying with the media, "I find it is always best to hear any news and announcements from the horse's mouth. That way there can be no— shall we say... Chinese whispers. I have recently entered the beginnings of a new relationship with a wonderful woman. She makes me feel alive in ways I never believed possible." Noah paused and laced his fingers through Eden's hand. He noticed her eyes glistening and quickly caught a tear escaping down her cheek. "I mean every word. Frankly, I don't care who knows about us. Nevertheless, that is your call." Once again, he adopted his professional voice and concluded his interview with Eden.

"My boss will be thrilled. Thank you for doing this, Noah. You really didn't have to do that." She leaned forward and pressed her lips to his.

"Yes, I did. I needed you to know how serious I am about you— about us. I did it more for you than anyone else."

Eden felt humbled by Noah's words. *I have already decided to come clean to Blake and confess to him that I am the mystery woman. I know I am putting my career at risk; however, Noah is worth it. He has stepped outside of his comfort zone and spoke publicly about his personal life for the first time in his lifetime. I feel even closer to him now. I am falling in love with him...* she concluded.

Noah extended his arm, reached for her laptop, and closed it shut, "Now come here," he ordered while pulling her close to him.

Eden raised the hem of her dress and slid on top of Noah. She gyrated against him slowly and teasingly, feeling him growing beneath her. Tingles ran down the length of her spine. Noah eased himself inside of her and felt a rush of sublime pleasure course through his veins. The feel of Noah deep inside of her excited Eden further and she began a slow sensual gyrating of her hips. Noah groaned beneath her and gripped her buttocks, firmly encouraging her movement faster. He could take it no more and without warning flipped her over and entered her deeper and faster. His hands cupped her breasts while he felt the rush building ready for the subliminal explosion. Eden gripped his back while digging her fingers in, swaying her hips sensually as she too climaxed. Noah moved down the length of her body, circling her belly button with his tongue, and then kissed her stomach. Eden's body relaxed. She wrapped her hands around Noah's neck, pulling him to her. Her tongue found its way to his. She enveloped his back with her long legs. Noah lay down on the bed and kissed her lithe, toned body from head to toe, familiarising himself with every inch of her. He searched her eyes and paused, taking her in and cherishing the moment, "Where have you been all my life?"

Eden smiled and brushed his cheek with a sweep of her hand, "I wish we could stay here like this."

"So why don't we?" Let's stay here tonight. We can get Bella, grab a takeaway and spend the entire night here in the woods!"

"Now that's an offer I cannot refuse. But first, I need to report back to my boss by 5 p.m. and then I am all yours."

Noah jumped up. "Sounds like a plan. Let's go. The sooner we get the mundane stuff out of the way, the sooner we can be right back here, alone, just the two of us "

Eden and Noah took a quick shower together before locking up the lodge and heading back to the house with Duke.

"I shall be back around 7 p.m. Does that work for you?" asked Eden.

"Perfect and don't forget Bella or Duke will be grumpy all night!"

Eden smiled, climbed into her car, and then headed straight for the office. She was feeling excited and nervous. After discussing her decision with Noah, she knew that her life from tomorrow would never be the same again. She parked her car and made her way into the office building.

Blake spotted her and hurried over, "Am I glad to see you. Come into my office."

Eden followed Blake swiftly and closed his office door behind them.

"So, what do you have for me?" blurted Blake.

"I need you to sit down, Blake. I have one hell of a story for you." Blake sat down and fidgeted excitedly in his chair. Eden took a seat opposite and inhaled a deep breath before continuing, "I know who the mystery woman is..." she paused.

Blake chimed in, "Well done. So, who is it?"

"Me..." Eden studied Blake's face, displaying disbelief!

"Excuse me!" he gasped.

Eden inhaled slowly and continued, "Noah took me by surprise. We had an immediate connection. It just happened. I wasn't expecting to fall in love with our client. We both fought our feelings initially. Strange as it sounds, our dogs brought us together romantically. I mentioned earlier about Noah having a dog called, Duke. Well, Duke and Bella hit it off immediately. I know this was unprofessional of me. Nevertheless, it was not intentional. After fighting our feelings, Noah and I gave into them. We have thought this through." Eden shifted nervously in her seat, awaiting Blake's response.

Blake did not respond straight away. He read her official write up for the magazine first.

"I can't believe this, Eden," piped Blake. A smile formed on his face, "This is incredible and beautifully written. So, is it the real thing?" he pressed.

Eden nodded, feeling relieved, "I think so. As I said, it took us both by surprise. It was never my intention. I am prepared to offer my resignation as soon as possible. However, I cannot give up Noah. I know I may lose my job and I accept that. I am so sorry. I did not want you to find out by other means. I wanted to be honest with you."

Blake remained silent while pacing the floor and massaging his temples. "Look, Eden, I can't promise that you will keep your job. It is not just up to me. I need to call a meeting with the board and put it up for discussion/vote. However, that said, they will respect your honesty as I have. There are few people who would have been so candid. You are a talented journalist, Eden. I will do what I can for you. Whatever they think of your relationship with Noah Ainsworth, they cannot deny that this issue will be the top-selling issue of the year and maybe even the decade. I will call you tomorrow after I have spoken with them. You did well and found love too. I am happy for you. Really, I am. I just hope the board will see it my way."

I feel relieved now that I have confessed everything to Blake. I have no idea if they will print my complete interview with Noah, which reveals me as the mystery woman at the finish. If they do, then the whole of England will know who I am by Thursday Morning. The very thought of this makes my stomach churn. I am not sure if I am strong enough to deal with such publicity. Nevertheless, this will be a big part of my life if I am going to be with Noah, she mused. Eden handed Blake the flash drive and left the office, not knowing whether she had a job to go back to the following day.

TWELVE

*A*fter collecting Bella and throwing a few things into her overnight bag, Eden left for the lodge. She followed Noah's instructions to the letter, bypassing Ainsworth House and heading down a rarely used country lane at the far end of the woods. She parked up, locked her car securely and began the short trek to the lodge through the back end of the woods. As she neared, she could see the smoke spilling out of the chimney. Discreetly lit, the lodge looked beautiful amidst the glow of the moon and enveloped by the dense woods. Eden smiled and crossed the wooden bridge to the entrance with Bella. The door to the lodge swung open and Noah greeted her in nothing but a pair of jeans. His bare chest caught her immediate attention. Her eyes trailed over his contoured form. He inched closer to her as she approached, picked her up and swung her around.

"Good evening, Miss Marshall!" he teased while leaning her back and kissing her neck softly.

"Now that is what I call a welcome." A beautiful aroma wafted from the kitchen teasing her taste buds, "Something smells good?"

"That is my culinary masterpiece. Made to perfection just for you." Noah laced his fingers through hers and led Eden into the lodge. Bella was already in and sitting beside Duke. Noah took her jacket and led her through to the kitchen where a table for two was laid out to perfection with a bottle of Moet & Chandon, White Gold Champagne chilling in a silver ice bucket.

Eden's eyes rested on the table. "I cannot believe you have gone to all this trouble, Noah. The table looks stunning."

Noah pulled out a chair for her and she sat down. She picked up the linen napkin and placed it on her lap. Eden wasn't used to this treatment. She glanced over the elegant bottle of champagne in the centre of the table, *I have had my fair share of champagne, but I have never seen this one before*, she mused.

Noah sensed her interest and sat down opposite her, "This is rather special. It has been sitting in my cellar collecting dust for God knows how long. This bottle of champagne is not just famous for its content but also for its bottle, which is contained in a plated white gold case featuring a laser-engraved Dom Perignon label on it," he educated while pouring Eden a glass.

Her eyes twinkled, "Seriously... And you opened it just for me. Honestly, Noah, I would have been happy with your average £30 bottle of supermarket champagne."

Noah's mouth curved into a smile. he leaned in and kissed her. I can't think of anyone that I would rather share it with."

"So, I am guessing this is very expensive then," she commented while taking a sip.

"Well, if you call £1,800 expensive, then yes."

Eden gasped and nearly choked on her drink, "Really? That is crazy! She took another sip and another, "Mmm, this is superb though. I can't remember the last time I felt so special." She felt the butterflies circle her stomach while watching Noah prepare dinner for them. He was perfect in every way, and she could not believe he was all hers. A part of her felt it was all too good to be true, *Things like this just don't happen to me. I hope I am not setting myself up for a fall.* Noah interrupted her thoughts and placed a dish of his Linguini special in front of her. The beautiful spices teased her senses and made her mouth water. She realised that she had barely eaten since breakfast.

Noah paused mid-meal and studied Eden's face, "Am I the first man you have dated since, well... since losing Jacob?"

Eden placed her knife and fork down on her plate. She fell silent while searching Noah's eyes. She knew at that moment that he was as genuine as they come. "Yes. I have not dated since I lost Jacob. It was a difficult time in my life and one I never saw coming or was prepared for." She turned away from Noah, contemplating her next words. She choked back a lump forming in the back of her throat.

"I found out after he died that he was unfaithful to me. He was seeing another woman, and she was pregnant with his child. It was a tremendous blow when she approached me at Jacobs's funeral. I had no idea—no idea at all. Jacob and I had been together four years and were due to go to Italy last summer, just weeks after his accident. The reason he died was because he was rushing to see me. He wanted to confess everything. He made a mistake, Noah, and he paid the ultimate price. The day of his accident, I held him in my arms and watched the life drain from him until the ambulance arrived. You see, he called me to tell me he needed to speak with me urgently. I left work early, and I was waiting outside of my office building for him to pick me up. He was in an emotional state, driving too fast, and sped around the corner head on into a lorry. It was awful, a day I will never forget. I watched it all unfold before my eyes. I ran over to his car and a stranger helped me to pull him out. Jacob looked at me with a knowing look in his eyes—he knew he was dying. His last word to me was, 'Sorry.' Jacob's sister eventually revealed the true nature of his urgent visit to me and that he was having an affair. He confided in his sister. He told her that he had made a mistake and he did not want to lose me. She encouraged him to come clean with me. It was so tragic. A needless death born from deceit. Nevertheless, I loved him for four long years. I thought we were happy together. But you can never really tell what is going on in someone else's mind." Eden took a sip of champagne, then another and another until her glass was empty, "Do you mind?" she asked while reaching for the bottle from the ice bucket.

"Of course not," Noah held out his own glass for a refill.

Noah reached across the table and took hold of Eden's hand, "I am not Jacob. I will never hurt you like that. You have my word. I will treasure you until my dying day," he promised.

Tears filled Eden's eyes and cascaded down her cheeks. She placed both of her hands over her face and sobbed. Noah leapt from his chair, picked her up, carried her over to the sofa, and lay her down. He lay down beside her, stroking her hair back off her face and kissing her lips. "I'm sorry that he hurt you."

Eden was lost in Noah's emerald eyes for the longest time. The words she was holding back escaped from her lips, "I love you!"

A smile formed on Noah's face. He cupped her face in the palms of his hands, "I love you too." He sat upright and began unbuttoning her blouse. It fell open revealing her breasts and Noah placed his face between them, bracing them while tracing his tongue all around them. Eden's head fell back as Noah worked his way down to her naval and circled it with his eager tongue. He unbuttoned her jeans and slipped them off, throwing them to the floor. His hands glided up and down the inside of her thighs and stopped while he took her knickers in his mouth and tore them clean off. Eden gasped and clawed gently at his back while Noah found his way inside of her. He felt Eden's inner warmth envelope him. This sent him into a wild frenzy. He could not get enough of her... Eden pressed firmly on his buttocks encouraging him to enter her deeper. She gyrated beneath him; feeling his hardness taking control of her entire being as they climaxed together. When they were finished, Eden did not want Noah to move. Pressing firmly down on his buttocks once more, she said, "Don't pull out. Stay where you are. I love the way you feel inside of me." Noah pressed his lips firmly on Eden's seeking her tongue out with his. No woman had ever had this much power over him before. A power so overwhelming he could hardly bear it.

Over an hour later, they emerged from the sofa. Duke and Bella were sleeping side by side and not in need of a walk. It was clear they were not going anywhere tonight.

Eden reached for one of Noah's white shirts from his wardrobe and threw it on. Her hair dishevelled and makeup kissed off her face. She strolled back into the living room where Noah was pouring them another drink with music playing in the background. Eden sat down beside him and placed her hand on his thigh, "Can I ask you something, Noah?"

He pressed play and the beautiful sound of Debussy echoed throughout the lodge. He turned to Eden, "Sure. What do you want to know?"

She cleared her throat and braved her question, "What happened to you three years ago? If you don't want to talk about it, I completely understand and will never mention it again. It's just that, well... whoever encouraged you to live such a solitary life must have done one hell of a number on you."

Noah stood up, swirled around with his back to Eden. She was regretting her question, wishing that she had said nothing at all. Noah turned around to face her but remained silent. It was evident to Eden that it was a painful time in Noah's life.

He rubbed his forehead, "No one really knows the truth of what happened to me three years ago. My team kept the press at bay and satisfy their need for a story with a watered-down version of events, shall we say." He paused, paced the room, and took a large gulp of his drink. He continued, "I was in a relationship with someone. We had been together for some time, however, after about a year into the relationship, I realised that she was not the woman I wanted to spend the rest of my life with. Unlike most men in my position, I do not have an inbuilt desire for many women—Just one woman. It was that one woman I was in search of. Stephanie, my girlfriend, was eager to take our relationship to the next level. However, I was not, and she could sense that I was distancing myself from her. I was waiting for the right moment to break it off. I knew she was fragile, and I was trying to be a gentleman about it. She was making it difficult at the time. She was telling anyone who would listen that we were to be engaged. Of course, this was not the case and no such conversation had ever taken place between us. Anyway, to cut an ugly story short, I broke off with her and she repaid me by trying to kill me. She waited for me to leave my office one night, knowing my day-to-day schedule at my London office inside out. I was living and working in London at the time. She waited patiently in the shadows, headlights off, and then ran me down like an animal. She did not get out of her car - she sped off and left me to die. I barely knew what hit me. I was put into a medically induced coma. When they eased out of my coma, my memory was intact, but my head was a mess. It had taken a critical hit, and I had to have life-saving surgery. I had a small steel plate put in my head. My ribs and legs were broken, and the list goes on. The press were having a field day. Speculating over this and that. Stephanie, it turned out, was unstable, to say the least. Anyway, it was put down to a hit and run accident. Stephanie was kept out of the press and placed in a psychiatric hospital by her family for evaluation. Although, there was speculation in the media about whether or not Stephanie was involved. My teams of lawyers insisted Stephanie's psychiatric evaluation as a condition of her not being charged with attempted murder. That would have served no one any justice. She needed help and the right medication. She was mentally ill. It wasn't until after the accident that her parents revealed her past problems to me. Her family were extremely wealthy and had no wish for the public to know what happened. That whole period was a complete nightmare for me. It made me feel vulnerable and untrusting. I have not seen or heard from Stephanie since. I am assuming she got the help she needed, or at least I hope she did. When I recovered from my injuries, I moved out of London to Ainsworth House. Very few people knew where I lived for a long time. I vowed never to allow anyone to get that close to me again. I have not dated since then – until now that is. The press was all over me at the time and I craved my freedom from them. Hence my choice of residence now. Like you said, Eden, you never know what is going on inside someone's head." Noah's revelation surprised Eden. She stood up and walked over to him. "I am so sorry you had to go through all of that. I cannot imagine what that must have done to you. It seems like we both have horror stories we would rather leave in the past." She took hold of his hands and searched his eyes, "Let's make a promise, right here tonight, never to mention the past again."

Noah nodded, "Agreed. Never to be spoken of again," he reiterated. Noah and Eden talked into the early hours of the morning before falling asleep in each other's arms.

THIRTEEN

*eams of light pouring through the blinds kissed Eden's face, rousing her from a deep sleep. Adjusting her eyes to the morning light, she stretched her arms above her head and turned to Noah– fast asleep beside her. Glancing at his naked body, she drew in a deep breath. *How did I get so lucky?* She ran her fingers over his toned stomach, leaning in; she kissed him gently until he stirred.

With his eyes opened, he pulled her close and kissed her, "Good morning, beautiful."

Eden smiled, pressing her body against his, "Good morning."

Noah's mobile phone rang and startled him. He picked it up and saw Max's number flash across the screen, "Sorry, Eden, I have to take this." Noah climbed out of bed and took his call downstairs.

Eden leapt out of bed, opened the blinds, and headed for the shower.

Noah paced up and down the lodge, furious. "I'm going to New York, Max. I will be on the next available flight. God help Jim when I get there. I will deal with this personally. Just make sure a car is waiting for me at the airport. I will forward you my flight details as soon as I have confirmation." Noah threw his phone down onto the sofa, grabbed his sweater and headed out of the door with Duke and Bella to clear his head.

He jogged through the dense woods, picking up his pace while his anger bubbled to the surface. After 20 minutes, he stopped in his tracks, placing his hands on his knees, bending down to catch his breath. *I needed that; Jim won't know what's hit him. I will make sure he never works in the industry again. Traitor...* he concluded. Noah straightened his back, inhaled a long deep breath, then turned around and headed back to the lodge.

* * *

Eden emerged from the shower feeling fresh and ready for her day. *I have never felt happier or more alive than I do right now.* She massaged cream into her face, brushed her hair and slipped into a pair of skinny jeans and a fluted baby blue blouse. She reached inside of her bag for her blue bally pumps. She slipped them on and ambled down the stairs. On the last step she stopped, glancing around the lodge puzzled, "Where did they go?" Quickly realising that Noah had taken Bella and Duke for a walk, she made her way to the kitchen and prepared breakfast. When Noah arrived with Bella and Duke, Eden knew something was wrong. He seemed different to her. "What's wrong?" she pressed.

"Something has come up. I need to fly out to New York this afternoon. I will be gone a few days. I'm sorry, Eden."

Eden's heart sank. She was hoping to spend the rest of the morning with Noah. "Hey, business is business right. I get it. You need to go. I will be here when you get back."

He tensed, "I need to take a shower and then we will have to leave." Noah ran up the stairs and left Eden in the kitchen.

Eden sensed Noah was furious about something, but she did not want to press the matter. "Come on Bella and Duke, let's feed you both before we leave."

After taking his shower, Noah was ready to head back to Ainsworth House. He found Eden hugging a mug of coffee by the window. "I have to go now." He kissed her slowly and cupped her face in his hands, "I'm really sorry I have to leave like this. Just when you will need me the most right now, I must desert you. If there was any other way that I could deal with this, I would. I will call you as soon as I return from New York."

He took out a key from his jeans pocket and handed it to Eden, "This is the only other key to the lodge. It is yours. I get the feeling you will be needing it after the magazine hits the shelves today! The press will be all over you, Eden. This place can be your sanctuary if things get too much for you. Don't forget to lock up when you leave." He glanced at Duke, ruffled his ears, and then turned back to Eden, "I know this is a big ask, but could Duke stay with you and Bella for a few days?"

Eden looked at the two dogs and smiled, "I wouldn't have it any other way. Now go, have a safe trip and I will see you soon."

Noah leaned forward and stole one last kiss before hurrying out of the door.

"Well, it's just us then," said Eden while watching Bella and Duke rolling around playfully on the floor. Eden tided up the lodge and left an hour after Noah. As she climbed into her car, her phone buzzed in her jacket pocket. She pulled it out and saw Blake's number flashing across the screen, "Hey Blake, so... how do it go with the board? Do I still have a job this morning?"

"Morning Eden. I am pleased to inform you that your job is safe. Although, I must warn you, the board were not overly happy with your revelation. That said, they accepted that you were an asset to the company and saw enormous benefits to your newfound relationship with Mr. Ainsworth."

Eden laughed down the phone, "I see, well, as long as I am not expected to share Noah's personal life with the magazine, I am happy to stay. But yes, you are right, Noah has many contacts, and I am sure that he will send more business your way in the future."

"The magazine hit the shelves this morning, Eden. Apparently, the word is they are literally flying off–some shops have already sold out. Online sales have soared too. Views are climbing at an alarming rate. It appears that your relationship with Noah Ainsworth is hot news everywhere right now... Take a few days off until everything settles down. You are due a long weekend off, anyway. It will give you time to adjust to the publicity. I have to say, Eden, your interview with Mr Ainsworth is officially one of our most successful of the decade. Well done. You did an incredible job," praised Blake.

"I could certainly do with a few days off right now. Thanks Blake," finished Eden. Immediately after ending her call with Blake, a stream of messages flooded through. The only one she opened was from her friend, Angie:

Hey, Eden...

Wow! You kept that one quiet. Good for you, girl. You deserve to be happy. Just a heads up, our website nearly crashed this morning. There have been hundreds of comments from the public on your relationship with Noah—mostly positive, but there are one or two nasty comments. Don't waste your time reading them. Just a few jealous women. That is to be expected. After all, Noah is one of the top 50 most eligible bachelors in the UK. Cannot wait to catch up with you on Monday. Blake has informed me he gave you a few days off so enjoy them. You know where I am if you need me.

Eden started her car and made her way back home with only one thought on her mind—Noah. She had fallen hard, and it scared her. Noah captivated her in ways no one else ever had before—not even Jacob. Now she would be under scrutiny from the entire country. The speculative armchair observers who knew nothing about her or Noah would dissect and tear their every move apart.

Deep breaths, Eden, deep breaths... I can get through this. Noah is worth it. What did my grandma used to say, ah yes, today's news is tomorrow's fish and chip paper. I hope you are right, grandma, she mused. She drove down the street towards her cottage and slowed down. Stunned by all the photographers parked up outside of her house, she pivoted the car around and headed straight back to the lodge. *Oh my God, this cannot be happening. I am no one for God's sake. How the hell did they find my home address?* she thought. She stopped her car at a small newsagent that she visited regularly. She knew the shopkeeper well. It was a mile or so from the lodge. She climbed out of her car and glanced around. She knew there would be few people around here. It was a very remote village. She pushed the door to the shop open and noticed a couple of teenagers at the counter. They turned to Eden and then glanced down at the magazine in their hands, while whispering to one another. They paid for the magazine and left the shop giggling, not taking their eyes off Eden.

The shopkeeper smiled and commented, "Well, that was awkward.

I am sorry, Eden. So, it seems you are a celebrity now! I must say, I never saw that one coming."

Eden placed her groceries down on the counter and smiled at the shopkeeper, "I never imagined it would create so much attention, Pete. I am still trying to get my head around all of this."

"If you are happy, Eden, then just block out all the white noise and enjoy your new relationship for what it actually is—don't allow the media to penetrate your life and create doubt. If it's right, then it will all work out," advised Pete.

Eden smiled, "Thank you so much. I needed to hear that today."

Eden left the shop armed with the things she would need for a few days. She climbed into her car, turned to Bella and Duke whose ears pricked up, "Not long now and you can run around outside the lodge." She focused her attention on the winding road ahead until she reached the lodge.

FOURTEEN

*A*fter parking up outside the lodge, Eden let Bella and Duke out for a run-around. She sat on the front step and watched them frolicking for a while. Her phone had been buzzing all the way on the drive back to the lodge. She reached into her pocket and retrieved it. She paused, undecided. *Just turn it off*, she urged herself. After much thought and consideration, she flicked through her phone. There were hundreds of messages and new friend requests on Twitter and Facebook. *Now people want to be my friend. I don't think so...* she mused while flicking through her twitter feed. The Twitter trolls were on form. They commented that Eden was not good enough for Noah Ainsworth. They believed that Eden was only after his money. *People have no bloody idea what they are talking about! I knew I should have turned my phone off.* She caught sight of a message from her mum asking her to call back urgently. "Damn it, of all the people I should have told–my mum," she cursed aloud. She swiped her mum's number and waited for her to answer.

"Hey Eden - is it true?" her mum blurted.

"Yes, it's true. I am so sorry, mum. It all happened so fast that I have hardly had time to think. I should have called you."

"Don't worry about that. Are you sure he is worth all of this publicity?"

"I am absolutely sure, mum."

"I'm worried about you, Eden. You know, after what happened last year?"

"I am more than ready now. I need to move on with my life. I wasn't expecting to meet Noah, but I did, and he is the best thing that has happened to me since Jacob passed."

"Well, as long as you are sure. You know I am always here for you, right?"

"I know. Just so you know, you may get a few calls from the press and God knows who else, about me. I just want you to be prepared."

"Well, that's why I left you a message to call me. There were two photographers outside my house this morning. My phone has been ringing off the hook. I don't know what to say to them, Eden. It's making me anxious."

"I am so sorry. Did you know who Noah was before today?"

"Of course, I did. Everybody knows who Noah Ainsworth is. I need you to tell me what to say to get them off my back."

"Okay, just satisfy their need for a story giving nothing personal about me away. Not that there is much to give away. For instance, yes, it is true; my daughter is dating Noah Ainsworth. It is early days, and they are still getting to know one another."

Eden added, "I hope that they won't find out about Jacob. I could not bear for them to dissect that painful time in my life. So do not mention it, mum. If they do happen to bring it up then simply answer with, that was a painful and sad time in my daughter's life, and we do not wish to discuss it. That is all you need to say. Then ask them to leave. If they continue to bother you, then ask them to get in touch with me if they want to know more about me."

"Okay, I will. You are in for a roller coaster of a ride over the coming weeks, Eden. Are you sure you can cope with it?"

"I will have to. It will settle down eventually. Remember what grandma used to say about chip paper..."

"God bless her. Yes, I do. And she was right. In a few weeks, the hounds will be onto their next poor victim. By the way, you caught yourself a handsome fish. Nevertheless, he is the lucky one to have you and don't you forget that."

"I love you, mum. Call me if you have any trouble. I will be staying in an undisclosed location for the weekend, until Noah returns from New York. The press were outside my house this morning and all over my drive too. I could not believe it. This week's issue only hit the shelves this morning. News travels fast. Anyway, I am going Wi-Fi free for the weekend. However, I do have mobile data, but my usage is nearing my limit. I will call you on Monday," finished Eden.

"Love you too and take care of yourself. You know where I am if you need anything."

Eden felt less panicked after talking to her mum. *I can't help feeling guilty. I've not seen her much recently. I must make more of an effort*, she decided. Eden hauled herself up from the step and called Bella and Duke to her side. They came bounding up the steps, circling her.

"It's just the three of us for the next few days," she said, ruffling their heads while unlocking the door to the lodge. She slipped the door key into her pocket and headed for the kitchen. A knock at the door stopped her in her tracks. Her heart pounded in her chest, *No one knows I am here...* Cautiously, Eden headed towards the door, hesitating before opening it. "Jackson, you gave me a fright!"

"Sorry, Miss Marshall. Noah asked me to drop this over to you before he left. If there is anything you need then please call me." He paused, reached into his pocket, and took out a card. "This is my personal number. If you need anything, I will be here in a flash."

"Thank you, Jackson. Would you like to come in for a cup of tea?" invited Eden.

A half-smile appeared on Jackson's face. "Oh, no thank you. I better get going now." Jackson turned around to leave.

Eden stopped him in mid-stride, "Jackson, could I ask you a favour?"

"Of course, what can I do for you?"

"Noah informed me that only you, Betty and Carter know of this place, so I was wondering if you could ask Betty if she would drop by and visit me over the weekend. You see, I am kind of hiding out here alone for a few days. I am sure you have heard the news. I could do with some company," finished Eden.

"Of course, Miss Marshall. I will inform Betty of your request." Jackson turned to leave once more and Eden halted him again, "Jackson, Miss Marshall sounds so formal, would you be so kind as to call me, Eden. Everyone calls me Eden. The only person who ever called me Miss Marshall was a teacher I disliked in high school?"

Jackson's smile reached up to his eyes. He found Eden endearing, "Consider it done, Eden."

Eden watched Jackson drive off and then closed the door behind her. "Now what do we have here?" she said aloud while glancing at the beautiful bow-wrapped box in her hands. She lifted the lid on the large wooden box and gasped! Inside was a bottle of champagne, just like the one they had shared the night before—an extensive selection of cheese, exotic fruit, and a beautiful silk nightgown, accompanied with an impressive selection of Channel pampering products. She noticed there was a small note. She picked it up and read it:

Relax and tune out the world for a couple of days. Jackson will be on standby should you need anything—anything at all. Just relax and turn off your phone. We can figure everything out on my return. Love
Noah x

Eden smiled and clung to her nightgown. *I am going to take a hot bath, crack open the champagne and watch a movie,* she decided.

FIFTEEN

Friday night was a welcome relief for Blake. He took a large sip of his whisky and sat back in his chair overlooking the golf course. He always had dinner at his country club every Friday after work. There was an attractive woman a few tables in front of him smiling in his direction, catching his attention. Surprised, he glanced over his shoulder. *She must be trying to catch the attention of someone behind me.* But there was no one there. In fact, the clubhouse was rather quiet this evening. He plucked up some courage and smiled back, tilting his glass before taking another sip. To Blake's surprise, she stood up and walked over to his table.

"Hello, my name is, Eva. I noticed you were dining alone. Would you mind if I join you?" she asked boldly.

"No, not at all." Blake immediately stood up and pulled out a chair for her.

"Thank you. I just hate to dine alone. My friend stood me up at the last minute and I thought, well, as I was here, I may as well have dinner. Then I noticed you were alone. I hope you don't mind."

Blake smiled, "I don't mind in the least. I was just about to order dinner myself. So, Eva, are you a member here at the club?"

"Actually, no. But my friend is. It was my friend's suggestion to meet here. She raves about the food here all the time."

"I see. Well, I guess this is my lucky night. It's rarely a beautiful lady joins me for dinner."

Eva studied Blake while he placed their order. He had a kind, genuine face and she liked him. "So, what is it you do when you are not dining here?" asked Eva.

Blake shifted in his chair, "I own and run Imperial Home Magazine. Well... Me and three other partners. The magazine has been our family business since the late 18th century."

"Wow! Very impressive and a classy magazine too. I have read it often for design ideas and of course to observe how the other half live."

Blake steepled his fingers beneath his chin and glanced into her hazel eyes, "And you Eva, what do you do when you are not being stood up?" he teased.

Eva laughed, "I am a web designer. I work from home mainly. I love the freedom that running my own small business affords me. I am currently on a break since I have taken no time off for over a year now. Work got so busy, and time just ran away with me. Therefore, I decided to take a few weeks off just to relax and step away from my laptop. It's easy to forget there is an entire world outside of my house, if you know what I mean."

Blake liked Eva instantly. He loved her smile and how her chin dimpled when she laughed. "I know exactly what you mean. I cannot remember the last time I took a day off work, let alone a holiday."

Blake and Eva got to know one another over three courses. It was almost midnight when they were ready to leave. Blake stood up and made his way around to Eva's chair. Eva stood up. Her nose almost touched his. A brief silence descended.

"I know this sounds cliché but would you like a coffee back at my place. I only live down the road?" Blake asked, breaking the silence.

Eva pondered his question for a moment and then the corners of her lips curled, "Why not. Yes, I would love a coffee."

Blake was smitten with Eva. *It has been a long time since I have been in the presence of a woman on a personal level. When my wife left me, I swore I would never get close to anyone again. I still felt the pain of losing her to another man*, he thought while he drove.

Eva followed behind Blake's car all the way back to his place and parked behind him in his driveway. Blake climbed out of his car and headed straight over to Eva's car.

"Welcome to my humble abode," he greeted. She linked his arm as they walked up the path to the front door. Blake unlocked the door and stepped aside, allowing Eva to walk through.

"You have a beautiful home, Blake."

Blake smiled, "It doesn't feel like a home. It is empty; somewhere I lay down my head to recharge. A home is not a home when you live alone in my humble opinion. What do you fancy, coffee or wine?"

Eva pondered over his question, "I think a coffee would be the wise answer!"

"Exactly my thoughts. Two coffees coming up."

Eva observed Blake as he loaded his coffee machine. *For a man in his position, he was surprisingly humble. Unlike some that I have met in the past. There were no airs and graces with Blake*, she surmised. He was candid and open, and she felt comfortable with him. Blake handed her a coffee, and they sat down on his over-sized sofa.

"So, tell me more about yourself. Where do you call home?" asked Blake.

Eva placed her coffee down on the table and crossed her legs, "I live down the south of the country. I am spending time in Warwickshire to recharge my batteries and catch up with friends. I must say, it is doing me the world of good, and I realise now that I should have taken a break much sooner."

"The beautiful south. I spent some time down south many years ago when I was at University. I had the time of my life. So, where are you staying while you are up here?" asked Blake.

"A friend of mine has a house a few miles from here and I am staying there for a few weeks while she is working abroad."

"She sounds like a good friend," commented Blake.

"Yes, she is. The best. We have been friends since secondary school. More like sisters, really. She stepped up when I hit a tough time in my life and pulled me through. I owe her everything."

Blake studied Eva and put her at around 28 to 30-years-old. *I can't help wondering why such a beautiful woman like Eva is giving me the time of day*. At almost 50-years-old, Blake's hair was peppered, and his long-ago good looks were fading. Eva inched closer to him, took his coffee from his hand, and placed it down on the table beside hers. She searched his eyes briefly and then pressed her lips to his. Blake responded without question and loved the feel of her pressed against him. She sat back and immediately apologised, "I'm so sorry, I... well, I just wanted to kiss you. I am not normally so bold."

Blake took her in his arms and kissed her fervently. She reciprocated wantonly. Before Blake knew what was happening, they were naked and making love on his living room floor.

SIXTEEN

*E*den smiled while watching the Saturday morning sun breaking through the clouds. She threw on an oversized t-shirt and headed downstairs to attend to Duke and Bella.

"Come on, you two out we go." Eden walked out onto the veranda and sat down on the chair-swing while the dogs ran around excitedly. She wrapped her hands around her coffee mug and inhaled the fresh air. Her immediate surroundings were awe-inspiring, and she loved it at Noah's lodge. It seemed far removed from the rest of the world, peaceful and private. *I think I will take a morning run with Bella and Duke*, she decided. Eden nipped back into the lodge for a quick change. Five minutes later, she was jogging through the dense woods with Bella and Duke. Squirrels were abundant everywhere she turned, and the blackbirds added music to the scenery with their beautiful song echoing through the woods. She caught sight of a hare hopping through the woods and paused. *I have never felt more at peace than I do right at this moment*. She stopped by a bubbling brook and sat down to catch her breath before turning around and heading back to the lodge.

Betty was climbing out of her car when she approached the lodge. With a beaming smile, Betty greeted Eden, "Good morning. Jackson passed on your message to me. To be honest with you, I had already decided I was going to drop by and pay you a visit. Anyway, I hope you haven't had breakfast yet because I have cooked up a feast for you this morning." Betty reached into the back of her car and pulled out a food warmer. I took the liberty of preparing you a hearty breakfast. I thought you would need it to keep your strength up."

"Thank you, Betty. I am starving."

They made their way into the lodge. Betty wasted no time in setting out the table and serving a full English breakfast on two plates. They both sat down.

Betty began, "You are the best thing to happen to Noah in a long time, Eden. I knew from the first moment I met you that you were the woman for him. He has been hiding away in that big house of his for far too long and that isn't healthy for a young, handsome man."

"How long have you been working for Noah?" asked Eden.

"A long time now. Eight years, to be exact. He is like the son I never had. No one knows Noah like Jackson and I do. He has been through a lot in his young life-" Betty paused, realising that she might have said too much already.

"It's okay, Betty. Noah told me all about Stephanie."

Betty's brows furrowed while her face hardened. She placed her cutlery down on her plate and then looked into Eden's eyes. "That was a challenging time for Noah. It was difficult for Jackson and me too. He almost died, you know... That crazy woman almost killed him. Yet, he still protected her from the press and kept her out of prison. Which in my opinion was the only place for her? It didn't take long for me to suss Stephanie out. Her mind was broken, and it did not work the way most people's mind works. She could not cope with her emotions at all and most of the time she was overwhelmed by them. It drove her to do stupid things and make bad decisions. Of course, at the time, we had no idea that she had problems. Her family kept it quiet. They were more concerned about the family's reputation. Stephanie was a dangerous woman. I blame her mother, Charlotte. She had always known Stephanie was not right and yet chose to ignore the signs. I saw many sides to Stephanie while she was dating Noah. When he lived in London at his former home, he had a more... well, fulfilling personal life. He had friends that would visit often and dinner parties for his clients at least once a month. Therefore, the house was always full of life and it certainly kept Jackson and me busy. Until that fateful day, she almost killed him. I have never seen Stephanie since. They sent her to a psychiatric hospital for evaluation and treatment- Finley Park Hospital, I believe. A private hospital for the rich and famous. She had a lucky escape if you ask me and did not deserve the generosity that Noah afforded her. For reasons I will never understand, it was his decision and knowing Noah the way I do, I am guessing he wanted to help her realise that she was seriously ill and in need of help. I blame her parents, of course. If they had addressed her issues years before, then maybe Noah would not have ended up in hospital. Instead, Stephanie's parents always made excuses for her outbursts and putting it down to a temperamental nature. However, I knew- I had always known it was far more serious than they let on. You see, their family's reputation was everything to Stephanie's parents. They projected a perfect family image to the world around them, and nothing could impede that. They were often featured in the society columns and Stephanie's mother, Charlotte, thrived on that. The last thing she wanted was to admit she had a less than perfect daughter. Anyway, since then Noah was a changed man. He left London behind and moved out here in the middle of nowhere. He shut himself off physically from the world around him, choosing to run his empire from Ainsworth House. He rarely leaves the house unless an urgent business trip requires him to. A sad state of affairs for a young man if you ask me, no matter how rich he is. On the outside it may look like he has everything, but I know he has not been happy these past three years. That was until you walked into his life, Eden. You have brought a sparkle to his eyes again. A piece of advice from an old cook, keep digging and you will reveal a precious diamond. Noah is unique, once you have his trust and loyalty, it is for life. He is not like most men in his position, he is rare."

Eden listened intently to Betty while she spoke of Noah and his past. She already adored Betty. She smiled endearingly while she struggled with a slither of bacon. "It never intended to fall in love with Noah. I had been going through some emotional stuff myself. If anything, I was avoiding love at all costs. The trade-off, I thought, was not worth it after what I had been through."

Eden shared her own tragic story with Betty. Once she had finished, Betty leapt up from her chair and gave Eden a tight hug.

"Well, my dear, it seems you both found each other for a reason. Just do not allow outside influences to get between you both. Because believe me, they will try to. You are both going to have to be strong to get through the next few weeks. The press is already having a field day. They will try to get into every area of your life. They will want to know everything about you now. Just take it on the chin and maintain grace and decorum through it all, as I am guessing you will. Then you will come through these initial weeks unscathed. Before you know it, this will be tomorrows chip paper," finished Betty.

Eden gave a smile and placed her hand on top of Bettys. "Was it something I said?" queried Betty, puzzled.

"Yes, it most certainly was. You see, my grandma used to use that phrase about chip paper. She died a few years back. You just reminded me of her for a moment," confessed Eden, still sporting a smile.

Betty squeezed Eden's hand before standing up. "Well, I better get back to Ainsworth House, the food won't cook itself. I have an office full of people to cook dinner for today. Noah's employees love my cooking. Today they have Betty's hotpot. They have their own dining area on the top floor. Noah likes to keep them well fed; he said it makes for a more productive team. He is not wrong either, those guys would go to the edge of the earth for Noah. Anyway, here is my personal mobile number." Betty wrote it down on a scrap of paper from her handbag and handed it to Eden. "Anytime you need to talk, just ring me. I am not into all this texting malarkey. I can just about find my way to answering a call on one of these things," she laughed, waving her mobile phone in the air while making her way to the door.

Eden gave Betty a tight hug and watched her drive off. Something caught Eden by surprise, and she froze! Her eyes rested on the oak tree—there was movement. It was so fast she could not make it out. Shrugging it off as wildlife, Eden closed the door. *All this hiding out is making me paranoid*, she concluded. Duke and Bella started barking. It worried Eden. "What is it?" She was aware of someone– a shadow of a person peering from behind the oak tree. She gasped and immediately called Jackson. Within ten minutes, Jackson was at the lodge.

Eden rushed to the door and welcomed him, "Thank you so much for coming, Jackson. Something spooked me. I thought no one knew about this place?"

Jackson stepped into the lodge and closed the door behind him. "As far as I know, only Betty, Carter and I know about this place. However, Mr. Ainsworth's newfound placement in the world of coupledom will have raised much curiosity, Eden. It may just be a random stranger out walking and accidentally strayed onto Ainsworth Land. It happens from time to time. On the flip side, it may be a reporter. There is no telling. Did you catch a glimpse of the person's face?"

Eden shook her head, "No, I just caught an outline; they were dressed in dark clothing, which did not help. I could not make out whether it was a man or woman."

"I will look around. I am sure it's nothing to worry about," advised Jackson as he left the lodge and headed towards the oak tree. Eden watched Jackson while he searched the immediate area. A few minutes later, he returned. "Well, whoever it was, they are long gone now. As I said, it was probably a walker who accidentally strayed onto the land. Had it been a reporter, they would not have left, in fact, they would have knocked the door at some point to snap a picture of Mr. Ainsworth's new girlfriend," reassured Jackson.

Eden placed her hand on Jackson's arm, "Thank you for coming so quickly. I think being here alone has made me a little anxious and what with the press and everything."

"I totally understand. Would you like me to drop by this evening before I turn in, to check on you?"

"That would be great, Jackson. Thank you."

Now I feel silly. For goodness' sake, Eden, pull yourself together. Duke and Bella lay down on the floor by Eden's feet. She felt safer with them around. "Thank God for you two," she said, patting their heads. By nightfall, Eden was dancing around the kitchen and cooking up a storm. She spun around startled by Duke and Bella barking ferociously... She hurried to the living room and saw Duke and Bella on their hind legs peering out of the window, barking. Fear gripped her. With her heart pounding, she squeezed in between Bella and Duke. She looked around but could barely see anything. It was too dark for her. Bella and Duke stopped barking and moved away from the window. *Probably a fox or something. I am in the middle of the woods for God's sake. Get a grip on yourself, Eden.*

SEVENTEEN

*S*unday morning was a welcome relief after an unsettled night's sleep. *I think I need to go home. As much as I love this place, I am getting cabin fear.* After closing the lodge and informing Jackson that she was heading home, Eden rounded Bella and Duke up and drove to her cottage. She stopped at the top of her street. She searched all around, it was quiet and not a reporter in sight. *Thank God for that. Maybe they have moved on to their next victim already*, she concluded.

She drove slowly down the street, turned into her driveway, and parked up. "Home sweet home," she said aloud. Bella knew exactly where she was, and her excitement was evident. "Come on you two, out of the car," urged Eden. She locked her car and walked up the path to the door. Hearing her land line ringing, she hurried into the house. She reached for the land line while dropping her bag down on the floor.

"Hello," she answered.

"Miss Marshall, this is Warwick Simmons from the Daily Express. I was wondering if you have a quote for the paper, something for our readers on your relationship with Noah Ainsworth?" he pressed.

Anxious, she paused to gather her thoughts.

"Miss Marshall are you there?" pressed the reporter.

"Mr. Simmons, Noah Ainsworth and I are at the beginnings of a new relationship. We are taking it one day at a time. I hope that will satisfy your readers. Good day." She placed the receiver down and stormed into the kitchen. "Really... this is what they call newsworthy. With everything that's going on all over the world right now and they are chasing me down! This is a seriously messed up world," she cursed aloud while making a coffee.

Eden's mobile phone vibrated in her pocket. Retrieving it, she could see Betty's number flashing across the screen, "Hi Betty," she greeted.

"Good morning, Eden. Jackson passed on your message. I just wanted to check that you were okay. Jackson told me that something spooked you yesterday at the lodge. I was surprised to hear that you were heading home today."

"I couldn't sleep last night. The dogs were barking like crazy at one point, peering out the window as if they had seen something. I put it down to a fox or other wildlife. It is the woods after all. I decided I needed to come home, Betty. Reporter's or not. I am going to have to face them sometime. Therefore, I may as well get it over and done with. The longer I leave it, the more mystery it creates for them and the more determined they will be."

"If you are sure? You know where I am if things get too much for you. I know what these bloodhounds are like. You are a brave woman, Eden. Take care of yourself," finished Betty.

Eden drew in a long deep breath and sat down with her coffee in-hand. She had a stream of unanswered messages that she could not face right now.

Her land line ringing echoed through the cottage, "What now..." She reached for her phone and answered, "Hello."

Silence greeted her on the other end of the line.

"Hello?" Eden repeated.

A dull tone followed, indicating the person had hung up!

"What the hell... seriously!" She paid no mind to the silent caller and made her way upstairs. *I guess I will just have to get used to it for now. Haven't these people got better things to do than harass me?* she questioned.

Her doorbell rang. She peered out of her bedroom window and saw a young woman holding a bouquet of flowers. At the end of her driveway, there was a florist's delivery van. She smiled and ran down the stairs to answer the door.

The woman smiled, "I have a delivery for a Miss Marshall."

"Yes, that's me," confirmed Eden taking the enormous bouquet from the woman. She sniffed the flowers and closed the door behind her. She eagerly opened the card and read the message:

> Thinking of you
> I cannot wait to see you.
> Miss you.
> Love Noah xxx

She beamed, not taking her eyes off the elegant bouquet of 100 roses. They were the most exquisite, long-stemmed, large-headed red roses she had ever seen - a stunningly intense, opulent display, finished with a sprinkling of sparkling diamanté pins. The beautiful Naomi roses were expertly bound and finished with gift-wrap and ribbon.

She went into the kitchen and searched her cupboards for a vase worthy of such a grand display. "There it is," she said aloud while reaching for her crystal vase from the back of the cupboard. She arranged the display and placed them down on the centre of the table. Then she stood back to admire them. *I miss you too, Noah. I wish you were here right now.*

Eden took her coffee into the living room and turned on her television. It surprised her to see a discussion taking place about Caspian Communication and Ainsworth Global Communications on a morning show. The two men were debating the advertising war between the two giants and predicting the outcome. An image of Noah and Caspian appeared on the top right-hand of the screen. *I guess that's why Noah had to hotfoot it to New York. That Caspian guy is ruthless for sure*, she concluded. Then the topic changed. She leapt off her seat when an image of herself appeared on the screen! "Oh my God, this can't be happening!" She studied the image of herself for some time and blurted, "They could have found a better picture than that one." She turned up the volume and listened intently to the conversation led by Adrian Forester:

"Well, it seems everyone is talking about Noah Ainsworth's new beau! What do we know about Eden Marshall, well, she is a journalist for Imperial Home Magazine? The two of them met when Miss Marshall was instructed to interview Noah Ainsworth by the magazine she is working for. I am guessing that was some interview!" laughed Adrian Forester.

Arran benedict, the co-presenter, smiled mischievously, "It seems Miss Marshall got more than she hoped for. I mean... come on; she has bagged herself one of the top 50 richest bachelors in the UK. That must have been one hell of an interview!"

Eden turned off the television. She could not listen anymore. She paced the floor, feeling mad. Her land line was echoing through the house and she wanted to scream. She picked up her phone angrily, "Who is it?" she raged.

A long silence ensued.

Eden's heart sped up, "Hello," she pressed. There was nothing but a deafening silence. She placed the phone down on the receiver and felt a nervous stir in the pit of her stomach. She checked the caller's number, but the caller's ID was withheld. "I don't know if I can deal with all of this," she said aloud while pacing the floor. Duke and Bella sensed her anxiety and inched closer to her. "Hey, at least I have you two on my side. It seems the rest of the world thinks that I am not worthy of, Noah." Duke licked her hand and Bella nudged her arm. "Come on, let's go down to the river."

She grabbed her coat, keys, and hurried to her car. As soon as Bella and Duke climbed into the back of the car, Eden drove the short distance to the river. She glanced around and there was no one in sight. Most people were at work during the day, and it was always quiet. She sighed with relief and climbed out of the car. Bella and Duke ran off down the riverbank with Eden trailing behind slowly. It was a beautiful summer's day. The sky was clear blue and not a cloud in sight. Eden contemplated her future with Noah and knew that her entire world was changing. The privacy her life afforded her before Noah came into her life was long gone and she knew it. However, she could not imagine her life without him in it either. *I will just have to get used to it. Noah is worth it and eventually, things will calm down. They always do. I just need to get through these initial weeks. At least Noah craves his privacy as much as I do. Everything will be fine*, she convinced herself. Picking up pace, she caught up with Bella and Duke and a woman was fussing over them.

"Hello, I hope they are not bothering you," Eden approached smiling.

The woman raised her head and glanced at Eden, "No, not at all. They are adorable. What are their names?"

"This one is Duke, and this is Bella," pointed Eden.

She held out her hand and introduced herself, "My name is, Eden." The woman shook Eden's hand, "My name is, Eva."

Eva continued, "Well it was nice to meet you, Eden."

"Likewise, Eva," said Eden.

Eva excused herself then continued to power walk ahead.

Eden glanced down at Bella and Duke, "Well, it looks like you two gained another fan today!" Come on let's go home."

EIGHTEEN

*E*den was relieved to be back at work, although it wasn't her typical Monday morning at the office. Curious glances greeted her while making her way to the coffee machine.

"I tried to call you yesterday. I was worried about you and wanted to check if you were okay?" Piped Angie, jumping up from her chair, following behind Eden.

Eden juggled her coffee and mail while making her way to her office. She threw her jacket over the back of her chair and turned to Angie, "I'm sorry. It has been crazy since the news about Noah, and I broke. My land line and mobile have been ringing constantly. Someone who keeps ringing my land line and then hanging up on me has shaken me up. And to top it off, reporters have been pressing for details every which way they can. It's been driving me crazy. The worst of it is Noah is in New York on an urgent business matter. So, I have been dealing with it all alone." Eden slumped down in her chair and inhaled a deep breath.

Angie leaned forward, placing both of her hands palms down on Eden's desk. "Trust me, all of this craziness will pass. You are hot news right now because you have just taken one of the most sort after bachelors in the UK off the market. People will want to know how you did it, what do you have that they don't, and so on. You know what people are like. Noah

Ainsworth is hot news and so is anyone affiliated with him, whether it be business or personal. This is something you will have to accept if you are going to be the future, Mrs. Ainsworth," advised Angie.

"Seriously, Angie... we have only just met. Who said anything about marriage?"

"Well, you never know. Look, Noah is not going to go through all of this and put himself on the line for you if he wasn't serious about you. And I am guessing you feel the same way, or you would not be with him. So, just lie low for a while, ride this whole media circus out until people are bored with it. And they will get bored eventually, trust me on that. May I add, you are one lucky lady, Eden Marshall. However, Noah is the lucky one. I mean it; Noah is truly the lucky one."

Eden gave Angie a tight hug, "Thanks, I needed a pep talk today."

Right after Angie left her office, Blake came in, "Good morning, Eden," greeted Blake while closing the door behind him. With a cheesy grin on his face, he sat down opposite Eden.

"Okay, out with it," pressed Eden.

Blake forked his fingers through his hair, "I have met someone!"

"Seriously... you too! That's great news. When did all this happen?"

"We met at the country club last Friday. We just seem to hit it off straight away. It was effortless. We have practically spent every waking minute together since. It has moved quite fast since then."

"Well, it seems we are both heading for a change in our lives right now. I am pleased for you. You look genuinely happy," said Eden.

"Thanks. Look, the reason I came in was to invite you over to dinner this evening. I thought while you were alone and what with everything that's going on right now that dinner with friends is just what you need."

"Blake, that is the best offer I have had in days. I would love to come."

"Great. I have invited a few others from the team too, Angie is one of them. So, make sure you are hungry because we are cooking up a storm tonight," said Blake, as he leapt from his seat and stood in the doorway. "See you later," he finished.

Eden was surprised at Blake's revelation. *I have not known Blake to go on a date, let alone find himself in a relationship since his wife left him. It looks like cupid is busy right now!* She mused.

Eden busied herself with paperwork for the rest of the day. She avoided the curious glances from her colleagues and remained in her office for most of the day. By 5 o'clock, Angie was ready to leave and popped her head around Eden's office door, "Do you want me to pick you up tonight or will you make your own way to Blake's house?"

"I will make my own way. Thanks for the offer."

Angie nodded, "Okay. I have to say, I am rather curious to meet Blake's new girlfriend."

Eden's eyes crinkled, "Yes, me too. She is clearly good for him right now. He has been beaming all day," she chimed in.

"Well, my working day is over. I am heading home to shower and change. I will see you there," finished Angie.

Eden finished what she was doing and left the office 30 minutes later. When she reached home, she fed Bella and Duke, then let them into the garden while she showered and changed. By 6.45, she was in her car and on her way to Blake's house. *I am looking forward to this evening. It's good to see Blake so happy, he deserves it.* She parked up behind Angie's car and made her way to the front door. She paused for a moment to straighten her dress and ruffle her hair, then rang the doorbell.

Blake greeted her with a beaming smile and stepped aside to let her in, "Thanks for coming. Just make your way through to the living room. Everyone else is here."

Eden meandered into the living room and glanced around. Her eyes rested on the face of a woman she assumed to be Blake's new girlfriend. There was a moment of recognition. Eden's eyes trailed the woman admiringly. She wore a beautiful shift dress, showing off her perfect figure to perfection. Her hair was a sleek Chinese bob and her skin glowed. She looked completely different to the first time she saw her. Eden made her way over to her, "Eva... I believe we have already met!" introduced Eden.

"What were the chances of this happening," piped Eva while gripping Eden in a tight hug. Blake stood at the far end of the room looking puzzled. He made his way over to Eva. Eva turned to Blake,

"We met the other day while I was out power walking. Eden was walking her dogs, and they came bounding over to me," revealed Eva.

Blake looked surprised, "Well... what were the chances-" Eva cut him off, "I know right."

Eden smiled and instantly took a liking to Eva. She was exceptionally beautiful and much younger than she thought Blake's new girlfriend would be. Yet, she was open and engaging and made everyone feel comfortable.

"Come on everyone, let's get seated and I will serve up dinner."

They all sat around a large oval dining table while Eva disappeared off into the kitchen. Angie turned to Eden and whispered, "Well, I wasn't expecting that. Eva is stunning. Not that Blake isn't a good catch. But, Eva... well, she is something else don't you think?"

Eden fell silent while glancing through the living room door. She had a direct view through the open door into the kitchen. She noticed how lovingly Blake and Eva interacted and smiled at the sight of them together.

"You know what, Angie, I think they are perfect for one another. I realise Eva is younger and clearly beautiful. Nevertheless, Blake is an amazing man and very handsome for his age, not to mention he has acquired a great deal of wealth in his own right over the years. They seem good together. I just hope it works out for Blake as I cannot recall ever seeing him so happy."

Eva came bounding into the dining room with two, large, platters of salmon surrounded with new potatoes and asparagus spearheads. She placed them down on the table and sat down herself. Blake came out of the kitchen armed with two bottles of wine. He made his way around the table and poured everyone a glass.

Angie stood up and raised her glass, "I would like to propose a toast to Blake and Eva and this delicious dinner they have prepared for us this evening."

Everyone raised their glasses in unison and toasted. The night flowed with ease. By the end of the evening, Eva had found her way into everyone's affections. She was a great host and cook. After dinner, Angie talked to Blake about a new project and Eden was helping Eva to load the dishwasher in the kitchen.

"It was lovely to meet you, Eden. Blake tells me you are dating the mysterious Noah Ainsworth..." Eva paused, studying Eden's expression.

"Yes, it's all quite recent and we are still getting to know one another. That said, I know he is the one. I feel like I have found my soul mate. We get each other if you know what I mean?"

Eva broke eye contact and peered out of the window, then turned back to Eden, "Yes, I do know. Once you have found your soul mate, there is no going back. No one else will do."

Eden sipped at her wine, "I know exactly what you mean. I can see how well suited you and Blake are. He is a genuine man, Eva. You will be hard-pressed to find anyone like him. I am happy for you both. We should have a toast, "To new beginnings," toasted Eden.

"To new beginnings," repeated Eva.

Eva poured herself another glass, "Would you like a top up?"

"No, thank you. I am driving. Speaking of which, I really need to get home. I have an early start in the morning." Eden placed her unfinished drink down onto the worktop and reached for her jacket. She then made her way into the living room over to Blake and Angie, "Blake, thank you for an amazing night. I need to head home now. Dinner was lovely."

"Hey, hold on for a moment. I will leave with you," piped Angie picking up her handbag.

"Blake, it was an amazing night and Eva is delightful. Thank you."

Eva walked into the room, "Thank you both for coming. It was lovely to get to know you?"

Blake chimed in, "A successful evening, I would say. We must do it again soon."

Eva walked over to Angie and Eden, giving them both an impromptu hug. "The pleasure was all mine." Eva stepped back and stood next to Blake, who placed his arm around Eva. They watched on the doorstep until Eden and Angie had driven out of sight.

"You have lovely friends. They seem genuine and easy to talk to. We must do this again sometime, Blake."

"Agreed." They closed the door behind them and headed straight upstairs to the bedroom.

NINETEEN

*I*t relieved Noah to be back in the UK. After dealing with Jim Peters personally, he made sure that no one in their industry would hire him again. He was satisfied with the outcome and left behind a powerful message–betray Noah Ainsworth expect to pay the price. He requested Jackson pick him up from the airport.

Jackson waited for Noah as agreed and spotted Noah exiting arrivals.

"Jackson, good to see you."

"I trust you had a successful trip," greeted Jackson.

"I would say so. Let's just say that I ironed out a wrinkle or two! Come on, I need a decent cup of coffee before we head home." Noah led the way to the coffee shop at the airport. He purchased two coffees and sat opposite Jackson.

"So, come on then, fill me in. What have I missed while I've been away?" pressed Noah.

Jackson shifted in his seat. He took a sip of his coffee before responding. He said, "As I mentioned to you on the phone, Miss Marshall left the lodge on Sunday morning. I think she got spooked. She thought she saw someone hanging around, but then convinced herself it must have been a fox or something. The press have been hanging around outside of Ainsworth gates since the news broke about you and Miss Marshall. Carter chased a reporter from the inside of the gates last night. I have no idea how he managed to get in."

Noah steepled his fingers under his chin, pondering his thoughts. "Okay, well, I need to tighten security around Ainsworth House. I am guessing they want a glimpse of Eden and me together. Therefore, that is what they will get. Maybe that will satisfy them, and they will back off a little. How has Eden been dealing with it all while I have been away?"

"She is an intelligent woman. However, it's clear all of this interest in her is taking its toll."

"Did she receive the flowers?"

"Yes. As instructed, 100 red Naomi roses."

"Thank you, Jackson. Sometimes, I don't know how I would manage without you."

"It is no trouble, no trouble at all," piped Jackson.

Noah sipped his coffee and fell silent. He knew what he wanted to do. "Let's go, Jackson. Can you drive me to Eden's house please?"

"Of course, Mr. - I mean, Noah."

Noah smiled, "See, I told you that you would get used to it, eventually. None of that Mr. Ainsworth - its Noah to you Jackson. Remember that."

Eden was glad to be home with Bella and Duke. *It has been a long day at work, and I am glad it is over.* She wrapped her hands around her coffee cup and snuggled on the sofa with Bella and Duke vying for her attention, "Hey guys, give me some room, you are crushing me!" Bella grumbled and jumped off the sofa swiftly followed by Duke who ran to the front door barking. Eden stood up and made her way towards the door. She almost jumped out of her skin when her doorbell rang. She opened the door, her jaw falling open. She ran into Noah's arms and wrapped her legs around him. "I have missed you so much. Why didn't you tell me you were coming?"

"I wanted to surprise you." Duke nudged between them and stood on his hind legs, placing his paws on Noah's shoulders. "Yes, yes, I have missed you too, Duke," said Noah, ruffling Duke's ears. Eden closed the door and they walked through to the living room and sat down together on the sofa. Noah felt his primitive side spring to life and pulled Eden close to him. He jumped up, grabbed Eden's hand, and led her upstairs to the bedroom, closing the door behind him. They fell onto the bed together.

"You have no idea how much I have missed you. The flight back home seemed to take forever," confessed Noah. Eden inched closer and pressed her lips to his. Noah's lips parted and their tongues entwined. Eden lay back while Noah unzipped his trousers eagerly. He tore off his shirt and threw it aside. Eden studied his toned form. Her eyes lit up. She wanted to discover something about him that no woman ever had. Eden slipped off her dress and straddled him. He laid back, a willing hostage beneath her. Eden's hands coasted his torso; her fingers trailed his mysterious scars—scars he was yet to talk about. He flinched and she paused. He smiled and for the first time, he encouraged her fingers to circle his scars—in that moment, she knew that she had discovered his heart in a way no woman ever had. She unzipped his jeans and tore them from his body. She eased herself down onto him slowly revelling in the pleasure of him deep inside of her. She began a slow sensual swaying of her hips and sent Noah into a wild frenzy. He could take it no more and flipped her over. He inched deeper inside of her while clasping her hands above her head. She groaned in pleasure beneath him as they climaxed together.

Noah turned on his side to face Eden, "You have no idea what you have done to me. How have I lived all these years without you?" He brushed a stray hair from her face and kissed her gently on the lips.

"I'm here now. I am going nowhere." She buried her head in his chest, fighting the tears escaping from her eyes.

Noah glanced down and placed her head in his hands lifting it up. "Hey, what's wrong?"

"I'm sorry, I promise you, they are happy tears. I wasn't expecting this, Noah. You have consumed me in every way possible. I feel so happy and yet vulnerable too. I am just overwhelmed right now. So much has happened in such a short space of time. I think it has all finally caught up with me."

"I feel the same way too. No woman has ever made me feel the way you do. I never believed I would find a love like this. One that was so immediate and all-consuming. You have quite simply taken my breath away."

Noah placed his lips on Eden's lips with a passionate need she had never experienced before. His arms enveloped her, pulling her as close as physically possible. Her body trembled like never before. His tongue parted her lips and danced with hers. She was completely under his control. Her heart lost to him. Noah slipped on top of her and parted her legs, entering her once more. Eden felt the rush ignite throughout her entire body, contorting beneath him as they climaxed eagerly together.

Eden lay beside him, catching her breath. She turned to face him and remained silent as her fingers traced the deeply etched scars on his chest. "What happened to you?" she asked.

Noah stood up, threw on his shirt and slipped into his jeans. Then he sat down on the end of the bed with his back to Eden. She wrapped the sheet around her and moved closer to Noah slipping her hands around his waist and resting her head on his shoulder.

"Let's just say I didn't have the best childhood. It was tough, a time in my life I would rather forget and leave it where it belongs–in the past." Noah paused and then continued. "My father was a religious man, and he was also an alcoholic. His alcoholism was a deeply kept secret from his friends and the church where he attended with my mother. My mother bowed to his every need and was afraid of him for good reason. I often heard him beating her when he returned home from a drunken spree. I was too young to do anything and often faced his wrath myself. Nevertheless, one day, he went too far. I tried to protect my mother from one of his beatings. I failed. I will never forget the way she was lying on the floor bleeding from her head and unconscious. I thought he had killed her. He then turned on me and began beating me with the same poker stick until I was on the floor, unable to move myself. A neighbour alerted the police after hearing the screams. Following that night, my father did some time in prison. My mother recovered and then divorced him. We moved away from the town and started a fresh in a new town. My mother reverted to her maiden name, and it was just the two of us thereafter. My mother worked hard to put me through university, and I will always be grateful to her for that. My father died several years after he was released from prison.

The drink got the better of him in the end. My mother died five years ago from cancer."

Eden brushed a tear escaping down her cheek and hugged him tighter. "I am so sorry. You have been through so much. Your mother sounds like an amazing woman. I wish I could have met her."

Noah turned to Eden and placed his hand on her cheek. "You are a lot like her in some ways."

A loud noise outside startled them. Bella and Duke began barking ferociously at the front door. Noah jumped off the bed, "Stay here," he demanded while heading towards the door. Eden wrapped herself securely in the sheet and listened intently to the chaos unfolding downstairs. Hearing the front door slam, she ran to the top of the stairs, "N-O-A-H, she shouted.

"Hey, it's okay. I think I scared them off. Looks like someone was snooping around in your garden. They won't be back anytime soon. All this intrusion will die down in a few weeks, trust me. Come on, it's nothing to worry about. Let's go back to bed," he said.

Eden propped herself up against the headboard. Noah's revelation of his past playing on her mind. She observed his face for some time. "I will never betray you. You can count on me," she blurted.

"I know I can. Now you know everything about me. No secrets from one another, okay?"

"It's a deal," agreed Eden.

TWENTY

*E*den's life had been turned upside down over the last several weeks since Noah revealed their relationship to the press. The media circus had calmed down after Noah and Eden posed for several pictures. Eden was now comfortable with her new placement in the world of coupledom, and she was used to her more public life with Noah. She learned to avoid the comments and speculations about her relationship and took them for what they were. She spent more time at Ainsworth House and found that she preferred to be there than at her cottage. She enjoyed the privacy it afforded her and Noah. *It makes complete sense to me now, why Noah chose Ainsworth House. It is far removed from the outside world and no one could get past the tight security Noah has in place.*

Eden finished her breakfast while Betty was kneading dough and humming a tune to herself in the kitchen.

"I'm going to walk the dogs, Betty. I shall be no more than an hour. They need a good run this morning."

Betty spun around, her hands covered in dough, "Will you be around for lunch today? I am preparing my special casserole!"

Eden slipped on her jacket and turned to Betty, "Sorry Betty, I am heading into town to meet Blake today. He has a new client lined up for me, so we are discussing it over lunch."

Betty sighed, "That's a shame. I will plate some up for you. Maybe you can have some later. Will Noah be back today?"

"No, he is in New York until Friday. I miss him when he's gone. I can't wait for him to come back. I'm just taking Bella and Duke for a walk before I head out to meet Blake. I shouldn't be too long."

Eden headed out of the door with Bella and Duke. The sky was a clear blue and not a cloud in sight. She ambled through the fields, lost in her thoughts for some time. Her future with Noah dominated her mind. *I can imagine having a family with him and seeing our children running through Ainsworth House causing mayhem for Jackson and Betty.* She realised that she had walked too far and for too long. She glanced at the time on her phone and gasped, realising that she had been out for almost two hours. She frantically searched all around her for Bella and Duke, calling out their names. However, there was no response. *Where the hell are they?* she wondered.

She found herself deep in the middle of a densely wooded area. "B-E-L-L-A, D-U-K-E, she yelled. She stopped dead in her tracks and listened intently for a sign—no response. Feeling panicked, she continued walking. She stopped when she heard a snapping sound behind her. Her eyes darted all around, but there was nothing. She continued walking picking up her pace. The panic elevated within her. She felt as if she was being followed. Again, the sound of snapping twigs startled her. She spun around, her eyes widening on sight of a masked stranger behind her. She attempted to run to no avail. The blow to her head forced her to the ground with a thud and everything went black.

* * *

"What is all this commotion?" cursed Betty, disturbed by the scratching and barking at the kitchen side entrance. She opened the door. Bella and Duke darted past her. Betty searched all around for Eden, but she was nowhere to be seen. "I am guessing she is trailing behind." She left the door ajar for Eden and made her way back into the kitchen to feed Bella and Duke. "What's wrong with you two, pipe down," urged Betty.

Jackson walked through the door and glared at the dogs, "What's up with them two? I have never seen Duke like this before."

"I have no idea. Eden took them out for a walk hours ago. I was getting worried until these two turned up a few minutes ago. However, Eden is not with them. I figured she was trailing behind them. But she has not turned up yet. Maybe you should go out and look for her. Eden said she was meeting her boss in town today, I'm worried she may have tripped and hurt herself," advised Betty.

"Good idea. I am sure she is fine, Betty. She probably stopped by the lodge. I will head over there now." Jackson headed straight out of the door and across the fields. Eden was nowhere to be seen. Jackson reached the lodge and searched all around. He knew Eden had not been there. He traced the land in every direction, but there was no sight of Eden. Panicked, he called Max.

"Max, it's Jackson. We have a problem. Eden appears to have disappeared while out walking the dogs. The dogs turned up alone after several hours. Eden was not with them."

"What time did she leave?" pressed Max.

"It was several hours ago. She told Betty she would be an hour at most as she had a meeting with her boss in town. I have searched the fields and woods." Jackson was cautious not to mention the lodge. He knew Noah did not wish for anyone to be aware of it.

"Thanks Jackson. Have you tried calling Eden?"

"Yes, it's going straight to her voice mail."

"This is not good. Not good at all. Jackson, come back to the house. I will need you here."

Max made a phone call to Noah. He felt dread setting in with the news he was about to impart. As soon as Noah answered the call, Max said, "Finally, look Noah, Eden seems to have gone missing. She took the dogs out for a walk after breakfast. She was only supposed to be gone an hour. Several hours later, the dogs turned up barking and alone. Eden has not been seen since. Jackson searched the land and woods, but nothing. I'm going to call the police, but I just wanted to check with you before I did anything. Look Noah, shall I reach out to your contact in the force, we can trust he will be discreet and won't leak anything to the press at this stage?"

There was a long pause before Noah replied, "Yes. Do you still have Hanson's direct number?"

"Yes, I do."

"Good, call him now. Reiterate the need for discretion, Max. After what happened three years ago, the last thing I need is a media circus on my doorstep. All they do is make things worse. I will be on the next flight out of New York. Max–please find her."

"Don't worry, we will find her."

Max searched his contacts and he stopped at Detective Hanson's number and swiped to call.

"Detective Hanson, speaking."

"Hanson... It's Max."

"Well, this is a surprise. I wasn't expecting to hear from you again. What brings you to me?"

"I'm guessing you've heard about Eden Marshall, Noah's new girlfriend."

"Yes, it's been all over the press, hard to miss really. What does this have to do with me?"

"She's gone missing. She disappeared while walking the dogs on Noah's land. She left this morning after breakfast. The dogs turned up at Ainsworth House alone several hours later. Eden has not been seen since. She said she would be no more than an hour as she had a meeting with her boss in town early afternoon. She is not answering her phone either. Something is wrong. Noah instructed me to call you directly. He values your discretion and wants to keep the media at bay for as long as possible."

"What is it with Noah and the women in his life? Look, Max, you know the drill. You can file a missing person's report after 24 hours. However, it must be 48 hours before we can make the missing person's details available to other UK police forces. Leave it with me, Max. I will investigate it. Do you have Eden's home address?"

"Yes, I will text it to you when we are done talking."

"Good, I will send an officer around to her house, get him to sniff around see if anything turn's up. In the meantime, keep me updated on any further developments."

"Thanks, Hanson. I really appreciate it."

Max ended the call and searched for Eden's number. Once again, it forwarded to voice mail. *Where the hell are you, Eden?* he wondered.

Jackson walked into the kitchen, kicking off his muddy boots. He placed them down on the doormat, exhausted after his second detailed search.

Betty hurried over to him. She worried, "What could have happened to her, Jackson?"

Jackson remained silent, shaking his head. Betty placed a hot cup of tea in his hands, "I have a bad feeling about this."

"Best not to speculate, Betty. We don't know anything at this point. It is too early."

"Oh, for God's sake, Jackson, too early, really? This sort of thing does not happen on Ainsworth land. Eden is in trouble, I know it. She takes the dogs out walking this morning and the dogs return alone. It is almost 5 o'clock. It has been more than seven hours already. I think the police need calling now," urged Betty.

"Calm down. Max has already called them. It is in their hands now."

"About time too."

Jackson remained silent and left the kitchen. He found Max in the atrium on the phone Jackson waited patiently for Max to finish his call.

"What is it, Jackson?"

"Any word from, Eden?"

Max shook his head, saying not a word. He paced the floor. He then turned around to face Jackson, his brow furrowing. "I don't know what else to do. You have searched all over the land. I have called Detective Hanson. There is nothing else we can do at this stage, except wait. Noah is on his way back from New York. He will need collecting from the airport later. Just be there for him. His flight arrives at 11.10 assuming there are no delays."

"Ofcourse,leaveitwithme."

"Thanks Jackson, you're a good man."

TWENTY-ONE

*E*den's eyes struggled to adjust to the darkness enveloping her. Her heart pounded in her chest when she realized that she could hardly move. Her breaths quickened and panic was setting in fast. She could just about move her arms. She extended her arm above her and felt around. She was enclosed... Fear consumed her. Her body trembled. She screamed–but her cries were ignored. She utilised all the force she could muster in the tight space. She tried to push the top of the box, but all that achieved was a rush of loose soil slipping through the cracks, covering her face. She shook her head vigorously, feeling the impending danger. Her lower lip trembled. Her eyes were gritty and sore. She sobbed. *Who would do this? What is happening to me? Where am I?* Her eyes widened, aware that someone was there... She froze. The person is silent – not a sound. Then all she could hear was the sound of footsteps fading into the distance.

* * *

Noah leapt out of the car, leaving Jackson to carry his bags. He ran into the house, shouting Max's name at the top of his voice, alerting everyone in Ainsworth House. Upon hearing the shout, Max flew down the stairs.

"Any news?" blurted Noah.

"Nothing, sorry," apologised Max.

"What the hell is going on, Max. Who would do this?" Noah paced the atrium, his fists clenched, and his mind engulfed by rage.

Max added, "I have no idea. This has surprised us all."

"Well, I can't just sit on my hands and do nothing. I am heading out to the woods. Eden can't have just disappeared off the face of the earth."

Max placed his hand on Noah's arm. "I'm coming with you," he insisted.

Noah tensed, shaking his head, "No, I need you here in case Detective Hanson tries to contact you. Mobile connection in the woods is poor. I will take Jackson with me."

Jackson appeared with Noah's bags, "I will take these up to your room."

"No, put them down here, we are heading straight back out," demanded Noah.

Jackson did as Noah instructed and followed him to the kitchen. "Betty, pass me two torches from the drawer. Jackson and I are heading out to the woods."

Betty's brows snapped together, "Jackson has combed the land and woods twice, Noah."

"Just pass me the torches, Betty– NOW. We are searching again. She must be somewhere. This makes no logical sense whatsoever. As I said to Max, I cannot just wait around hoping she will turn up. I need to do this."

Betty nodded and passed the torches to Noah. She watched from the back door, while Noah and Jackson headed off into the night.

It was pitch black in the dense woods. There was nothing for miles around, and Noah was worried. "Jackson, did you search the lodge?"

"Yes, twice. Inside and out. There was no sign of her being there today."

"It makes no sense, Jackson. I cannot think of anyone who would want to hurt me like this."

"What about, Caspian?" piped Jackson.

"This is even beyond Caspian's repertoire. It's not his style, Jackson. No–this is personal."

Noah and Jackson spent hours searching to no avail. Eventually, they turned around and headed back to Ainsworth House.

Once Noah had showered and changed, he called an urgent meeting with Max and Luke. Noah paced his office and then turned to Luke, "I need your best men on this, Luke. Use everything you have to trace Eden's digital steps along with anyone who has been in contact with her over the last 48 hours."

Luke nodded, "Consider it done."

"Max, the police can only do so much. We need to go underground for this. I need you to contact the boys, get them to conduct their own discreet investigation. If anyone can find out what is going on, they can. Someone somewhere knows something..."

TWENTY-TWO

*B*lake sat back in his chair, drumming his fingers on his desk and pondering the news Noah had imparted. *I cannot wrap my mind around it. Eden is missing...*

Blake informed Angie that Eden would not be in for a few days without explanation, complying with Noah's instructions. Blake's office door swung open, and a concerned Angie stood before him.

"Sorry to burst in like this. Is Eden okay?"

Blake's eyes widened. He shifted uncomfortably in his chair, "Eden has taken a few days off. After all, she is owed a backlog of holiday. Please can you rearrange her calendar and distribute her appointments between the rest of her team. Thanks. Oh... and could you divert all her calls directly to me."

Angie raised her brow, "Oh... I see. It's just that, she normally informs me if she is not going to be in."

"Angie, I am busy. Please, close the door on your way out," snapped Blake.

Blake swivelled in his chair to face the large windows overlooking the city. *I am worried – very worried*. His phone rang and alerted him. He spun around and glanced at the number flashing cross his screen. It was Eva. "Hi, this is a welcome surprise," answered Blake.

"You sound funny. Is everything okay?" queried Eva.

"Yes, everything's fine. It's just one of those days. Anyway, are we still on for tonight?" asked Blake.

"Sorry, Blake. Something has come up. How about Saturday, are you free?"

"Saturday is fine. Looking forward to it more than you know."

"Me too. I have to go. I will call you tomorrow. Miss you," finished Eva.

"Miss you, too."

Blake could not concentrate on his work. He grabbed his jacket off the back of his chair and was ready to leave. He informed Angie that he would be out for the rest of the day then left the office.

Angie watched him leave. She tried to understand what was going on. *Something is not right. I am going to give Eden a call.* She decided. She called Eden's number—no one answered it. She left a brief message and hung up. *What is going on?* She worried. There were several calls waiting to be answered. Angie answered line one, "Good morning, Imperial Home Magazine, how many I help you?"

"Angie, it's Jennifer, Eden's mum. Can you put me through to her, please? I have been trying to get hold of her since yesterday to confirm our lunch date tomorrow. However, she is not picking up her calls. This is unlike her."

Angie fell silent, not knowing what to say.

"Angie, are you there?"

"Yes, sorry. Eden has taken a few days off work. I am sure she will call you soon. I think it was a last-minute thing." *I feel awful. I can sense the concern in Jennifer's voice. I have my own concerns right now too*, thought Angie.

"Oh... I see. Well, if you hear from her first, will you please ask her to call me? I know how close the two of you are?"

"Of course."

"Thanks, Angie. Speak soon," finished Jennifer.

* * *

The sound of footsteps alerted Eden. She felt a sense of dread. She had no idea what time or day it was. "Hello... Who is there? Please help me." Her pleas were ignored. The footsteps stopped directly above her.

A shiver ran down her spine. A shadow cast her box into partial darkness. "Please... why are you doing this. I am nobody?" Eden heard a rustling sound. Her eyes darted to the top of the box and widened. Something was poking through the crack in the box and nearing her arm. She flinched, attempting to flatten herself against the base of the box. Frightened, she tried to wriggle to the left. She failed in her attempt and could not avoid the syringe puncturing her arm. Her body fell limp. She could not move a muscle— he was paralysed.

TWENTY-THREE

*N*oah pushed open the door to Eden's cottage and threw his keys down onto the hallway table. Bella and Duke ran past him. He had no idea where to start and felt as if he was invading Eden's privacy. *Sorry Eden, I have to do this, if it will lead me to a clue as to what is going on.* He began his search in Eden's small box office. He sat at her desk and pulled the top drawer open. He rummaged through Eden's personal papers, but there was nothing out of the ordinary. He sighed, then pulled out the second drawer and did the same. Halfway through searching, he paused. There was an envelope. He pulled it out and studied it. It was personal—not business. He took out its contents and gasped, *What the hell...?* He opened the card and read it:

To Eden,

Take your time. There is no rush. I have all the time in the world. I know this is hard for you. It is hard for me too. I was not expecting to meet you either. I keep thinking about last week—he best two hours of my life. I understand what a struggle the past few weeks have been for you. I cannot imagine being thrust into the limelight like that. I am just glad that you felt you could open up and talk to me about it. Anyway, I am off on a business trip and should be back the week after next. I hope that we can see each other then and decide where we are going with this.

Always on my mind–J.S.

Noah leapt from his seat in anger. It took him several minutes to process what he had read. He slipped the card back into the envelope and then put it into his top right-hand pocket. He slammed his hand down on the desk. *Why, Eden? Why? I thought what we had was real and that you were different. How wrong I was.* Noah filled up with rage while rifling through Eden's personal documents. Nothing of interest showed up. He closed her office door behind him and made his way upstairs to her bedroom. He flung open the bedroom door and paused for a few moments. *J.S. who is he?* Noah could not erase those initials from his mind. *Damn you, Eden.* He searched through her bedside drawers and found nothing of consequence, just a few books and Imperial Home editions. He turned to the wardrobe and was impressed at how everything was set out perfectly. He pushed back her clothes on the rails, creating an opening and glanced down at the floor. His eyes widened when they fell upon a pair of male boxer shorts. He picked them up and glared at them. He let out a harsh breath. Then he threw the shorts down. *I have seen enough. I need to get out of here*, he decided.

He headed downstairs, calling Bella and Duke to his side. "There you are. Come on you two, it's time for us to go." Bella whined and lay down on the floor beside Eden's boots, placing her head between her paws. Duke sensed her distress and lay next to her placing his paw on Bella's leg. Noah felt the pull on his heart and knelt down. He brushed Bella's head with his hand to comfort her, "Don't worry, Bella. Eden will be back before you know it. Come on girl, we need to go now. He got to his feet, and opened the front door. Bella and Duke climbed to their feet and they followed Noah out of the door to his car. Noah was confused; *Eden never indicated there was anything wrong, quite the opposite in fact. It makes sense—nothing makes any sense to me.* Noah thought to himself, feeling confused.

Noah pulled up outside Ainsworth House and climbed out of his car. He opened the passenger door to allow Bella and Duke to jump out. They ran ahead of him to the main entrance.

Jackson opened the door and greeted Noah, "Noah, Max has been trying to get in touch with you. There has been a development."

"Where is Max?" pressed Noah.

"He is in his office."

"Thanks, Jackson, can you feed the dogs for me and ask Carter to walk them too. I have not had time to walk them today."

"Of course. I shall attend to them immediately. Is there anything else?"

"No, that will be all for now," finished Noah.

Noah took the stairs two by two. He flung the door of Max's office wide open. "Max, what is going on?"

Max leapt from his chair and emerged from behind his desk. Thank God, where have you been? I have been trying to get hold of you for hours."

"My phone was in the car. Sorry, I stopped by Eden's house to see if there was anything I could find that may give me a clue as to what has happened to her."

"Look, Noah, you may want to sit down for this."

"For God's sake, Max, just spit it out," demanded Noah.

"Detective Hanson called. Eden is in the hospital. A dog walker found her unconscious down by the river this morning. It looks like someone purposely left her there to be found."

"Which hospital?" urged Noah.

"City Hospital. Come on, I will drive you," insisted Max.

"Is she okay?"

"She is unconscious. They gave me little information. Hanson said she might have been drugged. The nature of the drug is still being determined. This was a message for you, Noah. Whoever did this, if they wanted to kill Eden, they would have. They were sending you a message. Now we need to find out whom?"

"I don't know anyone who hates me enough to do this, Max."

"What about Caspian's men?"

"No. Absolutely not. It's not his style." With his mouth snapped shut, Noah glanced out of the window.

"What is it, Noah?"

Noah ignored the question.

"Noah?" pressed Max.

"It's nothing, really," snapped Noah.

"Well, there is something on your mind. If you know anything or anyone that could be connected to Eden's disappearance, then you need to tell me."

Noah spun around, his face twisted. "I'm not sure it is anything. However, I discovered Eden has been seeing someone recently." Noah reached into his top pocket and pulled out the card he had found in Eden's house, then handed it over to Max.

Max pulled over and read the card. His forehead creased, "What the hell... No, this can't be right. I saw what you two were like together. Eden wouldn't do this to you."

"Well, I guess you never really know someone. And she did do it, Max."

"So, what now?"

"I don't know. I need to talk with her when she wakes up; I need to hear it from her mouth. I think all the publicity was too much for her. I told you before, she is not like most women that I have come across before. She hates the limelight and all that pretentiousness. I just didn't realise how much until now."

"I'm sorry, Noah. This must be painful for you. I know how hard it was for you to open up and let someone into your life again, after what happened before."

"You're not wrong there. Come on let's get to the hospital. I need to get her moved to my private hospital. The press is going to be all over this."

"Ah, yes... that was the other bad news. It was all over the news an hour after they found her. They must have been tipped off, for it to have spread that quickly."

"Well, an unconscious body on the riverbank will do that. Not something we could have contained."

Max pulled up at the hospital entrance and let Noah out of the car. He parked up while Noah rushed to the reception desk. Max caught up with him and they followed the receptionist instructions to ICU. Noah stopped in his tracks before entering Eden's room. He turned to Max and asked, "Can you give me some time alone with her. Get us a coffee."

Max nodded and left. Noah entered the room and gasped on sight of Eden while clamping his hand over his mouth. His eyes trailed the surface scratches on her face and the bruise on her eye. The one side of her face was swollen and overlapping her eye. He glanced at her fingers - two nails had been torn clean off. The tips of her other fingers were red raw. *What happened to you, Eden? Who would do this?* His eyes flashed with anger as he surveyed her fragile body lying still in the bed. He sat beside her, brushing the tears from his face. "I promise you that I will find out who did this."

A woman he did not recognise entered the room. She stopped in her tracks on sight of Noah. An uncomfortable silence ensued. The woman rushed over to Eden. "My poor baby. What have they done to you?" she cried.

Noah reached over to the woman, guessing she was Eden's mother. He placed his hand on her arm, comforting her. The woman spun around, her eyes reddened, and her face soaked in tears.

She choked back her tears hard. "Hello, you must be Noah Ainsworth. I am-" she paused, choking back a lump in her throat. Then she continued, "I am Eden's mother, Jennifer."

Noah extended his hand courteously, "Pleased to meet you. I just wish it could be under better circumstances."

Jennifer could not contain her tears. She turned her attention back to Eden and gasped as her eyes trailed over her, "My baby...?" she cried. She took Eden's hand in hers and rested her head on top.

"We will find whoever did this. I promise you," said Noah.

Jennifer continued sobbing, unable to utter a word.

Noah placed a card in Jennifer's free hand. "I will leave you alone for a while. "If there is anything you need–anything at all, just call me."

Jennifer nodded, closing her fingers around the card in her hand.

Noah headed for the door. A nurse entering the room startled him, "Sorry, I need to change her drip. I won't be a moment."

"How is she? Do you know what happened to her?" pleaded Noah.

"I'm sorry. We are waiting for the toxicology report. Eden has been through the mill though. She is dehydrated and weak. I can tell you that nothing is broken. We are more concerned with the toxicology report at this stage. Then we can determine the next step forward," advised the nurse.

Jennifer spun around, her face twisted, soaked in tears. "I am Eden's mother; would you mind if I stay here a while longer?"

The nurse smiled, "I don't see why not."

Max entered the room with two coffees. He glanced around and caught Noah's eye. Noah raised his eyebrow and glanced at the door, indicating for Max to leave.

"Ah, got it!" said Max. He turned on his heels and waited outside the door.

Noah bid goodbye to Jennifer and followed swiftly behind Max.

"Here you go. So, what did the nurse say?" piped Max.

Noah drew in a deep breath, "They are waiting on the toxicology report. There is nothing they can do until the results are in. She was extremely dehydrated and unconscious when she was found, and that is all they know. She hasn't woken up yet. God Max, she has been through hell. How could I have let this happen?"

"You can't blame yourself, Noah. There was no way you could have anticipated this. No one could have."

"We have only been together a brief time. I have spent half of that time in New York. She needed me here when she was being hounded by the press and dealing with rogue calls. I am used to it, but I never took into consideration the impact it would all have on Eden. So yes, I blame myself. I should have been present a lot more than I was these last few weeks."

Sadness clouded Max's features. "You won't help Eden by beating yourself up. Focus on what we can all do to help her right now."

Noah raised his head and turned to face Max, "You are right of course. I need to focus on whoever did this. Eden was so still in there, Max. That is some drug she was given. She did not deserve that." Noah paused, lost in his thoughts for a moment. He added, "I swear, as God is my witness, I will find out who did this and make them pay. That will be my focus."

Max asked, "So, who was that woman beside Eden?"

"That was Eden's mother. Not the way I imagined our first meeting to go. She is devastated. No mother should ever have to see their daughter like that." Noah stopped halfway down the corridor on sight of Detective Hanson.

"Noah, how is she?"

"Not conscious yet."

"Look, we are doing everything we can. We have our best team on the case. As soon as I know something you will."

"Thanks, Hanson."

A doctor approached Noah, "Hello, my name is Doctor Matthews. We will keep Eden in ICU for the next 48 hours at least. She remains in a critical but stable condition. As soon as the toxicology report come in, we will let you know immediately."

"Thank you," responded Noah.

Max, let's go, there is nothing I can do for Eden here. I need to speak with Luke, see what or if he has found anything."

TWENTY-FOUR

*E*den's eyes opened wide and darting around the room frantically. She sat bolt upright screaming! Two nurses ran into her room and comforted her, "Hello Eden, it's okay, you are safe now. You are in City Hospital. The nurse placed her hand behind Eden's head and reached for some water. Here, drink this."

Eden was confused. The nurse buzzed for the doctor. "Doctor Matthews will be here shortly, Eden."

"How did I get here?" asked Eden.

"The doctor will tell you everything you need to know when he arrives. In the meantime, just lie down and relax."

"Noah..." she blurted.

"Would you like me to call him for you?"

"Yes. I need to see Noah."

"Okay, I will call him. Just stay calm. You are safe now," the nurse, reiterated.

Doctor Matthews entered the room and pulled up a chair beside Eden's bed. "Hello, Eden, how are you feeling?"

"Weak and disorientated."

Doctor Matthews nodded, "That's to be expected. You had us all worried for a while."

Eden shifted position to relieve the pain in her leg, "What happened to me?"

"That is what we are trying to determine. What do you remember about the last couple of days?"

"The last couple of days?!" repeated Eden.

"Yes. You were missing for two days."

Eden shook her head. A tear trailed down her cheek. "I remember walking Bella and Duke through the fields. I had been walking longer than I intended. I searched around and could not see them. That is all I remember. Until I woke up in a box. I really thought I was going to die...," she cried.

"It's okay, Eden. You are in the best hands possible. Nothing will happen to you here," assured Doctor Matthews.

"Who found me?"

"A man out walking his dog found you on the riverbank a couple of miles outside Acton Village."

"How is that possible? I was nowhere near the river. I was in the woods searching for Bella and Duke?"

"I'm afraid that's all I know. Detective Hanson will be able to tell you more later. In the meantime, you need to rest."

A nurse entered the room and whispered in Doctor Matthew's ear. "I'm sorry, Eden, I will be back shortly to check on you."

Doctor Matthews closed Eden's door and turned to the nurse handing him some papers. He stood quietly, assessing Eden's toxicology report. "Poor woman. Her bodies' been through hell. I'm surprised she's awake at all with that amount in her system."

"Right nurse, the patient needs activated charcoal to absorb any of the drugs in her digestive system. We need to place the patient on a full detoxification programme, to prevent fatal withdrawal symptoms from occurring. Keep a close eye on her vital signs and if her respiratory rate increases put her on oxygen. She will need to remain here for a few days at the very least."

"On it," replied the nurse.

Doctor Matthews re-entered Eden's room, "Hello Eden," he said, pulling up a chair beside her.

Eden remained silent waiting for Doctor Matthews to continue.

He continued, "Your toxicology report has come back. I am afraid it's not good news. It shows us that someone drugged you with Rohypnol. It is a trade name for the drug Benzodiazepine and forms part of the Valium family. Only, Rohypnol is by far stronger and at least ten times more potent. The tests show us that a great deal of this drug was administered to you and that is why you were unconscious for so long." Noting the worried expression on Eden's face, he continued, "We are going to place you on a full detoxification programme to ensure every last trace of the drug is cleaned out of your system. However, this will take a few days. So, in the meantime, you will have to remain in hospital so that we can closely monitor you."

"Rohypnol... but I thought it was illegal in the UK?" blurted Eden.

"It's not illegal in the UK. However, it is only accessible via prescription privately. Possessing it any other way is illegal.

"That's insane. I don't believe this," she cried.

"I promise you that we are doing everything we can. The nurse will be in shortly to attend to you. If there is anything you need, Eden, then don't hesitate to call. There is a buzzer right above your head."

Eden clutched her chest, "Will I be okay?"

Dr Matthews gave her a reassuring smile, "Yes. You are going to be just fine."

A nurse entered the room just as Doctor Matthews was leaving, "Detective Hanson is waiting for you in your office."

"Thank you, nurse."

The nurse attended to Eden while Doctor Matthews hurried to his office. He swung open the door and Hanson stood up, "I believe the toxicology report is in."

"Yes. Take a seat, please."

Doctor Matthews handed the report over to Hanson. Hanson glanced through it with a fine-tooth comb. "Wow! How is she awake?"

"That was my first reaction when I viewed the report!"

"Does she know?"

"Yes, I have just come from her room."

"How'd she react?"

"As expected, she is confused and fragile right now. She has no real concept of what happened to her from what I can gather. Her memory is confused, which is to be expected with this type of drug. We will keep her in for a few days."

Hanson swept his brow, "We will need to perform a forensic medical examination."

Doctor Matthews nodded, "I was coming to that. Until we received the results, we had no idea what we were dealing with. This type of drug is often used in rape cases. I will let you discuss that with my patient. Unless you would rather I did?"

"No, I will talk with her as this is her decision to make. Sometimes, victims of this sort of crime do not want to know if they were raped. It is rare, but it happens. Let me speak with her and we shall take it from there. Do you have a specialist nurse, trained and available, should Eden agree to the examination?"

"Thankfully, yes we do."

"Great. I will go and speak with Eden and then we will know where we stand." Hanson stood up and left.

Eden's mind was working overtime. She tried to recall what happened to her. All she remembered was walking through the woods, waking up in a box and the debilitating fear that consumed her. Everything else in between was a blur. Her eyes darted to the door when Hanson entered.

"Hello, Eden. I would like to talk to you if you are feeling up to it?" Eden took in a sharp breath and nodded, "That's fine."

Hanson pulled up a chair beside her. "I have just come from Doctor Matthew's office. He informed me that you have a large amount of Rohypnol in your system. I don't know any other way to say this, so I will just come out with it... Rohypnol is a popular drug used in sexual assault crimes. Now, in order for us to determine what exactly has happened to you, it would be advisable to have a full forensic medical examination. However, this is your decision to make. You don't have to go through with it if you don't wish to. I won't lie to you Eden, it will feel intrusive, and the process can last up to four hours. You will be prodded and poked, swabbed, photographed in all the places you might have been assaulted. The forensic nurses are specially trained. If you agree and halfway through want them to stop, then you just have to say the word. We need to determine why you were kidnapped and what if anything else happened to you. But it's your call Eden."

Eden swiped the tears blanketing her cheeks. She choked back a lump forming in her throat.

"Would you like some time to think about it?" asked Hanson.

Shaking her head, Eden looked into Hanson's eyes, "No. I want to do this. I need to know what happened to me."

"You are a brave woman, Eden. I will speak with Doctor Matthews and get the ball rolling."

"Is there anyone you would like me to call?"

"My mother. I need her here with me."

"Leave it with me."

"Thank you," choked Eden.

Hanson left the room and headed straight for Doctor Matthew's office.

TWENTY-FIVE

*N*oah ran through the hospital corridor to Eden's room, then paused. He inhaled a deep breath and pushed the door open. "Hanson!" blurted Noah.

Hanson spun around, "I was just leaving. Look, can I have a brief word with you outside?"

"Sure." Noah glanced over to Eden, "I won't be too long."

They both stepped out into the corridor. Hanson spoke first, "A sizeable amount of a drug called, Rohypnol was found in Eden's system." Eden has agreed to a forensic medical examination. In my experience, cases like these are usually indicative of a rape crime," Hanson paused allowing his words to digest.

Noah's hands balled into fists, "RAPE!" raged Noah.

Noah added, "Who would do this to her?"

Hanson placed a comforting hand on Noah's arm, "Let's not jump to conclusions just yet. At this point, it is just a formality to determine what might have happened to Eden. You need to keep it together, for Eden's sake. She has been through a tough time and now she must go through the ordeal of a full forensic medical examination. She is very fragile. We will know more when we get the results," advised Hanson.

"You are right. I need to keep it together. Thanks. Keep me posted," finished Noah. He took a moment to compose himself, swallowing down a gulp before re-entering Eden's room. He pulled up a seat beside her and took her hand in his.

She winced, pulling back her hand. "Sorry, my fingers are really sore," she apologised.

Noah's eyes rested on her fingers, "No, I'm sorry. I should have realised. How are you holding up?"

"I'm not. I have just lost two days of my life and I have barely any memory of what happened to me. Now I find out that I may have been raped too." Eden turned away from Noah, fighting back her tears.

"Hey, look at me. I am here for you. You are not alone in this."

Eden's glossy eyes searched Noah's face, "What happened to me, Noah? Who would do this?"

Noah shook his head and stood up, turning to face the window. He did not know what to say. He had no answers. Feeling his anger bubbling to the surface, he drew in a harsh breath to suppress it.

"Noah, are Bella and Duke okay?"

"Yes, they are fine. They found their way home the day you went missing. That was what alerted us to the fact something was wrong. You were only supposed to be gone for an hour. It was several hours later when Bella and Duke turned up. They were barking frantically at the kitchen door. Betty worried immediately as she knew you had a meeting with your boss. At first, everyone thought you might have slipped and hurt yourself. We searched the entire land and woods twice. Nevertheless, you were nowhere to be found. I have never felt so scared in my life. The thought of losing you sent me crazy."

Tears trailed down Eden's cheeks. Noah leant forward and wrapped his arms around her. "I promise I will never let anything hurt you again. I am going to have you moved to a private hospital later today."

"No... please, I want to stay here. I cannot bear to be moved now. The nurses have been amazing. Doctor Matthews is a great doctor—compassionate. Please, Noah, leave me here."

"Okay, as you wish. Do you remember anything about the last few days—anything at all?"

"All I remember is that I was lost in my thoughts while walking the dogs. You know—daydreaming about our future together. I was happy. I had been a little longer than I intended. I had wandered off your land and when I realised where I was, I frantically searched for Bella and

Duke, calling out their name-" Eden paused mid-speech, a look of terror flashed across her face...

"Eden, what is it?"

"There was someone behind me. I was not alone. There was someone there... The next thing I remember, I was waking up in a box. I could not move. I was screaming for help. That is all I remember. I have no idea how I got to the riverbank where I was found. I have no memory of that at all."

A nurse entered the room and glanced at Noah, "We will need you to step out of the room for a while now."

Noah looked at Eden, "Do you want me to stay? Just say the word."

"No. My mum is on her way. I need her here with me. You understand?"

Noah leaned in and kissed her forehead. "Of course. Your mother should be with you. I will be right outside if you need me," he assured.

"Noah–I love you."

Noah smiled but did not reciprocate. He left the room as the nurse pulled the curtain around Eden. Noah's lack of reciprocation was not lost on Eden. But right now, she had other things to worry about. Without warning, the door flung open again, "Mum, thank God."

"Don't worry. I will be here with you every step of the way."

The nurse chimed in, "Hi, my name is Cara banks. I am a specialist nurse, trained to examine victims of sexual assault crimes. We will perform a full forensic medical examination today. My colleague will be along shortly to assist. There are various steps we need to take you through this afternoon, Eden. We need to collect as much evidence as we can. I would like to brief you on exactly what we do today. I won't lie to you; this examination can feel invasive. We need to collect as much DNA from your body as possible. Whether you were raped or not, any evidence we collect is crucial and could help the police with their investigation." Nurse Banks glanced down at her sheet.

Eden was feeling vulnerable. Her chest rose and fell with rapid breaths. She squeezed her mum's hand tight. Jennifer searched Eden's face and wanted to scream aloud. Her heart was breaking for what her daughter had been through. Remaining silent, she held it together for Eden's sake.

Nurse Banks continued, "We will need to take internal swabs from both your vaginal and anal area. Are you okay with that Eden?"

Eden cleared a lump in her throat. Choking it back, she nodded, "Yes, I need to do this. I need to know what happened to me."

Jennifer stepped back, allowing the nurse to get closer to Eden and begin.

The nurse placed her hand on Eden's arm and gave it a squeeze, "You are very brave, Eden. Photographs of any injuries will also be taken and may be used in court at a later date. Should your case go to trial? Do you understand?"

Eden brushed a lone tear escaping down her cheek, "Yes, I understand."

"You are doing great. Remember, you can pause this examination at any time."

The nurse glanced over to the chair in the corner of the room, "Are those clothes on the chair yours?"

Eden nodded.

"Were those the clothes you were wearing when you were brought into the hospital?"

"Yes."

Nurse Banks stood up and walked around to the chair. She picked up the clothes and placed them in a bag, labelled it and sealed it.

"Have you had a shower or strip down wash since being admitted to City Hospital?"

Eden looked at the nurse confused, "Mmm, I have no idea. Not that I am aware of. You would have to ask the staff nurse attending to me."

"Okay. That's not a problem. I can ask them later. Now, before I continue, I just want to inform you that at any time during this examination you can stop or pause for a break. We can continue at any time. You just have to let me know. I know how hard this is. But the more evidence we collect, the more it will help your case."

"I understand."

"While we wait for Nurse Cowell, I am going to go through some paperwork with you. Medical questions any medication you may be taking and so on. Are you okay with that?"

"Yes, that's fine."

Nurse Cowell wandered up the corridor and stopped when she saw Noah perched outside of Eden's room. "You okay?" she asked.

"Yes. I'm just waiting to see Eden Marshall," he said, pointing to her room.

"Well, I'm afraid you will be waiting for some time. This is not a quick examination. It can take several hours. If I were you, I would go home and come back this evening. You will serve Eden better by returning freshened up later today. That is when she will really need you."

Noah thanked the nurse, then left.

Nurse Cowell entered Eden's room with a wide comforting smile on her face, "Hello, Eden, my name is Nurse Cowell, and I will assist Nurse Banks today," she greeted.

Eden gave a half-smile and remained silent. Her nerves had got the better of her. She was trembling. Fear enveloped her. She retreated to a place in her mind, no longer hearing the nurse's voices around her. She moved, sat up, stood up, and nodded robotically when instructed. Nevertheless, emotionally she was somewhere else for the following hours.

TWENTY-SIX

*N*oah paused outside Eden's hospital room. *I am dreading the results of her examination. Please God, let them be in her favour. I am not sure I could handle the worst-case scenario*, he prayed. He flung open the door and glanced over at Eden. She turned to him; her eyes were red and bloodshot. He sat down beside her– silent. He clasped her hands between his tightly. Searching her face, he brushed a rogue tear from her cheek.

"It's too soon for the test results, Noah. The nurse advised me there were no visible signs of rape, though. She said the usual signs in a case of rape were not visible anywhere. She thinks it highly unlikely that I was raped. However, we need to wait for the results to confirm that." Eden burst into tears.

Noah wrapped his arm around her, clearing a lump in his throat. It hurt him a lot to see what Eden was going through. He did everything he could to suppress his anger. Eden pulled away and reached for her glass of water. Noah stopped her, "Here, let me," he insisted, passing the water to her.

She looked into his tear-filled eyes, "When I was told there was Rohypnol in my system and what it was generally used for in cases like mine, I was convinced-" Eden broke off and clasped her hand over her mouth to quell her cries. Noah pulled her close to him, not saying a word.

"I pray the results confirm what the nurses think. But it makes no sense to me. I have been lying here thinking who would do this to me. I don't know anyone who would want to do this to me. At first, I thought it might be someone to do with your business world or someone wanting money from you. Then I brushed that thought away because there was no ransom demand. So, kidnapping for ransom was out of the question. They deliberately left me on the riverbank to be found, Noah. Why? To what end? There is no logic to it."

Noah nodded in agreement, at a loss for words. He said what Eden needed to hear right now to comfort her. "Right now, all you need to worry about is getting better. The police will find the underlying cause of this. They are working round the clock, I promise you," reassured Noah, unconvinced by his own words. But it was important that Eden believed him. He vowed to himself to find out whoever did this. J.S came to the forefront of his mind, dominating all other thoughts. *I need to know who this J.S guy is.*

"I have placed a security guard outside of your room. He will remain there until they discharge you. It is just cautionary. But I need to keep you safe."

Eden's eyes widened, "Do you think whoever did this, will come after me again?"

Noah shook his head and squeezed her hand, "No, but I am taking no risks." Noah spun around when a nurse entered the room. He stood up and kissed Eden on the forehead, "I need to head back to Ainsworth House. I will come back first thing in the morning. Is there anything you need me to bring for you?"

Eden smiled, "A toothbrush would be great."

"Consider it done. And remember, you are safe here. Simon is just outside the door. He is one of my best and most trusted security guards."

Noah left, leaving the nurse to attend to Eden. He could not shift the unsettling feeling circling his stomach. Something was not right. *Whatever is going on was not over. Max is right; this is personal and aimed directly at me. But why and who?* he wondered.

Unaware that he was being watched, Noah climbed into his car and drove out of the hospital car park. The car behind him followed him most of the way home, keeping a suitable distance behind Noah, stopping short of Acton Village. Noah turned right down a narrow lane and then a swift left until he reached Ainsworth House.

Max rushed out of the main entrance doors while Noah was locking up his car. "Thank God you are back. We have a situation."

Noah swiftly followed Max into the house and straight up the stairs to the boardroom. Max closed the boardroom door behind them, "You might want to sit down for this, Noah."

Noah's forehead puckered, "What the hell is going on, Max?"

Max cleared his throat, "Our systems have been compromised," blurted Max.

"Compromised! What do you mean compromised?"

"Basically, someone has hacked into our system. We were offline for over an hour. Once Luke managed to get the system up and running again, he revealed that someone had been searching your personal files. Luke is still working on the lead source to trace the hacker. If anyone can find them, Luke can."

"I don't believe this. How can this be possible? I have the best tech team out there. Ainsworth Global is practically impenetrable. Luke assured me of this. Where is Luke? I need to speak with him right now," demanded Noah.

"He's in his office trying to find the underlying cause of this nightmare. He hasn't left his computer since it happened."

Noah stormed out of the boardroom, across the hall, turned right and then left until he reached Luke's office. He burst through the door and startled Luke. "Start talking?" roared Noah.

Luke's mouth twitched, "I'm sure Max has filled you in. I am trying to figure out how the hackers got into our system. They are good, Noah—very good. They certainly knew what they were doing. So far, I have found nothing. They covered their tracks well. Leaving no trace behind. I can see what they were looking at—your personal files, specifically your itinerary for the next month. But why, who and where? Is a mystery. It is going to take me some time to figure this one out. What I am certain of is that nothing was downloaded or deleted. That is all I can assure you of at this time."

Noah slammed his fist down onto the desk, "I want you working on this around the clock, Luke. Where the hell is Sean?" Noah turned to Max, "Get Sean in here, in fact, get your whole God damn team in here. I want answers—tonight."

Noah stormed out of Luke's office, leaving the door wide open. Max raised his eyebrows at Luke and left the room. Noah headed down the stairs towards the library. Noah halted at the library doors and turned to Jackson. "I want to be left alone. I need to think."

Jackson nodded, remaining silent as Noah entered the library closing the doors behind him. The library was the only place in Ainsworth House where he could think clearly and figure out the solutions to his problems. He slumped down into a chair and drew in a harsh breath, placing his fingers on his temples while applying a little pressure to ease the tension building. *None of this makes any sense. Who is behind this and why?* he thought. Noah jumped off his seat with a start and fumbled in his jacket pocket for his phone. *Grasping at straws I may be, but I need to know!* he mused. He waited for Charlotte to answer his call. *Come on, Charlotte, answer your bloody phone.*

"Hello, Charlotte Chambers. Who may I ask is calling?"

"Charlotte, its Noah. I know this is unexpected, but I need to speak with you in person. Can I drop by this evening? It is really important."

Silence ensued. A moment later Charlotte answered, "Well, Noah Ainsworth... I must admit this is a surprise. I was not expecting to hear from you again. Does this have something to do with the kidnapping of your new girlfriend?"

"Yes, it does. Please, Charlotte. You owe me a few minutes of your time at least."

"Fine. However, if you think my Stephanie had anything to do with this—you are wrong. She is happy now. Moved on and found someone else. She got the treatment she needed and should have had years ago, I confess. So, I don't know how talking with me is going to help you."

"Just a few minutes of your time face to face. I can be there in less than two hours. Does that work for you? I promise I will not keep you long."

"Sure. I guess it won't hurt."

"Thank you, Charlotte. I appreciate it. See you soon." Noah rang off, pulled his car keys from his jacket pocket, and headed out of the library. He stopped in his tracks and turned to Jackson heading towards the kitchen, "Jackson, I am heading out. I will be gone for several hours."

"I shall inform Max on your behalf."

"Good man, Jackson."

Noah left the house with an urgency that worried Jackson. *I have a bad feeling about everything that is going on. I know there is something sinister we are missing in all of this*, thought Jackson.

* * *

Max gathered up most of the team and sent them to Luke's office. He popped his head around the conference room in search of Sean. He was not there. *Where the hell is he?* Max closed the door, turned to the back offices, and saw Sean heading up the corridor, "Sean, where have you been? I have been looking for you everywhere. Noah wants you in Luke's office now. All hands-on deck for this monumental fuck up. He wants answers tonight."

Sean nodded and headed straight for Luke's office, where the rest of the team were frantically tapping away and butting heads.

TWENTY-SEVEN

*C*harlotte pulled back the curtains and observed Noah climbing out of his car. She quickly swivelled around to her desk and fumbled with some papers, attempting to look busy. Her housekeeper answered the door and showed Noah through to Charlotte's office. Charlotte stood up and emerged from behind her desk. "Noah, I must say you are looking very well under the circumstances." She extended her hand, "Please, take a seat." Charlotte glanced at her housekeeper, "Grace, please would you organise a tray of tea?"

Grace nodded obediently and scurried out of the room. Charlotte took a seat opposite Noah and placed her hands on her knees. "So, why are you here, Noah?"

"I need to rule out Stephanie. I do not want to hurt your family. I did everything I could to help Stephanie get the help she needed three years ago. I think you will agree that I went above and beyond. So, now I need your help. Are you still in contact with her?"

Charlotte's brow wrinkled, "I am her mother– of course I am in contact with my daughter. Look, Noah, Stephanie remained in psychiatric care for over two years. She is on regular medication and it works well for her. Her mood swings are under control now?"

Noah chimed in, "Mood swings? Really, Charlotte–she was

144

psychotic. I think even you can admit that it was more than mood swings."

Charlotte raged, "Let's not get hung up on labels. Labels are damaging. She is not a threat to you anymore. She has long since got over you. She has a new love interest, and she is very happy. To be honest, I don't see much of her these days. However, we do speak on the phone or via face time at least once a fortnight. You know that she left the UK and moved to France, don't you?"

A flash of surprise crossed Noah's face, "No. I had no idea!"

Charlotte added, "Yes, she moved there with her partner just over six months ago now. She pops back every once in a while, but I have been unable to travel to France due to ill health."

"I am sorry to hear that. So, Stephanie rarely returns to the UK then?"

"That's right. After she was successfully treated, she wanted to forget what happened and get on with her life. She harboured a lot of guilt for what she did to you, Noah. She has always regretted it. But like I said, at the time, she was not in her right mind. I feel partly to blame, as I always knew there was something not quite right with Stephanie. I should have addressed it sooner. Anyway, I hope that I have put your mind at rest where Stephanie is concerned. Whoever did this to your girlfriend – I can assure you that it was not my daughter. She rarely leaves France. Stephanie and her partner bought a small vineyard, and they are living a peaceful life out there. Of course, you can check it out for yourself. The results will remain the same."

Noah sighed and placed his head in the palm of his hands for a moment. He then stood up. "Thank you. I just needed to be sure. You know... after what happened three years ago."

"I get it, Noah. In your shoes, I would have asked the same questions. Come on, I will show you out." Charlotte watched Noah until he drove out of sight. She remained standing on the steps for some time, before heading back into the house. Seeing Noah again, brought it all back to her. A time she never wanted to relive. Her losses were great, and she was reeling from the pain.

Feeling confused, Noah drove slow and steady all the way back home. After he had ruled out Stephanie, his focus turned back to J.S. *I need to find out who this man is. Something does not make sense. I can't raise the issue with Eden yet. At least not until she is out of the hospital.* Noah made a mental note of any suspected enemy he might have. *The only ones I can come up with are my business rivals and even they would not stoop to this level. My personal life until I met Eden was practically non-existent. The only person I vaguely suspected has now been ruled out following my visit with Charlotte.*

Noah was relieved to see Ainsworth House coming into sight. He pulled up and climbed out of his car. Jackson met him as he entered the house. "I wasn't expecting you to still be up, Jackson?"

"I had trouble sleeping. So, I came down for a nightcap."

"Are the team still here?" asked Noah.

"Yes. They have not left Luke's office all evening."

"Thank you, Jackson."

Noah headed straight up the stairs to Luke's office and flung the door open. Max stood over Sean and Luke. There eyes were firmly fixed on the screen in front of them.

"Any news?"

"Noah, you're back!" blurted Max.

"It's not good news, I'm afraid. Whoever hacked our system knew exactly what they were doing. All we know is that whoever did this was clever enough not to leave a trace. Luke has spent the last several hours securing the system."

Noah turned to Luke, "How can this have happened? You assured me we were secure, and no one could hack into this system."

Luke fell silent. He had no answers for the problem, and this was alien to him. Never in his entire career had he faced a technical issue he could not solve. Luke had an unpopular suspicion and not one that he was willing to discuss in front of the team. "Noah, can I speak with you privately?"

Noah nodded, "Step outside, Luke."

Luke followed behind Noah. His feelings on this matter were just gut instinct.

"Out with it, Luke." demanded Noah, standing with his arms folded.

Luke stood before his boss, nervously shifting from one foot to another. He knew that what he was about to say could unleash an assortment of problems within Ainsworth Global Communications.

"Noah, in my opinion, having spent four hours trying to get to the bottom of this, I have come to the only conclusion possible – it has to be someone on the inside. Someone who knows our system almost as well as I do. Whoever did this, broke through my encryption codes and accessed all the passwords, which are almost impossible to locate within the system unless you know exactly what you are doing."

"So, let me get this straight, you are telling me that this could be someone inside Ainsworth Global—someone in my employ?"

Luke nodded. Noah turned his back on Luke and began pacing the corridor. When he was done thinking, he turned around to face Luke, "Follow me."

Noah stormed off towards the secure, locked room at the far end of the corridor—a room reserved only for Noah, the most secure room in Ainsworth House. It was completely soundproof. He looked into the digital box and waited while his retina was scanned. The lock clicked. Noah pushed open the door. Luke followed behind curiously. "Sit down, Luke."

Luke sat down and glanced around the room in awe. *Wow! Finally, I get to see inside of this room*, he mused. He turned to Noah, "I always wondered what was behind this door."

Noah sat opposite Luke, ignored his comment and steepled his fingers beneath his chin. "Have you discussed your thoughts with anyone on the team?"

Luke shook his head, "No one."

"Good. I don't want you to mention your thoughts on this to anyone—not even Max. Only you and I will be privy to this. Any further discussions, thoughts or revelations will only be spoken of in this room. Is that understood?"

"Understood," repeated Luke.

"Start talking. I want the names of people who you think are capable of this and the names of those that may have a motive for wanting to do this. Do not trust anyone with your thoughts and I mean no one. Right now, let us assume everyone is under suspicion until we can rule them out. No one will be exempt from the investigation. It is now your job to find out whom. I want you to do a thorough search of everyone's laptop. But be discreet, override their passwords and anything that appears suspicious then bring it to me. Do not bring this to the attention of anyone - just carry on as normal.

If anyone asks what you wanted to talk to me about, just tell them it was about securing the system with the possibility of updating our software completely following the hack. Is that clear, Luke?"

"Crystal clear?"

"Just to reiterate, no one can find out that we suspect it could be someone on the inside."

"I got it, Noah. Trust me, no one will find out from me," he assured.

Noah paused and placed a hand on Luke's shoulder, "You are one of my most trusted employees, Luke. You have been with me longer than Betty and Jackson. I know you can get to the bottom of this. I have full faith in you," finished Noah.

Luke headed back to his office. The team were shaking their heads, sporting puzzled expressions.

Sean turned to Luke, "What was that all about?" he pressed.

Luke raised his eyebrow, "I wanted to pitch an idea for a new system. I thought now was a perfect time considering what's happened with our current system."

Sean gave a nod, "Cool idea. Well, I don't think we are going to find any answers here tonight."

The team fell silent and turned to Luke. "I guess you're right. We will have more luck in the morning if we go home and get a good night's sleep. Let us continue with fresh eyes first thing tomorrow. Go on get out of here. I will square it with Noah." The team did not need telling twice. It was gone 1 a.m. and they were exhausted.

"Are you coming, Luke?" asked Sean, standing in the doorway.

"I won't be far behind you. I just have a few things to do."

"Do you want me to stay?" offered Sean.

"No, there is nothing you can do here tonight. You can serve me best by going home and getting a goodnight sleep. I will need all hands-on deck in the morning."

"Whatever you say, Luke." With that, Sean left the office.

Luke remained in his office working. He caught a few hours' sleep in the staff guest bedroom and was up before the team arrived the following morning.

TWENTY-EIGHT

*E*den was feeling a lot better, albeit weak. Her system was successfully flushed out and clear of Rohypnol. Her vital signs now regulated, and her headaches had subsided. She was out of bed and ready to go home. Noah entered the room and Eden beamed on sight of him. "It is so good to see you. Can you get me out of here now? I just want to go home. I don't think I can stand another day of hospital food!"

Noah enveloped her in a hug, "Leave it with me. I will speak with your consultant and see if we can get you discharged this morning. How are you feeling today?"

"Better. Confused about everything. But relieved that the forensic exam results were negative. It's one less thing to worry about. I am trying to focus on the positive and that is –

I am alive. It could have been a lot worse."

"I don't want to even think about that," chimed in Noah while squeezing her tight.

Eden pulled away. "You just missed my mum. She is so worried about me. She was insisting I go and stay with her for a few days. However, I said that I needed to be with you. I don't want to be away from you another day."

Noah searched her eyes, "To be honest, I am glad that I didn't bump into your mother today. Not the best of places to get to know her. Did she mention that we met already? She seems like a lovely woman. She was so worried about you. It was hard seeing her like that. There was nothing I could say to ease her pain."

"She did mention it. She thought you were more handsome in person! She said the same thing, that she wished she had met you under happier circumstances. There will be plenty of time for the two of you to get to know one another in the future. Anyway, how's Bella?"

"Bella is doing fine. In fact, Duke has been looking after her very well. She has been a bit sad. She knows something is wrong. Duke has not left her side these past few days. I think she rather likes Ainsworth House though."

"I cannot wait to see her."

"On that note, let me go and see about getting you discharged today. I won't be long." Noah left the room in search of Dr Matthews. He found him buried in a pile of paperwork in his office. "Have you got a minute," asked Noah, tapping the door as he entered.

"Any minute away from all of this red tape is a welcome relief. What can I do for you?"

"Eden is up and anxious to go home. I believe her treatment has finished?"

"Yes. It was successful and Eden responded well to it. I don't see any reason to keep her in now. Let me sign her discharge papers and I will get a nurse to drop them to Eden shortly. By the way, the events have shaken Eden. The nurses have informed me that she has been suffering from nightmares and screaming out in the night. I have suggested that she see a counsellor, someone who specialises in cases like these. I have some recommendations that I will attach to Eden's discharge papers. I think it will help her recovery over the coming weeks. Physically, she is healing well. However, mentally, may take longer. She is traumatised and needs after care to help her through this."

"Sure. I understand. Don't worry, I will make sure she gets all the help she needs. Thank you for everything."

Noah headed back to Eden's room with the good news. He walked in sporting a smile.

Eden's eyes widened, "I can go home?" she blurted.

"Yep. So, let's go."

Eden was already dressed and threw what few things she had in her overnight bag. "I cannot wait to see Bella and give her a big hug."

A nurse walked into the room and handed Eden an envelope.

"Thank you," said Eden.

"Dr Matthews also enclosed some contacts for you. Should you need to speak with someone?"

Noah picked up Eden's bag and they left for the reception. Eden handed her discharge papers over to the receptionist while keeping hold of the contacts supplied by Dr Matthews.

Noah turned to Eden, "Come on, let's get you out of here."

Eden linked Noah's arm and they headed for the exit. Noah's security men followed behind, cautiously sweeping every direction with their vigilant eyes. Noah was taking no risks, and Eden's safety was his top priority.

TWENTY-NINE

*L*uke had his suspicions, but he did not want to alert Noah, until he uncovered proof. He was in his office two hours before his team arrived. Mason and Carl walked through the doors just after nine. Luke acknowledged their presence with a nod of his head, then continued with what he was doing. Sean turned up an hour late and Luke scoffed at him.

"What's your problem, Luke?" blurted Sean.

"You are an hour late. With everything that we are dealing with right now, I would have expected you to be on time this morning," roared Luke.

"So, what... you my timekeeper now?"

Luke stood up, kicked his chair back and squared up to Sean, "I am your superior. I head this team in case it slipped your mind."

Sean raised an eyebrow, "In case it slipped your mind, Luke, I am marketing manager with a tremendous knowledge of IT, hence, the reason Noah brought me in to help you guys out with this monumental fuck up. Not to mention I am more than capable of managing my own time."

"Yes, I am fully aware of your position. However, you clearly need reminding that I am an Associate Director for Ainsworth Communications and I oversee marketing and IT."

Sean's brows wrinkled, "I see... pulling rank on me now - Touché."

"I needed you here on time this morning. You wander in here without a care in the world. When we are amidst a crisis. Correct me if I am wrong, but your time management needs addressing."

Sean fell silent and scowled at Luke.

"Noah wants answers, and he wants them yesterday. So, if I were you, I would cut your tone and get to work," demanded Luke.

The rest of the team watched as Sean grunted while logging on to his laptop. They had never seen Luke react this way before to any of the team.

Noah burst through the door and walked straight over to Luke. "Any news?"

Luke spun around, "Not yet. Give me a little more time. I think I may be on to something." Luke's eyes darted to Sean and then back to Noah.

Sean glared at Luke squirming in his seat. He turned back to his laptop and continued with his work.

"I want to know as soon as you do, Luke," said Noah.

"You can count on it," finished Luke. Luke stood up, left the room, and made his way to his office. *I need privacy this morning and as much distance from Sean as possible*, thought Luke.

Sean was the newest addition to Ainsworth Global Communications. He had been in Noah's employ for 12 months. Luke always thought him to be too arrogant for his own good. During the past 24 hours, Luke had been doing some research into Sean's past and found something he needed to clarify, and soon. *I knew there was something off about Sean He held back a few vital details during his interview process, details that would not have come up during Noah's employee search at the time. Noah will not like this. I need clarification before I go to Noah with my findings*, he thought. Luke called the number written down on a scrap of paper and waited for someone to answer.

"Good morning, Blake Hill College, how may I help you?"

"Hello, I am enquiring about one of your former students, a Sean Mendes. He would have attended your college around 2006. I just need confirmation. He has applied for a position within my company, and I am carrying out the necessary checks."

"I will need to place you on hold while I check the system. If he attended this college then he will be on my system. Luke was placed on hold for some time before the secretary returned to the call, "Hello, sorry for the long wait. I am sorry to inform you that no one by the name of Sean Mendes has ever attended Blake Hill College."

"Thank you for your time." Luke placed his phone down on the table and Steepled his fingers beneath his chin remaining in quiet contemplation.

Without warning, his office door burst open. "Sean, what can I do for you?"

"I need to take an early lunch break. I will be back in an hour or so."

Not wanting to raise Sean's suspicions, he nodded, "Fine. See you later."

Luke spent the next hour on his laptop until he had found what he was looking for, "There it is—I've got you!"

He kicked his chair back and exited his office in search of Noah. He found him in the middle of a heated discussion on his mobile phone. Noah spun around and raised a finger, indicating he was finishing. Noah finished his call and turned his attention to Luke. "Follow me." Luke followed Noah to the top floor. Noah scanned his retina and they entered Noah's secure room, closing the door firmly behind them.

"Who is it?" demanded Noah.

"Sean."

Noah remained silent, turning his back on Luke for a while. He spun around, his jaw tightened.

"How?"

"He had people in place to cover him. The contact numbers he provided for previous employers were not actually his previous employers. They were acting on Sean's behalf. You would not have known this. I had to dig deep and hack a system or two myself. He never attended Blake Hill College and nor did he attend Warwick University.

I hacked into his laptop I was on it all night and then again, first thing this morning before the rest of the team arrived. I found a back door that he had used to hack your personal files. He was very clever, and I don't think anyone else would have discovered it. Sean just never figured on me. His biggest mistake was underestimating me. Mind you, I have never been too open with regards to my genius techy capabilities!" he boasted.

"Luke, you are an absolute genius. Where is Sean now?"

"He said he needed to take an early lunch." Luke glanced at the time on his phone. He added, "That was nearly two hours ago. He must be back by now."

"Do not alert Sean to the fact we are on to him. Just act normal. Leave the rest to me."

Luke made his way to the team's office and glanced around. "Is Sean back yet?"

Mason shook his head, "Nope."

Luke tried to call Sean, but no one answered the call. He then left a brief message and hung up. "Where the hell is he?" he mumbled.

THIRTY

*E*den hugged a mug of coffee while peering out of the window. Bella had not left her side since she returned to Ainsworth House. *Why didn't he say he loved me back at the hospital? Has he changed his mind? He seemed distant with me but not in an obvious way. Something's wrong, I can feel it*, she concluded.

Noah burst into the room, "Sorry I have been elusive today. There is a whole heap of shit unfolding upstairs. How are you feeling?"

"Better – a lot better. Very confused though. I think it will be a while before I venture out of the house by myself. I feel anxious all the time and I am not sleeping – or rather, I am too afraid to sleep. The nightmares are bad."

"I noticed you were tossing and turning a lot last night. I almost woke you up but then you quietened. It is to be expected. You have been through a traumatic experience and it will take time. You need to allow yourself time to adjust and come to terms with what happened to you. Have you given any more thought to seeing a therapist?"

"I have and I think it will be good for me. I have already made my first appointment for next week."

"That is great news. I really think it will be good for you. Sometimes, it is easier to discuss problems with strangers than it is with people close to us. They are neutral. They can see things from a different perspective and one better able to help you."

"I guess you're right. We shall see."

Noah clasped his hands together. Eden sensed his agitation. He paced the floor and then turned to face Eden. "Are you happy – with us, is what mean?"

Confusion crossed Eden's face, "Of course I am. Where is all this coming from?"

"I understand that being with me is not easy. What with the publicity and everything? I just wanted to give you the chance to speak candidly about any reservations you may have about us." Noah studied her face. However, Eden gave away nothing. *She is good, I will give her that,* he thought.

Colour drained from her face, "What's this all about, Noah?"

Noah turned his back for a moment then spun around, "Do the initials J.S. mean anything to you?"

"J.S... No, why should they?"

Noah's expression dulled. His demeanour guarded, "I see." He reached into his pocket and pulled out a letter then handed it over to Eden.

She glanced at the words, shocked, and confused. She raised her head and glared at Noah, "Is this some kind of a joke?"

"It's no joke, believe me. What is going on, Eden? I trusted you. I let you into my life believing you were the one and you do this to me. I thought you were different."

Eden's jaw dropped. She could not make sense of what she was hearing. "Noah, there is nothing going on. You are the only person I have been involved with since Jacob died. Where did that letter come from?"

"Your cottage."

Eden's eyes widened, "My cottage? That is impossible. It makes no sense. I have never seen it before. And what were you doing searching through my private things anyway?"

"You were missing, Eden. I was desperate to find anything that would give me a clue as to who would do this to you. Therefore, I decided to search your property. I had to do something."

"And you found that letter. Well, I have no idea where it came from. I have never seen it before."

"I would have believed you. That was until I saw a message flashing across your mobile phone in the hospital from J.S." Noah paused and then continued. "Please, explain to me how that is possible if you have no idea what is going on here, Eden. Because it all seems pretty clear to me." Noah placed her phone down on the table and walked over to the window.

Eden rushed over to the table, picked up her phone, and glanced through the messages from J.S. "Noah, I have no idea what this is all about." Eden fell silent. She could not explain to Noah what was going on. She shook her head and walked up to Noah, "Please, Noah, I love you. I almost lost my career for you. Surely, that says it all. I am not seeing anyone else and I have never seen these messages before. I don't recognise that number." Tears shimmered in Eden's eyes.

Noah glanced into her eyes with coldness. "I'm sorry Eden. I think it would be best if you stayed with your mother for a while. I think we both need time apart to get our heads around this. I have other serious issues to attend to here at Ainsworth House. I will instruct Jackson to drive you to your mother's house." Noah left the room without a word.

Eden stood there confused and in disbelief. She put her mobile phone back in her pocket and picked up the letter off the table. She reread it through. *I have no idea who this person is. What the hell is going on and how did it end up in my cottage. Someone is setting me up... If Noah is ready to believe all of this without giving me a chance, then I don't want to be with him. How could he think I would do this to him?* she cried. She brushed the tears from her cheeks, stormed out of the room and up the stairs to the bedroom. She packed her suitcase and headed straight back down the stairs. She searched for Bella. She came running from around the corner closely followed by Duke.

"Hey Bella, I need to go to my mum's house for a few days. You cannot come with me. You know she is allergic to dogs. So sorry. I love you." Bella jumped up onto her hind legs and placed her paws on Eden's shoulders while licking her face. "I know Bella, I love you too."

Eden then turned to Jackson who was waiting for her patiently, "Jackson, can you please inform Noah that I will have to leave Bella here for now. My mother is allergic and cannot have dogs in her home."

"Of course. Leave it to me. Here let me take your suitcase." Jackson led the way to the car with Eden trailing behind and tears filling up her eyes.

Noah watched from his office as Jackson drove off out of sight. He felt the pain in his chest as Eden disappeared from Ainsworth House. *This feels like the end of something. I cannot reconcile with all that is happening. Nothing makes sense. Nevertheless, I need to be apart from Eden in order to find the root cause of everything,* he concluded.

THIRTY-ONE

*S*ean searched through his contacts. His finger rested on a number and then he swiped to call. He waited anxiously pacing the apartment, "About time too. Look, Luke is onto me. I know he is. I made my excuses and left. They won't find me. Nevertheless, it won't be long before they realise that I am not Sean Mendes. Don't worry, they have no idea about you. However, Noah has the best team at his disposal. They are working fast. Do you still want to continue?"

A brief silence ensued, "Yes. We shall stick to the plan. I am positive that your real identity cannot be discovered; I don't care how good Noah's team think they are. Did you manage to access Noah's personal files? What is his itinerary for the agreed day?"

"Yes. It was not easy though. Only Max and Luke have access to his daily schedule. Noah is very private. He ensures his staff are kept in the dark where is daily itinerary is concerned. Noah has serious trust issues. Noah is the keynote speaker for the Young People's Charity Gala at the Convention Centre. The gala starts at 7.p.m. Noah will be first on stage to deliver his speech. Noah will not remain at the event all evening. He does not like to hang about, you know how he is," finished Sean.

"That's enough talking. Meet me at our agreed place in an hour and we will discuss this in more detail." Sean heard the click at the end of the line.

He placed his phone back in his pocket, locked up the apartment and left.

*　*　*

Luke went in search for Noah and found him in his office. He tapped the door as he entered, "Noah, you are not going to like this-"

Noah halted Luke mid-sentence, placing a finger over his lips indicating for Luke to be quiet. Noah's forehead puckered. He kicked his chair back, walked from behind the table and extended his hand, indicating for Luke to exit his office. Luke walked into the corridor, he remained silent while following Noah to his secure room. Noah scanned his retina and the door clicked open. When the door was securely shut, Luke began. "Sean Mendes does not exist... Whoever he is – he is not Sean."

"How could this happen, Luke? This is not possible," roared Noah, slamming his fists down onto his desk.

Luke paled, "Whoever he was, he knew his stuff. He was clever, very clever. I'm sorry; I don't know what to say."

Noah's eyes narrowed, "I want him found. I want this man to pay. Who the hell is he and what did he want with Ainsworth Global?"

Luke chimed in, "I don't think his interest was with Ainsworth Global Communications. I think it was with you personally."

Noah fell silent; he paced the floor while massaging his temples. "I need to go back to my office." He opened the door and hurried down the corridor with Luke trailing behind. He sat behind his desk and reached for the phone.

Mason entered Noah's office. Noah put down the phone and glared at Mason.

"Sorry to interrupt, this is urgent. Our people have confirmed that Caspian Communications had nothing to do with Eden's disappearance or our systems being compromised," informed Mason.

Noah's fingers circled his temples, pacing the floor in a rage, "What the fuck is happening here?" Silence descended. Then Noah turned to Mason, "That will be all, Mason." Mason left the room.

Luke piped up, "Noah, you may not like what I am about to say, but it needs saying. Until Eden came into your life, everything was running smoothly. Since the two of you got together, all hell has broken loose. It begs the question-"

Noah stopped Luke mid-speech, "Don't even say it, Luke. Eden has nothing to do with all of this. How could she? She was kidnapped and drugged for God's sake. I doubt that she did it to herself. How could you even suggest it?"

"I'm just saying that with the entry of Eden into your life, chaos has unfolded. Surely it has to be linked to her in some way?"

Noah did not respond. He digested Luke's words. Luke remained where he stood, silent and patient.

Noah spun around, his eyes widened, "Luke, I know you mean well, and you make a lot of sense. It may well be linked to Eden, but I don't believe Eden is involved. I need to go out. Keep on it and call me if anything else turns up. Noah grabbed his jacket off the chair then left hurriedly, leaving Luke standing there alone.

Twenty minutes later, Noah was pulling up outside Detective Hanson's house. He climbed out of his car and wrapped on the door. The lights were on, indicating someone was home.

"Noah, this is unexpected. What brings you to my house?" said Hanson, opening the door startled.

"I have a theory. I want you to hear me out and look into it," he blurted.

"Go on," urged Hanson closing his door behind him and stepping out onto his porch.

Noah filled Hanson in on Sean Mendes and handed him a file. "Also, I know Stephanie has been ruled out. I get it; she has moved on and is now living in France. I have already confirmed that with her mother and you confirmed that too through your own investigations. Nevertheless, whoever is doing this is doing it for personal reasons. The only person who could possibly have a personal issue with me is, Stephanie."

Hanson shook his head in disagreement, "Look, Noah, we already checked her out, she has barely been in the county these past few months.

There is no way that it can be her. We have nothing that links Stephanie to any of this."

"But it is possible – right?" urged Noah.

"I guess if you are grasping at straws there is a small possibility. However, highly unlikely."

"Please... humour me. Look into it. Check her out again. If for no other reason than to completely rule her out and remove that tiny possibility that is plaguing my thoughts right now."

"Sure. Leave it with me. And Noah, in future, please call me first. I don't like bringing my work home." Hanson's eyes darted to the window, noticing that his wife was peering through the window, he added, "It unsettles my wife."

Noah glanced over his shoulder and caught sight of a woman looking at them. "Got it. Thanks, Hanson. I owe you one."

"You owe me more than one, Noah!"

"I know. I appreciate it. Thanks again."

"If anything urgent comes up, let me know," requested Hanson.

Noah nodded and climbed into his car. Thoughts of Eden's devastated expression before she left taunted him. *She genuinely looked surprised. She is either a great actor or she is telling the truth and has no idea who J.S is. After everything that I have been through. I cannot trust her at this point*, he decided with a heavy heart. He arrived back at Ainsworth House and Luke rushed out of the main doors and greeted him. He said, "I have news. Sean Mendes is AKA Christopher Atkins. This took some detailed searching – and not the legal kind."

Noah held up his hand, "I don't want to know how you did it."

Luke gave a half shrug and continued, "Christopher Atkins started his career as a software engineer but get this, he then went solo – self-employed and made his way around the country installing and upgrading software for small businesses of all types. One of those companies was a private and expensive psychiatric hospital down south." Luke paused, waiting for the penny to drop.

Noah's eyes widened, "So, let me get this straight, Sean, I mean Christopher, installed new software at Stephanie's psychiatric hospital around the time that she was residing there?"

"Yep. He was there during the last couple of months before she was discharged."

"We have her. I knew it. The bitch. It all makes sense now. She certainly has the money to carry through with all of this. So, where is she? And if she is reported to have not left the country at the time Eden was kidnapped there is no way we can tie her to any of this."

"But we can link Christopher to Stephanie. That is enough to take it to Detective Hanson. The link between them cannot be just coincidence. It's all making sense now."

"Luke, can you find Max and tell him to meet me downstairs in 15 minutes."

"Consider it done," said Luke while hurrying out of the door.

Noah was not going to call Charlotte ahead of his arrival. He wanted to surprise her. He wanted to confront her raw.

Max appeared in the atrium, "Max, I need you to do something for me."

"Sure, whatever you need ask away."

He handed Max an envelope. "I want you to take this to Detective Hanson. You must hand it to him personally. Is that understood?"

"Understood. You mean right now?"

"Yes, right now. I will be gone for most of the night. If there are any developments, please call me right away?"

"Will do," agreed Max.

Betty came scurrying up to Noah, "Where are you going, Noah? I have cooked your favourite dinner?"

"Sorry Betty, I have to go out."

"Will Eden be coming back?"

"Betty, I am not having this conversation with you right now."

"Fine. But I think you are making a huge mistake, Noah."

"Thank you for your words of wisdom. Good night Betty."

Betty stood beside Jackson and watched as Noah sped away. Jackson glared at Betty shaking his head.

Betty furrowed her brows, "What, Jackson?"

Without saying a word, Jackson walked off.

"Jackson, don't you walk away from me," blurted Betty, following behind him.

Jackson stopped in his tracks and turned around, "Betty, sometimes, you just need to know when to silence yourself."

"Really? Well... someone has to put Noah on the right track." She stormed off in a huff. A smile appeared on Jackson's face as he watched her disappear off into the kitchen. *Betty is cute when she is mad with me. As fond as I am of her, she does not need to know that...*

THIRTY-TWO

*C*harlotte grunted at the sound of the doorbell. Climbing out of her chair, she made her way into the hallway. She straightened her dress while Grace answered the door.

Noah barged in.

Charlotte raised her chin, "Noah, what is going on?"

Noah did not acknowledge Grace. He stormed passed her and up to Charlotte. "I need to speak with you – now, Charlotte."

"Not here, come through to my office," she demanded.

Charlotte closed the door behind her and sat down behind her desk. "I do not appreciate your unannounced visit, Noah."

Noah studied her anxious face, "You have not been completely honest with me, Charlotte. Where is Stephanie?"

Charlotte leaned back in her chair with her arms folded, "I have no idea what you are talking about. How dare you barge into my home like this? What gives you the right?"

"The kidnapping and drugging of my girlfriend gives me every right. Now where is she, Charlotte?"

Charlotte averted Noah's glare. Rising to her feet, she turned to face the window, "I told you, I don't see her often. I am unable to travel these days due to my health. Since David died, my health has not been good."

Noah looked confused, "I am sorry. I had no idea." "Why would you?" scoffed Charlotte.

Noah fell silent, contemplating his words, "Please... Charlotte, someone is going to a lot of trouble to ruin my life. I need to find out who before someone gets seriously hurt."

Charlotte spun around and her eyes met with Noah's, "I am sorry all this is happening to you. The truth is that I have not seen Stephanie for months. As I said, we speak on the phone from time to time. Our contact is minimal. She is changed; she is not the woman she was. She went through a great deal and the loss of her father broke her heart. Three years ago, after everything that happened with Stephanie, it all became too much for my husband. He could not cope with what Stephanie had done. Eventually, it killed him. He died of a heart attack. The pressure of it all got the better of him." Charlotte swiped a tear escaping down her cheek, then continued, "You have no idea what that did to my family. I have lost the love of my life. Since David passed, I fell into ill health. It has been hard. David took care of everything. I feel as if I have lost them both. Stephanie is living her own life now. As I said, she emerged from her treatment a completely different person in every way. I am sorry but I cannot help you. What I can tell you with all sincerity is that Stephanie has no interest in you or whom you are dating. She never talks about you or mentions the past. She is a changed woman – and for the better."

Noah shook his head. He was surprised to find himself sympathising with Charlotte. He could see how broken she was. "Can you at least tell me the name of her boyfriend, any information you can share would be useful?"

"Look Noah, who Stephanie is dating, is no concern of yours. As I said, Stephanie is living her life now and far away from here. It is not my place to discuss her personal life with her ex-boyfriend. I am sure you understand my position." Turning away from Noah, she added, "I think you should go now. There is nothing more that I can tell you other than you are barking up the wrong tree. I will say it again and for the last time; Stephanie has nothing to do with your troubles. She rarely visits the UK these days. She certainly has not been in the country these past few months. There is nothing more for you here, Noah. Now please leave."

Noah picked up his keys off the table and stood up to leave. When he reached the door, he stopped and turned around, "I am sorry for your loss, Charlotte. David was a good man."

"Noah, please don't call or visit me again," advised Charlotte, not turning around while staring out of the window.

Noah left Charlotte's house unconvinced. *She is covering for Stephanie. I just know it. There is no way Charlotte could cope with any more scandal attached to her family name. She is not going to offer up her daughter readily that much I do know.*

He sat in his car and swiped through his messages. He stopped on a message from Eden, opened it up and read it:

Hi Noah, we need to talk. You need to make sense of all this for me. I love you. No one else. I would never betray you. Please believe that. Do not let this be the end of us. Something is amiss and I don't have an explanation for what is happening. Please believe me. X

I cannot, speak to Eden right now. Not until I find the underlying cause of all this, he decided. His heart felt heavy. *I love you Eden that is undeniable, but I need to be sure that I can trust you.*

Noah slipped his phone into his pocket, belted up and began the long drive back to Ainsworth House.

His thoughts drifted back to the tragic events three years ago. *I am saddened to hear of David's heart attack. I liked David. He was a good man. His only fault was allowing his life to be ruled by Charlotte. She was a hard-driven woman that's for sure. One thing I am sure of, Charlotte will do anything to protect her family name. Nevertheless, it was clear that she loved David very much. They were the ultimate power couple of their generation. They came from old money and had doubled their families' fortune over the years. Stephanie had access to an extremely generous trust fund, which afforded her the luxury of living her life any way she chose to. I am guessing this newfound life of hers in France was courtesy of her trust fund,* he mused.

After a long, thoughtful journey home, Noah sighed with relief when Ainsworth House came into view. He parked up and then made his way to the side entrance and into the kitchen. He turned on the lights and Betty's famed hotpot teased his senses. Realising he had not eaten for hours, he took the dish out from the oven and plated a sizable portion for himself. He placed it in the microwave for a minute and then took a seat at the centre island. He sat silently eating until he had cleaned his plate. Bella and Duke rushing through the kitchen startled him. "Hey, you two," The door creaked open again. He glanced up and saw Eden stood in the doorway. "Eden!"

Eden stepped inside closing the door behind her. She paused, brushing a stray hair from her face, "Hi. I needed to see you. I did leave you a message. I could not sit at my mum's house with all this weighing on me. So can we talk? I know it's late, but I am not sleeping. I am miserable without you. I feel as if I am losing you. I love you Noah and I would never hurt you."

Noah melted on sight of her. He noticed her eyes glistening. He saw the truth pouring out in her tears. The naivety he loved so much about her displayed on her face. He walked up to her realising just how much he had missed her. He wrapped his arms around her and pulled her close to him. "God, I have missed you. I am so sorry. I should have believed you. I know you were telling the truth now."

Eden pulled away and searched his face, "I love you, Noah. I knew what I was getting myself into when we started seeing one another. I knew how much my life would change when we made it official, and I accepted that. I was overwhelmed, yes, but not scared. I have no idea who this J.S. is or how that letter came to be in my property. All I can tell you with absolute honesty is that it is not me and I have no idea what is going on. I totally understand why you stepped back from me. I think that in your shoes I would have done the same. We have both been hurt and betrayed in the past. However, I need you to trust me. I need you to believe in me."

Noah took her face in the palm of his hands and pressed his lips firmly on Eden's lips. He had missed the feel of them. "I promise I will never doubt you again. Someone is going to great lengths to destroy everything I care about. That includes hurting us. Nevertheless, they will not get away with it. Anyway, let us forget about all that for tonight. Come on, it's late.

Let's go to bed, there is nothing I want more in this world right now than the feel of you beside me." Bella barked loudly and jumped-up Eden.

"Sorry Bella, you can stay with Duke. This is not something you want to see!" laughed Eden.

THIRTY-THREE

*oah stirred, opened his eyes, and smiled. The sight of Eden fast asleep beside him warmed his heart. He leaned across, kissed her lips and climbed out of bed. His mobile phone buzzing on his dresser alerted him. He picked it up and answered, "Hanson, what can I do for you?"

"Noah, I looked further into Stephanie. She has not been in the country for months. However, she is dating Sean Mendes – I mean Christopher Atkins. They met while he was installing software at the psychiatric clinic where she was a patient. One former resident who was close to Stephanie said they became close rather quickly."

"I knew it–" piped Noah.

Hanson cut Noah off mid-sentence, "Don't jump the gun. I can tie the two of them together, but I cannot tie either one of them to Eden's disappearance. The only thing we have is that Christopher accessed your personal files during his employ with you and operated under an alias. He did not access your business or monetary files, which has been established by your own team. He did not download or delete any files. And so that leaves us with an unclear motive at this stage."

"UNCLEAR! You have to be joking. It is as clear as day to me... Stephanie is out for revenge. She heard about my new girlfriend and flipped. She got Sean- I mean Christopher, to carry out her dirty work for her. She has the money and the motive to pull this whole thing off. There was no need for her to leave France – I mean... why would she? She is clever and there is no way she would implicate herself. She was always manipulative. You have no idea what she is capable of, Hanson. She almost killed me three years ago, remember," roared Noah.

Hanson chimed in, "Her record since then is exemplary and not even as much as a parking ticket can be attributed to her name. Your theory will be hard to prove, Noah, without any hard evidence. Bring me something that I can work with. In the meantime, we will try to locate Christopher. Although, it won't be easy as he has gone off grid."

"Gone off grid?" chimed Noah.

"Yes, disappeared without a trace. His pay-as-you-go mobile phone turned up in a dumpster outside a Chinese takeaway. He has not used credit or debit cards recently and the car he was driving was hired under his alias. He has gone underground. Now, Christopher is definitely a person of interest and we do need to speak with him. However, we have nothing substantial on him. Although, it is clear, that he has something to hide. What that is has yet to be determined. We find him, and then maybe we are closer to solving this. I am not ruling anything out, nevertheless, I need more to go on right now," finished Hanson.

"Sure. But I'm telling you, Stephanie is behind all of this."

Noah threw his phone down on to the chair and headed for the shower, shaking his head and cursing under his breath.

* * *

Christopher swiped across the only contact in his new phone. He paced the floor of the rental apartment impatiently.

"I told you not to call me. I cannot be tied to any of this, Chris. Noah is on to us. And knowing him, he will not let this go. He is like a dog with a bone right now."

"I know. Sorry. I have had to go underground. They have connected Sean and Christopher. You said there was no way that could happen?"

"Well, it has and there is nothing we can do about that now. They barely have anything of consequence on you. Nothing that could stick anyway.

A company would dismiss you for your actions nothing more. But you took yourself out of the equation by leaving anyway. We continue with our plans as discussed."

Christopher asked, "So tomorrow night as agreed?"

"Yes. There can be no mistakes. I am relying on you. I trust that you can pull this off?"

"Of course. My alibi is in place. You will not be connected to any of this at all. Your plan is genius, especially the alibi."

"People always make the mistake of underestimating me. You know what to do with the car once you are done right?"

"Yes. Are you sure the car is untraceable?" he queried.

"I am sure the car is untraceable back to you or me. Where it came from is not your concern. However, burn it anyway. Follow the plan to the letter and then nothing can go wrong. I must go. Get it done. Do not contact me by phone again. I will see you soon enough as planned. Oh... and Christopher, don't be foolish enough to go off plan and head over to France no matter how tough things get. Stick to the plan, don't buckle and we are home dry. It will be worth it in the end, I promise you. Understood?"

"Understood," repeated Christopher.

Christopher glanced around the empty rental apartment, *24 hours and all this will be over.*

THIRTY-FOUR

*E*den went in search of Noah and found him in his office. She stood silently in the doorway watching him work. Sensing someone was behind him, he spun around, "Hey you. Come here."

Eden walked over to him and he pulled her close. She hitched up her dress and sat across him, gently biting his lip. "You were gone when I woke up. Early start?"

"Yep. Too much going on everywhere right now. You smell amazing," commented Noah inhaling her perfume and changing the subject.

He added, "As much as I would like to throw you down on this desk right now, I can't! Give me a couple of hours and I'm all yours."

"It's a deal," agreed Eden. Climbing off him and straightening her dress. Eden left Noah alone to continue.

He paused and watched as she teasingly backed out of the door. He inhaled a deep breath and picked up the phone. "Hey Max, any news for me?" he asked.

"I was just about to call you. I will drop by your office in ten minutes. Just let me finish up here," said Max.

* * *

Blake opened his front door and he stood aghast. His eyes trailed over the devastation before him. He burst through the doors and went from room to room in disbelief. "What the hell-" he picked up his phone and called the police. After explaining what had happened, he made his way into his office. The drawers in the office were upside down. Someone went to a lot of trouble to break them open. He glanced at all the files scattered on the floor and his heart sank. His computer was upside down on his desk and the hard drive was missing. He made his way upstairs to his bedroom. His eyes roamed around the scene. The room was untouched. "Someone knew exactly what they were looking for?" he said allowed. Startled by the doorbell ringing, he spun around and headed down the stairs.

Two police officers stood before him. He stood aside and extended his arm indicating for them to walk through. He gave the officers a detailed account of what he believed to be missing. He had no enemies that he was aware of and had no indication who would have any reason to break into his home. After 45 minutes and filling out a statement. The officers handed him a crime reference number then left.

Blake sighed and took as many pictures as he could for his insurance company. Then he began clearing up the mess. When he was finished, he was exhausted, confused, and angry. His mobile phone buzzed on the table. He glanced at the number and recognition flashed across his face. Smiling, he picked it up, "Eva, you have no idea how good it is to hear your voice right now."

"Is everything alright?" she asked.

"Not really. I have had a break in at my home. I came home to a right mess. The police left a couple of hours ago. They took my statement and filed a report."

"Oh Blake, I am so sorry to hear that." "Eva, can you come over tonight?"

A long silence ensued, "I am sorry Blake. I can't." I do need to speak with you though. Are you free tomorrow lunchtime?"

"Yes, tomorrow is good for me."

"Great. Meet me at the country club for lunch. See you tomorrow," she finished.

Blake slumped down on to his sofa with a heavy heart. *Something in*

Eva's tone bothered me. She wasn't her usual self at all, and I am disappointed that she couldn't come over. The night had got the better of him. His eyes were heavy. He turned off his phone and headed upstairs to bed.

THIRTY-FIVE

*E*den was looking forward to seeing Angie. She took a seat near the window in their favourite coffee shop. Right after dropping her off, Martin took a seat at the back -three tables behind Eden. Noah did not let his guard down. Martin was Eden's assigned bodyguard for now. Eden felt safer knowing Martin was close by. Ever since her disappearance, she had been too afraid to go out alone. She smiled on sight of Angie waving to her. She breezed through the coffee shop like a breath of fresh air.

"It's so good to see you. I have missed you so much," greeted Angie.

"I have missed you too. I took the liberty of ordering you a latte," said Eden.

"A latte works for me, but where is the cake?" laughed Angie.

Angie leapt from her seat and headed over to the counter, "Do you want one," she asked pointing to the Danish pastries.

Eden shook her head. "Not for me. I had a late breakfast."

Angie placed her order and sat back down. "Have you heard about what happened to Blake?"

Eden's eyes widened, "No!"

"His home was burgled last night. Whoever was responsible left it in a right mess, apparently."

"Poor Blake! How is he taking it?" pressed Eden.

"He is furious as anyone would be."

"I will call him later to see how he's doing," said Eden.

Angie placed her hand over Eden's arm, "How are you doing? I can't believe everything you have been through."

"One day at a time is how. I am confused and scared of my own shadow right now. I have not been out alone since it happened. I can't sleep and I am not eating too well either." Eden glanced over to Martin sitting at the back of the café. She raised her eyebrows and tilted her head towards him, "That's Martin, my bodyguard. I would not be here if I had to come alone," confessed Eden.

Angie glanced at Martin, "I can totally understand. At least you know you are safe with him a few feet behind you. I can't even begin to imagine what you must be going through."

"It's tough, but I will get there in the end. I have my first session with a therapist next week. I need it, Angie. I need to work through everything that has happened to me and make sense of it all if I am to move forward."

"Yes, you do. And going to therapy is a big step forward. You know, I am only a phone call away if ever you need to talk right?"

"I know. And I will hold you to that. Noah is going to great lengths to find out what happened. Although, he is keeping me out of the loop. Every time I bring up the subject, he changes it?"

Angie listened intently then chimed in, "He only has your best interest at heart. Clearly, he does not want you to worry. He just wants you to recover. Are the police any closer to finding out what happened to you?"

"I don't think so. Nothing concrete anyway. I overheard Noah speaking with Max the other day and he seems to think his ex-girlfriend is behind it. Of course, he had no idea I was listening. I just don't know what to think, Angie. Anyway, on a lighter note, how's everything going at the office?"

Angie's eyes crinkled, "Ah the office. Well, it seems romance is blossoming in the marketing department. Stacy and Jack have begun dating secretly. Neither one will admit to anything, but the whole office knows already. They have been spotted out several times recently up close and personal."

Eden's eyes widened, "Really... I would never have put the two of them together. I am happy for them. Cupid's been busy of late."

"Yep. Anyway, I must get back to the office. Lots to do. It was good to see you, Eden."

Eden stood up and hugged Angie, "Why don't you come to Ainsworth House to see me, next weekend perhaps. What do you think?"

"Sounds delightful. I have always wanted to see inside that glorious house. It's a date. Try keeping me away!"

"Great. I will call you to confirm in a couple of days," finished Eden.

She watched as Angie exited the coffee shop. She finished her latte and then left. Martin followed swiftly behind Eden to the car.

* * *

Eden sat in the back seat of the car and called Blake. She waited patiently for a response.

"Hello," he answered.

"Blake, its Eden. I have a new phone, so add this number to your contacts. I just heard about your break in. I am so sorry."

There was long silence on the line.

"Blake...Are you still there?"

"Yes. Sorry Eden. It has been a bad couple of days. The break in was a shock. It appears the only thing missing was my computer hard drive. Whoever took it left a mess behind though. Then to top of it off today, Eva broke up with me..."

"Oh, Blake, I am so sorry. You two were good together. She seemed so in to you too. It makes no sense?"

"I never really knew that much about Eva. I had never been to her home down south or the house she was staying at in Warwickshire while she was holidaying up here. I never met any of her friends. She was vague to say the least about her family. I am beginning to wonder who Eva was. She left my life as quickly as she breezed into it."

Eden could sense the heartbreak in Blake's voice, "Don't let all this beat you. We have both been through the mill recently. We just have to get on with it and don't let it grind us down."

"I am sorry, Eden, I am being selfish. After everything that you have been through recently and I have not even asked how you are coping. My troubles are nothing compared to yours. How are you?"

"I am coping. Noah is looking after me extremely well. He has assigned me a bodyguard. I still cannot venture out by myself because I am too scared. So, I welcome Martin, knowing he is watching out for me makes me feel safe. The police are still investigating what happened. The truth will out as the saying goes..."

"Yes, it will, Eden. You are a strong woman. You are approaching all of this with a positive attitude. It will help you greatly to come to terms with it all. Look, Eden, I need to go. I will speak to you soon. Thanks for calling. It means a lot," finished Blake.

Eden put her phone back into her bag and glanced out of the car window. *Poor Blake, he did not deserve all that has happened to him, thought Eden.*

THIRTY-SIX

Noah glanced over the agenda for the Young Peoples Charity Gala. He was the keynote speaker, and this was one event he would not cancel. It meant a lot to him personally. In addition, he refused to let the children down.

Max was impatient and attempting to hurry Noah along, "We will be late, Noah."

"Well, they cannot begin without me. So, stop fretting. We will make it." Noah fixed his bow tie and glanced over his reflection in the mirror, "I think that will do."

"You look great now let's go already," urged Max with one foot out of the door.

Eden stopped Noah mid-stride, "Hey, how about a kiss for luck!"

Noah pulled Eden close and kissed her. Are you sure I can't persuade you to come with me tonight?" he pressed.

"I am sure. It's too soon for me."

"I understand." He leaned in for one last kiss.

Max rolled his eyes and headed out the door.

Eden watched them leave, "I will see you later. Good luck for tonight. Do you have your speech?"

Noah patted his top-right hand pocket and smiled. He turned around and followed Max out of the door. They climbed into the car and Max drove off. They approached the security gates at the end of the long drive and waited for them to open. Max continued driving out of Ainsworth gates and headed straight down the road through Acton Village then passing through Shenley Village toward the City Centre.

Max was flustered and it began to irritate Noah, "Max, calm down. You are beginning to make me anxious. We have plenty of time to get there."

Max turned to Noah, "I do not like to be late. You know how I am. Better an hour early than a minute late. Only in our case, we will literally just make it with seconds to spare if we are lucky."

Noah turned and studied Max's face, "Max, from one friend to another, I think you have serious issues," he teased.

Max pulled up on Broad Street and let Noah out. "I will park up and join you in a few minutes, good luck," he said, winding down his window.

Noah walked speedily to the convention centre. The door attendants nodded and opened the doors while they greeted him. As Noah entered the hall, he received a round of applause. He walked on stage and took the microphone in hand. Max rushed through the doors and took a seat at the back of the room feeling relieved that they had made it on time.

Noah's speech was inspiring and impressive. The looks on the young adult's faces spoke volumes. At the finish, Noah received a standing ovation as he walked off the stage. The amount of money raised by the end of the evening was phenomenal. The ticket holders were more than generous. And that made Noah happy.

"I think it's fair to say that was a successful evening. And you stayed until the end too, a first for you," piped Max.

"Successful indeed. Will you collect the car? I am ready to leave now. I will wait for you on Broad Street, where you dropped me off."

Max left to collect the car while Noah said his goodbyes. Noah made his way around the hall and then left the convention centre. He stood on the curb waiting for Max. He studied the long queue of cars waiting to leave the car park up ahead. Realising Max would be at least five minutes or more, he took his phone out of his pocket and swiped through his messages. He was unaware that he was being watched further down the road while waiting.

Christopher left the headlights off. He revved up the engine of the old car while glancing out of the tinted windows. With force, he put his foot to the pedal. Noah was viewing his messages and did not see him coming. When he lifted his head up, it was already too late... Alerted by screams of a woman behind him, Noah spun around and gasped – there was no time to act. Christopher mounted the pavement and was feet away from Noah. A woman behind him screamed while witnessing Noah mowed down like an animal.

Christopher did not stop and drove off at great speed. People began running up to Noah lying limp on the floor. A stream of blood leaked from his body down the road.

A young man knelt down beside Noah and checked his vitals. "He's still alive!" confirmed the man. He then turned to the onlookers surrounding him, "Call an ambulance now," he shouted.

A woman shouted from the crowd, "I already have, they are on their way." Within minutes, an ambulance and the police were on the scene assessing Noah's injuries.

Max pulled out of the car park and saw the commotion on Broad Street – he knew... He panicked and leapt out of his car, running toward the commotion. He forced his way through the crowd and stopped behind a medic attending to Noah.

A man beside him shaking his head spoke, "Do you know him?"

"Yes. He is my friend. Did you see what happened?" asked Max.

The stranger nodded, handed Max a card, "If your friend needs a witness..."

Max thanked the stranger and turned to a police officer approaching. The police officer addressed the stranger beside Max, "I am going to need your statement. Did you witness what happened?"

Max stepped forward leaving the witness to be interviewed. He watched as the medics carefully lifted Noah into the ambulance. "Wait, I need to go with him, "shouted Max.

"Who are you?" queried the medic.

"I am his best friend."

The medic nodded and stepped aside allowing Max to climb in with them.

* * *

Christopher followed the provided instructions to a set of old garages behind the site of an abandoned industrial warehouse. As instructed, he drove the car into the garage, covered it in petrol and set it alight. He watched the car light up and then rushed to the garage at the far end. He lifted the garage door and as promised, there was a car waiting for him. It brought a smile to his face. He opened the door and climbed in. He took the keys out of his pocket and started the car, backing out of the garage. He drove off into the night feeling euphoric.

THIRTY-SEVEN

$\mathcal{N}$oah was rushed through A&E and straight into the emergency room. A nurse stopped Max from entering the room. "You will have to wait outside," urged the nurse, closing the doors behind her.

Frantically, Max took his mobile phone out of his pocket and ran outside. He called Detective Hanson and paced outside the entrance doors waiting for his call to pick up. "Detective Hanson," he answered.

"Hanson, have you heard about Noah?"

"Yes, I have just left the scene. I am on my way to the hospital now. Wait there until I arrive."

"Now do you believe Noah's theory. Stephanie is behind all of this. He was mowed down like an animal in the same way he was three years ago. He is barely alive in there. You better hurry," urged Max.

He did not give Hanson time to reply. He ended the call and swiped Eden's number. He was dreading this call. She had been through hell already and he knew this would tip her over the edge. Seeing Noah and Eden together reminded him that true love did exist. *I hope to find it myself one day. I just pray that Noah makes it through this.*

After he made all the relevant calls, Max paced the floor of the waiting area until Hanson burst through the doors.

"Max, how is he?" Hanson asked.

"Not good. He was barely breathing. I have no idea what's going on in there," he replied, pointing towards the emergency room.

"My officers are at the scene taking statements from witnesses. The CCTV footage from Broad Street bars and restaurants are being pulled as we speak." Hanson added, "What the hell happened out there, Max?"

Shaking his head and in a confused state, Max said, "We had just left the charity gala. Noah was waiting for me on Broad Street. It took me longer than I expected to exit the car park as there was a long queue waiting at the ticket barrier. When I came out, I saw the commotion and I knew straight away that something was wrong. There were many people about when it happened. Passers-by and people leaving the charity gala. It was mayhem. I rushed over as Noah was being lifted into the ambulance. The man who waited beside Noah until the ambulance arrived said it was no accident – it was deliberate. Several other people confirmed this too. He saw it for himself, a car running Noah down with force and speeding off into the distance. Max paused and reached into his pocket, "Here, take this. It's a business card from one of the witnesses."

Hanson took the card and glanced down at it before popping it into his pocket.

"The witnesses are being interviewed as we speak. One thing is clear, someone wants Noah dead..."

A surgeon emerged from the emergency room and Max rushed over to him. "Will he live?" pressed Max.

"He is alive. However, he is in a severe, critical condition. The next 24 hours are crucial. The good news is, he is a fighter and is hanging on. We are transferring him to the critical care unit now. We have put him into a medically induced coma. He has multiple fractures including a punctured lung caused by the pressure of his rib penetrating it. His left leg is broken, several ribs, his jawbone is fractured, and his left arm has two fractures. We won't know what or if there has been any brain damage until the results of the scan come in. It's a waiting game now. If he can make it through the night, then he will have a fighting chance of coming through this. His head took a blow but was not severe. It was a deep cut, which we have stitched up. However, he has a steel plate in his head from a previous accident, which raises a few concerns. As I said, he needs to fight his way through tonight. He will be under close observation throughout the night."

"Can I see him?" asked Max.

"Sure, but like I said, he is non-responsive. A nurse will call you when he has been transferred."

Max slumped down onto a nearby chair. Detective Hanson had a quiet word with the surgeon and then made his way back over to Max. "I am going to place an officer outside Noah's door. We cannot take any chances. Once the person who did this realises that he is not dead, they may attempt to come back to finish the job," advised Hanson.

Max nodded and placed his face in his hands.

"Max, I have to go now."

Max lifted his head in acknowledgement. He said, "I'm telling you that Stephanie is behind this."

Hanson placed his hand on Max's shoulder then left and exited through the revolving doors.

Max raised his head and his eyes widened on sight of Eden hurrying over to him with tear-filled eyes.

"Max, what happened? Is he going to make it?" blurted Eden.

"Truthfully, I have no idea. His body took a severe hit. He has multiple fractures a punctured lung and that is just for starters. His head took a hit too and that can't be good. They had to place him into a medically induced coma. The next 24 hours are crucial."

Eden let out a loud cry. The cry was so loud that it startled people in the waiting room. Max placed his arm over her shoulder to comfort her. She sobbed uncontrollably until a nurse approached them.

"You can see Mr. Ainsworth now. Please follow me," she urged.

Max aided Eden off the chair, and they followed behind the nurse. When they reached Noah's room the nurse pushed open the door and then stepped aside. "I will be outside should you need anything, "said the nurse.

Eden followed Max into the room. Her eyes fell upon Noah. Her jaw dropped. Her eyes trailed over the monitors and drips attached to him. Her eyes halted at his neck brace. She drew in a deep breath. Her eyes continued to roam. She winced at the sight of the cuts on Noah's face.

"Omg!" she blurted, noticing that Noah's left leg and arm were strapped up securely. Attempting to quell her cries, she placed her hand over her mouth. She pulled up a chair and took hold of his right hand. "I'm right here, Noah. I am not going anywhere. Please don't die. I need you."

Max turned to face the window, not wanting Eden to see his tears. He swiped them away and turned around approaching Eden. "I am going back to Ainsworth House, Eden. Noah is going to need a few things."

Eden looked into Max's reddened eyes, "Who would do this, Max?" Why?"

Max remained silent. There were no words he could share to ease her pain. "Just hang in there, Eden. Right now, the police are doing everything they can."

Eden turned her attention back to Noah and Max left the room.

THIRTY-EIGHT

Christopher wrapped on Charlotte's door impatiently. He shifted from one foot to the other as the large door swung open.

"Hello Grace, I have come to see Charlotte. Is she in?"

"Yes, she is on a call at present. Please come in and I will inform her you are here." Grace scurried off to Charlotte's office leaving Christopher pacing the grand hallway.

It was some time before Charlotte made an appearance. Christopher spun around, "Hello Charlotte."

"What a surprise," greeted Charlotte.

"Would you like some tea?" she asked.

Christopher raised his brow, "Maybe something stronger?"

"Of course. Come through to my office." Charlotte turned to Grace, "That will be all, Grace. I will call you if I need you."

Charlotte stepped aside as Christopher walked through the door, following swiftly behind him. Christopher paid note to Charlotte's personal assistant, typing away on her laptop at the back of the room.

"Oh, don't mind, Julia," piped Charlotte, noting the look of concern on his face.

Charlotte walked over to the mini bar and poured them both a scotch whisky. She dropped some ice in the glasses and walked over to

Christopher, "Here you go." Christopher took the glass from her hand and gulped it down.

Charlotte cupped her glass with both hands, "I believe you are heading back to France soon?"

Christopher once again, glanced over to Julia. "Yes, soon. I thought I would drop by and pay you an impromptu visit before I left."

"I am so pleased you did. I have a parcel for Stephanie. Would you mind giving it to her?"

"Of course, it would be my pleasure."

The ringing startled Christopher, forcing him off his seat.

"My, you are jumpy this evening?" intoned Charlotte.

Charlotte answered the phone, "Detective Hanson. What can I do for you?"

Charlotte began pacing the wooden floor. She glanced over at Christopher several times. Feeling uneasy, he squirmed in his seat and averted her glare. "I see. Well, I can assure you, Detective that my Stephanie had nothing to do with this. She is not even in the country. In fact, she was hosting a wine tasting tour at her vineyard this evening. I am guessing more than twenty people can verify her whereabouts at the time. This must stop, Detective. It is bordering on harassment." Christopher's ears pricked up. He climbed off his chair, walked over to the bar, and refilled his glass. "I'm sorry, but I have never heard of Sean Mendes."

Christopher spun around almost dropping his glass.

Charlotte paused and then added, "Yes, I know Christopher very well. He is my daughter's partner. In fact, Detective, he is here with me right now. Why do you ask?"

Hanson fell silent. The last thing he expected to hear was that Christopher was in London with Charlotte. "He is a person of interest. I need to speak with him?"

"Well, maybe you need to speak with him yourself, here, I shall pass the phone to him."

Charlotte walked over to Christopher, her brows furrowing, "Detective Hanson would like to speak with you..."

Christopher's eyes widened. He glared at Charlotte and then nervously took the phone from her hand, "Hello."

"I need you to come into the station to clarify a few things for me.

It would be in your best interest if you came into the station voluntarily," urged Hanson.

"And if I don't?"

Unimpressed, Charlotte glared at him.

Hanson continued, "Like I said, it would be in your best interest?"

"I see. Okay you got me, Detective. I am guessing this is about Ainsworth Global. Look, I know I should not have accessed those files. I was aware that I did not have level clearance. I was just being a nosey employee. No damage was done. I never took anything, and I never downloaded anything."

"Well, that is not for me to determine. I need you to drop by the station and complete a statement. By showing willing it will help you greatly."

Christopher smiled inwardly. *The plan was working perfectly. I know they have nothing concrete on me. Charlotte is my perfect alibi. There is no way they would believe I could have made it from Birmingham to London in the time frame needed to place me at the scene. A hacking charge at best was already configured into the plan. As a first offence, I am unlikely to serve time. Maybe a suspended sentence and a fine at best,* he mused. "Sure. I will drive up tonight. You can bank on it," finished Christopher.

Charlotte glanced over to Julia, then back to Christopher while choosing her words carefully. "So, Christopher, it seems you have gotten yourself into some bother? I hope that this will not impact on Stephanie in any way?"

"No, I promise you."

"Well then, I don't need to hear any more. Whatever you have been up to is your business. Quite frankly the less I know the better."

"Let me go and get that parcel for Stephanie. I won't be long," said Charlotte leaving the room. Christopher glanced out of the window while Julia did not raise her head once. Charlotte re-entered the room several minutes later, "Here, Stephanie will love this."

Christopher took the parcel from Charlotte, "I need to head up to Birmingham now. I may not be going to France quite as soon as I thought after all! However, once this small matter has been cleared up, I will be out of this country for good."

Charlotte buzzed for Grace, "Grace, please show Christopher to the door." Charlotte turned her back on him and then walked over to Julia.

Christopher left Charlotte's house and climbed into the car. He placed the parcel on the back seat and smiled. He started up the car and then headed for Birmingham. *Perfect, just perfect. Everything is in place as planned. Just one more stop to make before handing myself in,* he mused.

THIRTY-NINE

ax finished his call with Hanson. He felt a surge of relief that Christopher was being interviewed at the station. He did not deny illegally accessing Noah's personal files. Hanson advised Max that there was no evidence that linked Christopher to Noah's near-fatal incident. The CCTV footage revealed no facial recognition of the driver. The windows were tinted. The license plate led to a dead end - a registered stolen car. They were two separate incidents. Christopher confessed that he often used an alias to gain employment as his educational history often held him back. Stephanie had been completely ruled out and witnesses confirmed her whereabouts on the night of Noah's accident. They had no other suspects at this time. *They are missing something. Something does not add up. I just know Stephanie is involved somehow. There is no way that this is all some coincidence,"* Max concluded, furious while heading to ICU. He pushed open the door and his eyes rested on Eden. She was fast asleep in the chair, slumped forward with her head resting on Noah's bed. He reached for a blanket off the back table, eased Eden back into the chair and placed the blanket over her. There was no change in Noah. Almost 48 hours had passed. He remained critical and his heart rate was erratic at best.

Dr Matthews entered the room, "Hello, Max. It is unbelievable what has happened. First Eden and now Noah." Dr Matthews walked over to Noah and reached for the clip board from the end of Noah's bed. He glanced at it for some time. "No change to speak of. The good news is that he made it through two nights with no complications. This is a good sign. He is not out of the woods yet though. How is Eden doing?"

Max glanced over at Eden, shaking his head. "Not good. She has been through hell and back recently. She is still coming to terms with what happened to her. This has affected her greatly. What are Noah's chances?"

"No one can answer that. What I can tell you is that it is looking good right now for Noah. He is a fighter. If he continues to fight, then he has a good chance. Truthfully, at this point, anything can happen."

Max sighed and noticed Eden stirring. She raised her head. Her eyes darted from Dr Matthews and then to Noah, "Is he alright?" she panicked.

"He is fine. He made it through another night. That is a good sign. As I have been advising Max, he is still critical, nevertheless, he is a fighter. But he has a long way to go yet."

Eden stood up, "Have the results from his scan come back?"

"No. I should have them later today. As soon I know then you will know. Right then, I have other patients to see. I shall be back later to check on him. It might be a good idea if you go home, get some proper rest and return later," advised Dr Matthews.

Eden shook her head, "No. Absolutely not. I am not leaving his side. I need to be here."

Max turned to Dr Matthews and arched his eyebrows. Dr Matthew smiled sympathetically then left the room.

Max turned to Eden, "You know, Dr Matthews is right. It will do you good to go home, take a shower and rest up."

"NO MAX," she shouted. Max held up his hand in defeat. Eden added, "I am sorry. I just can't leave him, Max. What if something happened while I was gone? I would never forgive myself."

"Okay, as you wish. Is there anything you need from the house?"

"Just a toothbrush and change of clothes."

"Consider it done. I shall be back later." The door opened and Betty burst through. Max's eyes widened on sight of her, "Betty!"

She brushed past Max, "I had to come. The boys will have to feed themselves today. How is he?"

"Not good Betty. He is fighting." Max did not want to go into detail about Noah's injuries. He knew it would tear Betty apart.

"Look, I shall leave you both to talk. I need to head back to Ainsworth House." Max said, making his way out of the door.

Betty pulled up a chair beside Eden, "He will make it. Noah is a force to be reckoned with. Trust me, nothing can keep him down. I noticed the police officer outside the door, at least that is some peace of mind."

Eden placed her hand over Betty's arm, "I am so glad you are here. I just cannot wrap my mind around all of this. It makes no sense to me."

Betty listened to Eden and remained silent. She had her suspicions. She did not want to worry Eden with them. In fact, no one was discussing the possibility of Stephanie's involvement around her. She had been through enough already and throwing a psychotic ex-girlfriend into the mix would not serve Eden well right now.

"Focus on the positive. He survived the night, and he will survive another night," assured Betty.

FORTY

*B*lake climbed out of his car and rushed through the A&E entrance doors. He stopped at reception for directions to Noah's room and continued off down the corridor. A nurse leaving Noah's room held the door open, as Blake walked in.

"Blake! This is unexpected."

"Hello, Eden. I called Ainsworth House to see how you were doing after hearing about Noah. Max told me you had not left Noah's side. I just had to see you and show you my support."

Eden stood up and hugged Blake, "Thank you. I cannot believe what has happened. It all seems like a terrible dream that I cannot wake up from."

Blake pulled up a chair and sat beside Eden. He studied Noah in shock. "Someone did a real number on him. I noticed the police officer outside the door. Do they think whoever did this will try again?"

"It is a possibility. However, it gives me peace of mind knowing the officer is there."

Blake shook his head, "This is all so unbelievable. I have no words right now, Eden."

Eden studied Blake's face and noticed a sadness in his eyes, "Are you okay?"

Eden could see how much Blake was hurting. She placed her hand over his, "It just wasn't meant to be for you and Eva. Fate has other plans for you."

"I guess. How are you holding up?"

"By a thread. I can't lose him, Blake."

Blake did not reply. There was nothing he could say. "Is there anything I can do for you, Eden?"

"No. You can pray for Noah's recovery. He needs all the help he can get right now."

Blake smiled, "Consider it done. I have to get back to the office. Take care of yourself too. Noah needs you healthy and rested when he wakes up."

Blake left Eden with a heavy heart. *The more I think about the burglary the less sense it makes.* He dashed his plans to return to the office and headed straight home.

Blake pulled up on to his driveway and climbed out of his car. He rushed through his front door and headed straight for his office. With clarity that eluded him on the day of the burglary, he searched through every file. Several hours later, he was about to give up when his eyes rested upon Eden's employment file. His eyes widened - it was empty. He opened the top drawer and searched for the flash drive containing Eden's interview with Noah – it was gone.

The penny began to drop; Blake shook his head and paced the floor while he derived a conclusion. "Eva..." he blurted. He continued pacing trying to make sense of his thoughts. "There is no other explanation. Nothing was missing. This house is full of expensive things and nothing was taken!" He sat back down at his desk and searched through the remaining files. His mind worked overtime. Slowly, he thought back to how he had met Eva... *I am an old fool. She planned it all. Luck had nothing to do with our meeting. A beautiful young woman like that would have no interest in me,* he concluded. He took his phone out of his pocket and swiped until he reached Eva's number. He opened his messages with her and there was nothing displayed – everything there had already been deleted "WHAT THE HELL..." he roared while frantically swiping. "Where are all the messages?" He called Eva's number.

A robotic voice answered, "This number is no longer in use."

Anger bubbled to the surface. "Damn you Eva – if that's even your real name." With more thought, he had no idea who she was at all. *She had never mentioned family or anything that could betray her real identity. I knew nothing about Eva's life. I fell for her so hard and fast, that all that stuff did not enter my head.*

He wasted no time in calling the police and asking for the lead detective on the Noah Ainsworth case.

FORTY-ONE

A week had passed since Noah's accident. Eden had finally left the hospital under advice from Dr Matthews. She divided her time between Ainsworth House and the hospital. And although she would not admit it to anyone, she felt better for it. Seeing Bella and Duke daily, lifted her spirits. Betty could not do enough for her. Martin followed her everywhere she went, remaining close always as per Noah's instructions before his accident. Max ensured it was business as usual and the team continued to run things as normal. Caspian retreated and pulled his advert, adding that it was inappropriate at this time. He publicly wished Noah a speedy recovery.

Luke updated and installed new software for Ainsworth Global Communications, and it was more secure than ever.

* * *

Detective Hanson's leads had run cold. Blake's revelation led to a dead end. *Eva was a person of interest; however, she had disappeared off the face of the earth. There is no trace of her to be found anywhere. Whoever she was - she had covered her tracks exceptionally well*, Hanson thought. He took the entire paperwork home, spent the whole night reading the files on

Noah Ainsworth and Eden Marshall, hoping he would find something that he missed. With Noah's case being high profile, the pressure was on. One of his intuitive feelings was consuming him and one that he could not push aside *The press are all over Noah's case. Speculation across social media is widespread, with everyone connecting Noah's previous accident with his current one. Although, it made sense, there is no evidence to suggest otherwise. Stephanie has been ruled out following a thorough investigation. Her alibi is rock solid. As for Christopher, he was with Charlotte that night. I am missing something here,* he concluded while turning over a file and reaching for the next in the pile. Noah's business rivals had been investigated and ruled out leaving nothing left to go on. A light bulb moment forced him off the floor. He grabbed his keys and headed out of the door. He called into the station to advise them where he was going and began the long drive down south. Hanson's mind was doing overtime.

* * *

Smiling, Eden watched from the library window while Jackson headed out across the fields with Bella and Duke for their daily walk. Bella and Duke were running rings around Jackson and he almost toppled over. She longed to take them walking herself, but fear consumed her, and she often wondered if she would ever be able to get over it. Her nightmares continued, forcing her awake during the night in a cold sweat. However, her biggest fear was losing Noah. She looked at a photograph of Noah on the wall and smiled, "I miss you," she whispered. She leapt from the chair and headed towards the kitchen for lunch. Betty always ensured she had a good meal before she visited the hospital. Martin was standing outside the library door when she exited. She turned to him and smiled, "I think I am quite safe in Ainsworth House, Martin."

"Just doing my job," he replied, following behind her as she made her way to the kitchen.

"Well then, you can lunch with me before we head off to the hospital." Eden pushed the door to the kitchen open. Betty greeted her with a beaming smile, "Just in time," she said. Betty glanced at

Martin and the corners of her mouth turned up. "Take a seat and I will plate up," she urged.

"Smells delicious, Betty," piped Eden.

"Today I am serving, Salmon Encroute."

Betty plated up lunch and served Eden and Martin. "Good to see you taking time out to eat, Martin. I am guessing Eden had something to do with that."

Martin raised his head and nodded while chewing.

Betty raised her eyebrows at Eden and continued pottering around the kitchen. Max burst through the doors huffing and puffing, "Have you seen Luke," he blurted.

Eden shook her head. "No sorry. I have not seen him today."

"What about you, Martin?"

"No. Not today."

"Well, if you see him, can you let him know I'm looking for him? I cannot get used to this new system at all."

Max left the kitchen cursing to himself.

Betty turned to Eden, "Looks like someone is in a fluster today."

Eden smiled endearingly at Betty. She was fast becoming one of Eden's favourite people in Ainsworth House and realised just how much Noah needed her in his life. *She was like a mother/grandma/aunt all rolled into one. Everybody needs a Betty in their life* she concluded.

Without warning, Jackson burst through the kitchen door with Bella and Duke. He looked exhausted!

"Jackson, are you okay?" pressed Betty.

"I am fine, thank you." He grunted as he made his way over to the sink and poured himself a large glass of water. They all watched him while he gulped down the water not pausing for air.

"Looks to me like the dogs took you walking!" laughed Betty.

Eden looked away from Jackson hiding her grin.

Jackson huffed and left the kitchen.

"I guess Jackson left his sense of humour in bed when he got up this morning," laughed Betty.

Eden smiled, "Betty, do you always tease him like that?"

"Of course, he may not realise it, but it does him good. He loves it really!"

"You are one of a kind. Right then, I need to go now. I am staying overnight, so I will be back tomorrow morning."

"Before you go, here take this." Betty handed Eden a plastic box. "To keep you and Martin going. I know what that hospital food is like."

Eden took the box from Bettie's hand, "Thank you." Martin smiled at Betty in appreciation and they both left.

FORTY-TWO

*H*anson walked along the elegant corridors of Finley Park Mental Health Hospital. The hospital was a private unit for the rich and famous. *Money can buy you just about anything*, he mused, taking note of the beautiful architecture. *This place looks more like a 7-star hotel than a hospital.* Hanson continued towards Dr Clay's office and paused.

"Hello, can I help you?" asked a nurse.

"I am here to see, Dr Clay."

"Do you have an appointment?"

"No." Hanson retrieved his badge from his pocket and flashed it at the nurse.

The nurse raised an eyebrow, "Please wait a moment and I will inform the Doctor you are here."

The nurse knocked on the door in front of them and entered, closing it behind her. A minute later, she emerged, "Dr Clay will see you now."

Hanson walked into Dr Clay's office and closed the door behind him.

"Please, sit down, Detective."

Hanson pulled out a chair opposite Dr Clay and sat down.

"So, what is all this about?" pressed Dr Clay.

"I am inquiring about a former patient of yours, Stephanie Chambers. She was admitted here three years ago and spent two years under your care. I am more interested in her visitors. What can you tell me about her regular visitors, Dr Clay?"

Dr Clay shifted uncomfortably in his chair. He shuffled some papers around on his desk and then cleared his throat. "Stephanie was an extremely interesting case. She was an intelligent woman. She responded exceptionally well to her treatment here at Finley Park. She was no trouble at all. She had one regular visitor, her mother. Her mother was a forceful woman, intolerable at times. Stephanie became close to a contractor towards the end of her stay here. He was employed to install and update our software. They both clicked according to the staff and although they advised against it while Stephanie was a patient, it did not stop them. I recall her mother kicking up a storm when she first found out, stating he was not good enough for her daughter. She blamed Stephanie's vulnerability at the time on her poor choice. Then unexpectedly, she endorsed their growing friendship. One of the nurses found it odd that the mother was often found in deep conversation with the contractor in the quiet room. There was gossip of course, you know how women are. The nurse's station was rife with speculation at the time, I recall," he revealed.

Hanson furrowed his brows. "Can you elaborate for me?"

Dr Clay rose from his seat and paced the floor, "The contractor spent more time with the mother here than with Stephanie. After his brief visit ended with Stephanie, he would then be seen talking at length in the car park with Stephanie's mother before heading their separate ways. Other times, they would head down to the public canteen and were often seen in deep conversations on several occasions. It struck the staff as odd at the time. The mother was so vehemently against the pairing in the beginning and then as if overnight, she had completely changed her tune."

"How is a patient allowed to strike up such a friendship with an outside contractor, Dr Clay?"

"Look, detective, our patients are some of the richest people from around the UK and Europe. This is not a high-security unit. Most patients are here of their own volition. There have been more than one or two romantic pairings over the years. People are human after all. Being sick does not remove such emotions. It is not a prison or a secure unit. Most patients can leave as and when they like. They are voluntary patients for the most part."

"Understood. Do you think the contractor's intentions were genuine?"

"Yes. I really do. He was smitten with Stephanie. The mother, however, seemed to have a lot of input. What that input was I have no idea. Nevertheless, the mother and the contractor had a lot to talk about each time the mother visited. The contractor was here daily for a couple of months and once the mother finished her visit with her daughter, she would seek out the contractor and spend over an hour talking privately with him. It was the talk of the halls for quite some time, I recall. Some were speculating whether the contractor was interested in both mother and daughter. However, it was none of our business. These rich people have an enormous amount of power and keep this hospital running with their fees. We must tread carefully. Stephanie was rather quiet, sad even. She spent a lot of time on her own and did not mingle with other patients, choosing to keep to her room for the most part. She liked to roam the gardens after breakfast before her daily classes began. Once we got her treatment right for her, she adapted fast and well. She is on medication for Schizophrenia for the rest of her life as I am sure you are aware. She adjusted well to the treatment. In fact, Stephanie was a model patient. There is no reason why she can't go on to live a normal balanced life as long as she remains on her medication."

"Is there anything else you can think of that I should know?"

Dr Clay sat back down in his chair and steepled his fingers beneath his chin, "I'm not sure that it helps but Stephanie's father died of a heart attack shortly after she was admitted here. I recall how hard that hit her. It set her back a few months. I believe Stephanie was close to her father. Nevertheless, it hit her mother harder. Her mother looked devastated for a long time. She broke down in front of a nurse one day, saying how she blamed Noah Ainsworth for the death of her husband. She believed that everything that happened to her family stemmed back to his rejection of her daughter. She was bitter about it. Stephanie's mother was one woman that is not easy to forget. She left a lasting impression here and not a good one. It was quite a relief when Stephanie was ready to leave. No one was sorry to see the back of the mother. Her visits here during Stephanie's stay were dreaded by my staff." Dr Clay paused for a moment then added, "May I ask, how is Stephanie doing now?"

Hanson replied, 'She is living in France now. Bought a small vineyard."

Dr Clay rose to his feet and extended his hand. Hanson shook the doctor's hand then left.

Hanson hurried to his car and made a quick call to the station before driving off to Charlotte's house. *All I have to go on is my gut instinct... Now I must prove my theory. I have no evidence whatsoever, but what I do have is - motive.*

He ordered his officers to re-interview Christopher while he paid Charlotte a surprise visit. He did not call ahead. He pulled up onto the vast driveway of Charlotte's house and parked up. He leapt out of his car, walked up to the entrance and rang the doorbell. The door flung open.

"Hello, how may I help you?" greeted Grace.

Detective Hanson flashed his badge; "I would like to speak with Charlotte Chambers please."

"I am sorry, Detective, Charlotte is not here. She took a trip up to the Midlands."

Hanson shifted impatiently on his feet, "May I ask the nature of her visit?"

A woman came into sight, "That will be all Grace." Grace scurried off. "My name is Julia. I am Charlotte's personal assistant. What is this all about?"

"I need to get in contact with Charlotte urgently. Can you tell me where I can find her?"

"Of course, she has gone to Birmingham to pay Mr. Ainsworth a visit. After discovering the tragic news of his accident, she wanted to visit in person. She knows him very well and was saddened by the news."

Hanson spun around and headed for his car, not saying a word. Julia stood on the porch looking puzzled as Hanson sped off into the night. He had a two-hour journey at most ahead of him. He called the hospital and was put on hold," Damn you!" he cursed.

He called again, but the lines were busy. He then called into the station ordering an officer to go straight to City Hospital.

FORTY-THREE

*C*harlotte waited patiently in the shadows for Eden to leave. She searched around and then stepped into the corridor. She approached Noah's door with flowers in-hand. The officer guarding the door halted her. "Good evening, officer. I am here to see Noah Ainsworth. I am an old friend of the family," she said. Dressed like a fragile elderly woman in her 60s rather than the power dresser she normally was. The officer smiled and pushed open the door.

"Thank you so much," said Charlotte.

Charlotte walked in and closed the doors behind her. She threw the flowers into the bin and walked up to Noah. Charlotte's eyes blazed as they trailed the tubes. Her hand reached out and her fingers traced one of the tubes. Her mouth twisted into smile. "All you had to do was marry Stephanie. However, no - she was not good enough for the mighty Noah Ainsworth. You broke her heart and in turn killed my husband. In addition, for what? That woman – that common woman. What the hell did she have that my Stephanie didn't have? You ruined all our lives with your poor choice. Eden Marshall is nothing. I should have left her in the ground where she belongs. And you - you should be dead.

She began to squeeze the tube feeding Noah's air supply. Closing her eyes, she felt a rush of adrenalin coursing through her veins. The corners of her lips curled as she prevented the air from reaching Noah's lungs. The sense of satisfaction consumed her. She leaned in close to Noah and whispered in his ear, "You don't get to live..."

The doors burst open; Charlotte continued squeezing the tube not turning around. She was in a daze while continuing to drain the life out of Noah's body. The officer ran up to her and pulled her away from Noah pressing the emergency button above his head. Charlotte made no attempt to escape. She coldly glared at Noah while the officer handcuffed her and read Charlotte her rights. The loud beeping sound alerted the nurse's station. Noah went into cardiac arrest. The crash team burst into the room. The officer left the crash team to do their job and escorted Charlotte out of the hospital.

* * *

Eden's screams echoed through Ainsworth House. Martin pushed open the door to the library and scanned the room.

Max and Jackson rushed to her aid and found Eden sobbing. "Eden, what's happened?"

Eden struggled to speak through her sobs, "It's Noah. He went into cardiac arrest. Max take me to the hospital..."

Jackson was in shock. Martin followed behind Max and Eden out to the car. "Hurry Max.

Please hurry," begged Eden.

Twenty minutes later, they were running through the hospital corridor towards Noah's room.

Dr Matthews was exiting Noah's room as they arrived, "Noah is alive. It was a close call though." Dr Matthews continued to his office. Eden and Max burst through the doors. Eden ran to Noah's side and clutched hold of his hand. "Thank God. You are alive and that is all that matters. I will never leave your side again," she sobbed.

Max walked over to Eden and placed his hand on her shoulder. "He is a fighter that's for sure. He will come through this Eden, you will see."

Eden did not respond. She placed her head on Noah's limp hand and sobbed.

Max exited the room. "What the hell happened here?" he asked the officer standing beside Martin.

The officer turned a crimson colour, "I'm sorry. She was an old fragile-looking lady; I had no reason to think that she was a danger."

Max roared, "Well she had you fooled." Martin placed his hand on Max's arm to curb his temper.

"Yes, I know, Martin," he said, pulling back his arm. While storming off down the corridor, he added, "Tell Eden I shall be in the canteen for a while."

Martin remained outside the door patiently. He looked up when Hanson appeared. He nodded in acknowledgement.

Hanson burst through the door. "Hello, Eden. How's he doing?" he asked.

Eden glared at Hanson, "How was this allowed to happen? Please... I need to know."

Hanson pulled up a chair, "I'm sorry. No one could have anticipated this."

"So was Charlotte Chambers really responsible for everything. Even my kidnapping?"

"Yes...yes she was." Hanson paused, placed his hand on top of Eden's. He continued, "Charlotte was an embittered woman who believed that Noah was responsible for her family's downfall. She blamed him. It consumed her. She wanted revenge for Noah rejecting his daughter and the premature death of her husband. Of course, she could not see that Noah was not at fault. She had it all twisted up in her head. She wanted someone to blame and so she blamed Noah."

Eden sat upright, "So what will happen to her now?"

"Well... She is being charged as we speak with kidnapping and two counts of attempted murder to list a few, along with her accomplice, Christopher. Charlotte was the puppet master – the mastermind behind it all. The saddest part of all this was that Stephanie had no idea what

her mother and her boyfriend were planning all this time. She was completely oblivious and innocent. Charlotte was very clever, until the end when she lost it. Noah was never meant to survive the hit and run. She wanted to finish the job. In the end, she did not care about getting caught. I must go to the station now. I will be removing the officer from outside Noah's door. Now we have the culprits in custody there is no need for him to be here." Hanson made his way to the door and Eden halted him, "Thank you. Thank you for everything."

Hanson smiled and left. Eden turned her attention to Noah. "I am right here. I love you. I love you more than you can ever imagine." She leaned forward and kissed him on the lips.

FORTY-FOUR

*S*tephanie reached for her bottle of pills and shook two pills loose into her hand. She gulped them down with a swig of water and meandered out onto her wraparound porch overlooking her vineyard to wait for her friend. Her lips curled into a smile as her eyes trailed over the vast vineyard set out before her like a tapestry.

A sadness emanated from her as thoughts of her mother dominated her mind. One month on from the revelation of what her mother did still made the hairs on the back of her neck stand on their ends. Still reeling from the shock, she drew in a deep breath and then leapt to her feet. The sight of her friend's car approaching caught her attention. She walked down the steps as the car pulled up.

Christy climbed out of her car smiling. "Stephanie, it's so good to see you," she greeted while leaning in for a hug.

Christy continued, "So, how are you holding up?"

Stephanie walked up the steps and slumped down into the chair. "I am still in shock at what my mother and Christopher did. It does not feel real. I cannot make sense out of any of it. I thought I knew Christopher – clearly, I had no idea who he was. Yes, he loved me, but he loved my mother's money more. She offered him more money than he ever dreamed possible. Now they are both in prison, and I am left with no one and that's what hurts the most. As for my mother, I always knew she had a dark side, however, I never anticipated she would do anything like this. She always held it together. Her reputation was everything to her even to the detriment of her family. To lose it the way she did in the end is something I will never reconcile with – not ever."

Christy inched her chair closer and reached for Stephanie's hand. "You have me, and you will always have me. I owe you my life and I have never forgotten that. I thought I would stay here for a while. Call it an extended holiday. I can keep you company while you come to terms with everything. I hate the thought of you being here alone."

Stephanie swiped a tear escaping down her cheek. She studied Christy for a moment and her face creased into a smile. She said, "That would be wonderful. You are the best. I am lucky to have you."

Christy chimed in, "No – I am the lucky one. I will never forget that first day you walked into primary school with your high pigtails. I remember you smiling at me nervously and I ran over to you and asked you to be my friend. Do you remember?"

Stephanie's eyes crinkled, "Of course I remember. I was so relieved I made a friend on my first day and from that day forth we were inseparable! Personally, I think we recognised each other's 'Crazy' and we just got each other!" she laughed.

"You're not wrong there! We were always different from the other kids, over emotional and too sensitive. But we found each other and here we still are."

"Yep, here we still are and thank God for that. I hope you are not going to disappear from my life any time soon?" piped Stephanie.

Christy placed a comforting hand on Stephanie's arm, "I am going nowhere. I will always be here for you."

Stephanie climbed to her feet, "Enjoy the view while I go and fetch us drink."

Christy swiped through her picture gallery on her phone while waiting for Stephanie. She looked at a photo she thought she had deleted. Her finger hovered over the delete icon, *Sorry Blake. You were a decent man. Nevertheless, you were a means to an end.* She studied the picture of herself and Blake taken at the dinner party. For a brief moment, she felt a twinge of guilt and then it faded away. *I rather liked being Eva...* She deleted the image and turned off her phone. *My job is done... And I was paid handsomely for it, although it was for Stephanie, I did what I did, not for you Charlotte. I owed Stephanie everything. It is a shame you lost it in the end. You just could not let it be and now you are paying the ultimate price.*

Stephanie startled Christy back to reality, as she appeared with a tray. "We have wine from my own vineyard, a selection of French cheeses, olives and grapes," said Stephanie placing the tray down on to the table.

"Wow! Now that is perfect. It's good to see you smiling, Stephanie. Things will get easier over time. Just focus your energies on the vineyard and your new life here in France. Oh, and me of course," laughed Christy.

"I don't know what I would do without you. You have been my rock this past month," confessed Stephanie.

"You were always there for me. You saved me once and I have never forgotten that. I will always be here for you. You can count on that," promised Christy.

Stephanie sat back in her chair sipping her wine while glancing over her vineyard. Noah flashed through her mind. *He did not deserve what happened to him. What was my mother thinking? Maybe I inherited my illness from her. After all, it is hereditary and her actions and behaviour over the years have been questionable to say the least. But I guess now I will never know. Just keep taking your medication Stephanie and everything will work out,* she concluded, while a sadness enveloping her.

FORTY-FIVE

Four Months Later

oah limped into the kitchen, "Have you seen Eden, Betty?"
"She skipped breakfast and went out for a run about 40 minutes ago."

Noah smiled, "Really!"

"Yes, really."

"All by herself?"

"I know. I was surprised too. It's a step forward, Noah."

"Wow! I wasn't expecting that."

Eden burst through the kitchen door, beads of sweat pooling on her brow, "I need a glass of water," she gasped.

Betty and Noah stared at Eden while she gulped down a pint of water.

"What's with you two?" Eden asked, spinning around.

Noah's eyes darted from Betty and then back to Eden, "Oh nothing. Just glad to see you back to your old self!"

"It felt so good to be running again. I feel free."

Noah walked up to her and enveloped her in a tight hug, "I have a surprise for you. Go and shower and I will meet you in the library when you are done."

Eden furrowed her brows and glanced at Noah and then Betty. Betty held her hands up and turned to face the worktop.

"What are you up to, Noah?" asked Eden.

"Like I said, it's a surprise."

"Okay, if you insist, I shall play along. Eden left the kitchen to shower.

Betty spun around, "Just relax, Noah. Everything will work out as it should," she winked and continued cooking.

Noah made his way to the library and paced the wooden floor. Duke and Bella were by his side and walking up and down the room with him, "Hey, you can't be nervous too! I need you to be strong for me!" he laughed. Duke jumped up and placed his paws on Noah's shoulders, "I love you too." Bella spun around Noah's legs. "And you too Bella."

Eden opened the doors to the library.

Noah shifted on his feet nervously. "I know you have just been jogging and probably don't feel like a walk right now. But I want to go to my lake with Duke and Bella."

Eden glanced at the dogs and then to Noah, "Jackson took the dogs walking this morning?"

Noah rolled his eyes, "I know, nevertheless, I want the four us to go. Please...just humour me this once?"

"What are we waiting for then, let's go?" urged Eden.

The dogs ran out of the library to the entrance doors. Smiling, Jackson opened the door for them and stood on the steps watching them walk across the fields. He spun around when he heard Betty's familiar footsteps behind him. "This is it then?" said Betty.

"Yes," smiled Jackson.

Noah laced his fingers through Eden's as they approached the lake. Duke and Bella rolled around on the bank. Noah paused mid-stride and spun Eden around. "This is where you captured my heart. That day you emerged from the lake soaking wet. I knew then that you were the woman for me. It took a while for my head and heart to agree of course! But deep down that is the moment I knew." He reached into his top right-hand pocket, retrieved a small box, and then knelt down before her.

The realisation of what was happening hit her with force. Her heart pounded through her chest. She gasped.

"Eden Marshall...would you do me the great honour of becoming my wife?" he paused and searched Eden's face. His heart was in his hands.

A smile reaching up to her eyes confirmed what he needed to know. "Y-E-S! she screamed, throwing her arms around his neck and kissing his face all over. "I love you so much. A life without you is unimaginable. I know that now. Almost losing you made me see that. Yes, yes, and a hundred more yes's!"

Noah chimed in, "Duke, Bella, she said yes!" Duke and Bella ran up to them running in and out of their legs. Eden kissed him with a passion he knew he could not live without.

"I have one last surprise for you."

"Really!"

"Yes, really. Come on, we need to head to the lodge."

Eden's curiosity was getting the better of her, "Please...just one clue?"

Noah shook his head, "We are almost there now." He stopped them in their tracks. "Okay, I need you to close your eyes now. Hold my hand and I will guide you up to the veranda."

He paused at the door of the lodge, "Keep them closed until I say open them."

He pushed open the door and led her into the lodge. "Okay, you can open your eyes now."

Eden was puzzled. She glanced around the lodge - it looked the same. She glanced at Noah.

"Keep searching," he encouraged.

She continued searching then her eyes fell upon a set of beautiful Louis Vuitton luggage. Her eyes widened when they rested on the airline tickets sitting atop them. "Seriously, Noah! We are going on holiday?"

"Yes. Everything has been arranged. It is my engagement present to you, to us. I felt we needed it after everything that has happened. Everything is packed. I took the liberty of packing them myself. I have our passports and we are good to go. Jackson is on standby to drive us to the airport," he confessed.

Eden ran over to the luggage and glanced at the airline tickets, "Bora Bora! Wow... I don't know what to say."

He took her hand in his, "You have already said the only word I need to hear and that was—YES!"

The End

AMNESIA - EXCERPT

(Romantic Psychological Thriller)

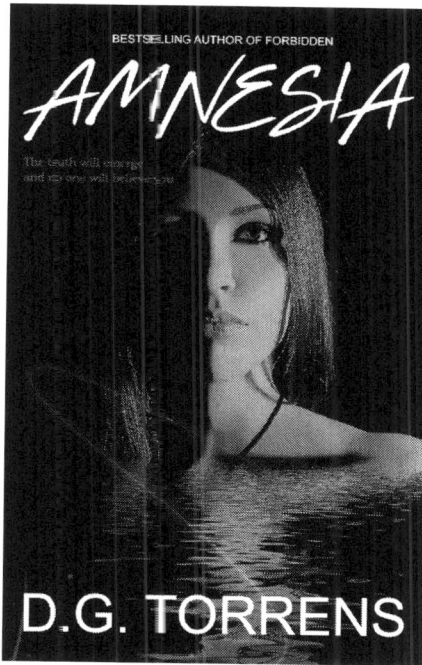

Cassie repeatedly rubbed her wrist until it was soar.

"Do you remember anything from that day, Cassie?"

The question unnerved her. She fixed her gaze on the window while contemplating her answer. Jennifer Clayton studied Cassie while patiently awaiting her reply. Cassie shook her head and dipped her eyes.

"That's okay. Your memory will return eventually. It has only been a few months. The brain is a complex organ and serves to protect us against trauma. Your mind has shut down and will return when you are better able to cope with the tragic events of that day."

Cassie looked up and observed Jennifer Clayton. A tall, slender woman with sleeked back hair tied at the nape of her neck. She wore minimal makeup and dressed in an understated trouser suit. Cassie thought she looked more like a teacher than a therapist.

"It's okay, Cassie. Anything you reveal in our sessions is strictly confidential. This is a safe place. You can trust me."

Jennifer observed Cassie's behaviour, noticing her arms cradling her torso. Cassie hunched her shoulders forward. *Classic shielding behaviour,* she noted.

Jennifer continued, "Post Traumatic Amnesia is more common than you think. This transient state of confusion occurs immediately following injury. What you are experiencing is normal."

Cassie shifted nervously in her chair.

"How are you sleeping?" asked Jennifer.

Cassie raised her head, "Not good. I have nightmares."

"Do you want to talk about them?"

Cassie's eyes lowered to the floor. Silence ensued.

Jennifer made some notes. "We don't have to talk about them today."

Cassie searched Jennifer's face, "I'm not ready. Sorry." She rose to her feet and slipped her bag over her shoulder, showing that she was cutting her session short.

Jennifer offered a sympathetic smile, stood up and walked around to the front of her desk and leaned against it. "Same time next week?"

Cassie offered a weak nod and left. She hurried down the stairs and burst through the doors into the street. She paused, inhaling a deep breath. Droplets of rain brushed against her skin. She felt terrible for lying to Jennifer. She did remember something.

Cassie battled the wind devouring the streets until she reached home on the outskirts of Warson Town. She wasn't sure of anything anymore. She paused at the foot of her apartment building, a converted industrial masterpiece. Her sprawling loft apartment rested on the top floor and sported exposed brick walls, large steel columns, sash windows that added to the charm of the light-filled, airy space. It was one of several industrial buildings in the large town successfully converted to upmarket loft apartments over recent times. The architectural history featured throughout was the draw for Cassie when she first viewed the loft and sealed the deal for her. She used the money that she received from her late father's will, deciding to invest the money in property, and it proved to be quite the investment. She entered through the large, glass doors, smiled at the Concierge, and headed for the escalator. The doors glided open on the 5th floor and Cassie stepped out. She paused at her front door, aware that Leo was waiting for her on the other side. An anxious feeling circled her stomach. *He has been so patient with me. I feel guilty for pushing him away. He has been my saviour over the last few months. Yet, I can't talk to him or confide my feelings with him. Why is that? I know he is desperate to help and make me feel safe. However, I want to be alone. I don't know how to tell him. I need to address this,* she worried

She turned the key and entered the wide-open space to her apartment. Leo was waiting for her, eager to learn how she'd progressed with her session.

He leapt forward and enveloped her. Cassie did not reciprocate and waited for him to release his hold. Leo stepped back, hurt by Cassie's frosty reception. "How did it go?"

Cassie walked past him, ignoring his question, heading into the kitchen area, and poured herself a glass of water. The smell of home cooking raised her curiosity. She glanced at the oven and then turned to Leo, meeting his gaze.

He smiled proudly, "I cooked us dinner. I thought you would be hungry."

"Thanks," commented Cassie.

"Well, are you going to tell me how it went today?"

Cassie turned away, "Nothing—I can recall absolutely nothing," she lied.

Leo extended his arm across the table and took her hand. "Maybe it's for the best. You are still fragile and need more time. You may never remember and that is okay too. I am here for you."

Cassie retrieved her hand from under Leo's and picked up her knife and fork. She took a mouthful of food and then placed her cutlery down.

"I'm sorry. I am not hungry. The truth is Leo, I think the best thing for me right now is to be alone. Since I left the hospital, I have not had a solitary moment to process what happened to me. I feel that is what I need right now."

Leo startled Cassie when he stood up and kicked back his chair, "You can't mean that. After everything I have done for you and now you want me to leave!"

Cassie shrank away from him, "Sorry. I need my space. Please understand."

Leo paced the wooden floor, "Well, I don't have a choice, do I?" he snapped.

Cassie lowered her eyes and shook her head.

"Fine, I will pack a bag and stay with my brother for a while. Rob has a spare room. I am worried about you, Cass. I don't think you should be alone right now."

"I will be fine, and you can still come around. It's not like I am breaking up with you. I just want a little time out from everyone, not just you. Please don't take it personally," she pleaded.

Leo caved, hugged her, and kissed her cheek. He took both of her hands in his, "If you need anything night or day you will call me?"

"I promise, you will be the first to know."

"I love you, Cass. Don't forget that, okay?"

Her eyes met his concerned look and smiled, "I won't."

Sadness clouded Leo's features. *Cass didn't reciprocate. I am losing her*, he worried.

Leo headed to the bedroom and retrieved his clothes from the wardrobe and slipped on his jacket. He picked up his bag, feeling disheartened.

Cassie sat on the bottom step of the staircase that leads to the open-planned bedroom, overlooking the entire loft space below. Leo climbed down the stairs and paused at the bottom, dropping his bag on the floor. He lowered his head and placed a kiss on Cassie's forehead. "Call me anytime, okay?" he reiterated.

"I promise. Thanks for understanding, Leo."

Leo retrieved his bag off the floor, hunched it over his shoulder and exited the apartment. Cassie rose to her feet and stood in the doorway, watching until the doors of the escalator closed, and Leo was out of sight. She sighed with relief as she closed the apartment door behind her. A sense of freedom rose inside of her. *I'm no longer sure of my feelings for Leo. I can't focus on our relationship. I know he cares but he is too much at times,* she mused.

Cassie headed upstairs to change. She undressed in front of the large mirror. Standing naked, she turned to the right, her eyes trailed the mangled scars embedded deep in her back. She shuddered and fought a rising panic. She turned away and paused before pivoting to look one more time before dressing. The scars arrested her emotions, evoking a sense of dread—the same feeling she experienced each time she saw them. *I have to accept my new body. It's not the end of the world. I will get used to it over time.*

After dressing, she retrieved her phone off the bed and swiped to call Anna, her long-time best friend.

"Hey Cassie," answered Anna.

"You're home! I wasn't sure if you would be yet?" said Cassie.

"I sneaked out of the office early today! Are you okay, Cass?"

"I guess. Well... no, not really. I asked Leo to move out for a while. That's why I'm calling. Could you drop by during your lunch hour tomorrow and apply the cream to my back. I can't reach all over?"

"Hey girl, consider it done. What's on your mind. You sound depressed."

She read her tone like a book and always knew when something was bothering her.

"Every time I catch a glimpse of my back, I shudder with disgust, Anna. I can barely look at myself. If I feel that way imagine what others will think. It changes things, like swimming for instance. I can't imagine going swimming again. The thought of people glaring at me in horror, makes me feel sick. Then there's our spa days, I loved having a back, neck, and shoulder massage and now it seems like a distant memory. I'm trying to come to terms with my scars but it's hard."

"Cass, you are still the same person. Your scars will fade a lot over time. I don't profess to understand how you feel. But I do know you, and you are the bravest person I know. It doesn't matter what others think. Shift your focus and concentrate on new goals and challenges. From today, set yourself new targets to reach. I will be here to support you. You are beautiful and nothing has changed that."

"I needed to hear that today. Thanks, Anna. You're the best."

"So, how did Leo react to being ushered out the door!"

"I shall fill you in on the details tomorrow."

"Sure thing. I should reach your house around one o'clock. Is that okay?"

"Perfect. See you tomorrow," finished Cassie.

AUTHOR TITLES

Biographies & Memoirs:
Amelia's Story – A childhood Lost (Memoirs 1.)

Amelia's Destiny - Finding My Way (Memoirs 2.)

Amelia the Mother – A Pocket Full of Innocence (Memoirs 3.)

Romance/Romantic Suspense
Broken Wings (Military Romance)

Tears of Endurance (Ferria/Fielding Novel 1.)

Whispers from Heaven (Ferria Fielding Novel 2.)

The Poppy Fields (Military Romance 1.)

The Poppy Fields-Eternity Bound (Military Romance 2.)

The Poppy Fields-In Life We Trust (Military Romance 3.)

A Soldier's Fear (Military Romance)

Forbidden (Hamilton/Sharma Novel 1.)

Dissolution (Hamilton/Sharma Novel 2.)

Unforeseen (Hamilton Sharma Novel 3.)

AMNESIA (Romantic Thriller/Suspense)

Poetry & Prose
Abyss – Journey Through Depression

Sonder – Thought Provoking Poetry & Prose

Military Boots – Anthology of War Poetry

Heart and Mind – Contemporary Poetry

Quotes:
Midnight Musings – 300 life quotes

ABOUT THE AUTHOR

D.G. Torrens is an international bestselling author of the Amelia Series—a true story that touched the hearts of people all over the world. D.G is a multi-genre author and has authored many books. These include romantic suspense, military romance, contemporary romance, romantic drama, biography & memoirs, and poetry books. If you enjoyed FINDING YOU, try the author's latest release, AMNESIA a psychological romantic thriller.

D.G. lives in Birmingham United Kingdom, with her husband and daughter. The author attends several book-signing events each year. To find out more about these book signings and dates you can follow the author below.

The author loves to connect with her readers. To connect with the author, you can visit her at the following links:

FACEBOOK: http://www.facebook.com/dgtorrens

TWITTER: http://www.twitter.com/torrenstp

INSTAGRAM: http://www.instagram.com/dgtorrens_author

WEBSITE: http://www.dawnsdaily.com

AMAZON: http://www.amazon.com/dgtorrens

AMAZON: http://www.amazon.co.uk/dgtorrens

Printed in Great Britain
by Amazon

60972606R00139